Letters

From

Hadley

Cassidy Bryant

Identifiers: ISBN 978-1-966698-00-5 (paperback) | ISBN 978-1-966698-01-2 (eBook) | ISBN 978-1-966698-02-9 (hardcover)

Library of Congress Control Number: 2025902503

Edited by Heather Moore and Meghan Zalar

Cover Design by Layla Brown

Warning: This book explores themes around death, grief, depression, anxiety, bullying, heartbreak, cheating, and suicidal ideation.

Find Cassidy Bryant online!

cassidybryantauthor.com

To Alex. Sorry for being the mean older sibling growing up. I think you're awesome, though, and I love being your sister.

Author's Note

Death, including suicide, is discussed in this book. Please take care of your emotional wellbeing while reading.

For a list of possible triggers, please see the bolded warning on the copyright page.

If you or someone you know needs support:

United States: Call or text **988**, or visit 988lifeline.org
United Kingdom: Call **116 123** (Samaritans) or visit samaritans.org
Canada: Call **1-833-456-4566**, text **45645**, or visit talksuicide.ca
Australia: Call **13 11 14** or visit lifeline.org.au

Letters
From
Hadley

Chapter

One

The bathroom door opened, startling me.

"Parker," my dad murmured, sticking his head in, "are you ready to go?"

I took a deep breath, then straightened my gray tie one last time in the mirror. "Yeah, I'll be right down."

"Okay." He hovered in the doorway like he wanted to say something else but didn't know what. He ran a hand through his salt-and-pepper hair, then pointed behind him. "We'll be in the car."

"Okay."

After my dad shut the door, I stared at myself—dark circles underlined my brown eyes. It had been days since the last time I'd had a full night's sleep.

I loosened the tie now. I didn't wear it enough to feel totally comfortable in it. I pulled it out for lacrosse banquets, semi-formal dances with my girlfriend, and that senior homecoming dinner my school put on a few weeks ago. Of course, those were happier events—events that marked a sort of coming of age, or whatever. But this wasn't a happy event. It was a funeral.

And it wasn't just any funeral. It was the funeral of Hadley García, my ex-girlfriend. A senior—like me. And so, I had to ask myself: was I really ready? Was I ready to see her parents and siblings, standing there without her, crying? Was I ready to see her lifeless body in a casket? Was I ready to face the fact that she was dead and never coming back? No. A hundred times no.

But did I manage to gel up my hair and brush my teeth this morning to prepare for the occasion?

Yes.

So, like I'd told my dad, yes. I was ready to go.

As I climbed into the back of my parents' SUV, my mom's voice flowed back to me, sweet like honey and just as nauseating for this early in the day. "Hi, Parker."

"Hey," I mumbled.

She offered me that soft, sympathetic smile that moms seem to have mastered. Like, they don't have any wise or comforting words to give but want you to know they care. Outlining her smile was some beige lipstick, and her curly brown hair—a genetic feature she had passed on to me—had been touched up. She was trying to look nice for the occasion, which I should have seen as a meaningful gesture, considering the fact that, to my parents, Hadley was just another one of my many past girlfriends.

I didn't have the energy to acknowledge that or smile back, so I turned my head to face the window. Outside, the leaves on the trees were bursting in hues of orange and red. It wasn't out of the ordinary for Oregon in October. For weeks now, people had been watching these leaves prove just how beautiful they could become before they died, shriveling up into brown clumps of nothing. Despite the vibrant colors trying their best to stand out, the overcast sky and fog-veiled mountains turned everything gloomy. But, again, not too out of the ordinary for this part of Oregon.

Hadley loved the gloomy weather. I thought it was a good match for her to be living in Copperton, Oregon. The cruel irony is that it was sunny the day she died.

I didn't find out about her death until the day after it had happened. It had seemed like such a normal day. I drove to school, then spent too much time trying to find a parking spot until I gave up and made my own next to someone's truck. On the way to the doors, I'd hoped it wouldn't be the day Administration decided to enforce the parking rules. When I got inside, I had about five minutes before class started. It had been enough time to talk to my best friend, Gage, at our lockers. Gage was being his usual cheerful self, talking about something one of our lacrosse friends told him as he ran a hand through his short, kinky hair. By the time his story ended, there was not enough time to see my girlfriend, Mallory, who would have already been off with her student council friends. So, I went straight to class and landed in my seat just in time for the final bell to go off.

I pulled my notebook out of my bag, said something to one of my teammates in the class, and then I saw it. My physics teacher, Mrs. Melton, had wet red eyes. And instead of greeting the class in the overly energetic fashion she was notorious for, she just sat behind her desk. Had to be something from her personal life, I figured.

But then the morning announcements started. Instead of Mallory's or Brittany's voice, it was Mr. Conley's, the principal. And his tone wasn't cheerful like usual either.

His voice was raspy as he chewed on each word. "Good morning, students. It is with a heavy heart that I make this announcement." The speaker crackled as he paused. "Hadley García—a senior here at Lincoln—passed away in a car accident yesterday."

My stomach dropped. The room spun. Surely I'd misheard him. Maybe there was another Hadley García, who was a senior here. Or someone with a name that sounded like hers.

"Hadley," he continued, "was a bright student. She was a light to all who came in contact with her. And I know I speak for all of us when I say she will be deeply missed."

He'd made a comment about counselors being available and then, just like that, Mr. Conley's voice was replaced by Brittany's. She was hesitant but peppy as she spouted off about upcoming assemblies and football games.

I looked around. Mrs. Melton was crying. Some students looked sad. Some looked bored. I probably looked deranged as I waited for the marching band to bust through the doors, yelling, "Surprise!" as they banged on their stupid drums. "Hadley's not really dead! But you know who's gonna be dead this Friday when we kill them in football? The Mountain View Mustangs!" Then, they'd step out of the way to reveal a living Hadley, and we'd all shoot streamers into the air and chant the fight song.

Not gonna lie, I half-expected the same thing as I walked into the church this morning. Hadley's birthday was only a few weeks away, so maybe this was some ploy to get everyone to dress up and come to her party. She'd just stayed home from school, pretending to be dead for a few days, and then once everyone arrived, she'd bust out of the coffin. Of course, Hadley wasn't that kind of person. But, at least this time, I hoped she was.

Beside the entrance of the chapel sat a table. It had a picture of Hadley smiling—her long, dark hair framing her face. There was also the flower wreath Mallory and her student council friends made in Hadley's honor and a stack of programs. I didn't know why, but I almost expected the newspaper reporting her accident to be stacked on the table, too. I'd seen the article pop up so many times over the last three days that I almost had it memorized—keywords haunted me as intrusive thoughts. *October 17. Head-on collision. Police and medical personnel arrived at the scene of the accident at 4:27 p.m. Teenager found dead upon arrival.*

"Parker," my mom said, gently running her fingers through my hair, "Dad and I are going to go take a seat. Take whatever time you need."

"Thanks."

Looking around, I couldn't help but notice all the people who'd come to her funeral. She never would have believed it. Hadley wasn't exactly a loner, but she wasn't the most popular person either. She was quiet and had a small circle of friends.

But the people who filled this church vastly exceeded a small circle. There were family members, friends, and even some classmates I didn't know she knew. And there were many people—Mallory and Gage, included—who weren't able to make it but wished they could have. So many people who loved her. So many people who were crying, agonizing over their loss. Under different circumstances, I wished she could have seen this.

Without meaning to, I made eye contact with Hadley's father. He smiled faintly and made his way over, giving me just enough time to straighten my tie again.

Mr. García came to America from Mexico when he was a kid. At about 5'9" he wasn't very tall, but that didn't stop him from being extremely intimidating. Even when Hadley and I were together, he made me nervous. Although he eventually warmed up to me, I was unsure of my standing now.

"Parker," he said. I'd almost forgotten the sound of his

voice. "Thank you for coming. I … I know Hadley would have appreciated it."

"Thank you," I mumbled. "I'm really sorry."

He looked down, arms folded. "Me, too." His voice cracked on *too*, and I almost swore I saw tears form in his eyes.

I hadn't cried up to this point, but seeing Mr. García like this nearly broke me. From what I'd seen and heard, Mr. García was a tough man. According to Hadley, he had a pretty rough upbringing that he says he overcame through hard work and perseverance. And because of the adversity he had to overcome at a young age, he didn't take excuses from his kids very well. He wasn't soft.

But now … now, I wasn't sure about that. Behind him, I watched his wife in the back corner, bawling her eyes out while a group of women took turns hugging her and rubbing her back. Standing near her was Hadley's older sister. I'd never actually met her, but I could tell who she was. She stood the same way Hadley often did, with one arm hanging down and the other one clutching it.

"Well," Mr. García said, clasping his hands together, "the service is about to start."

"Yeah, I should go find my parents."

"Tell them 'Thank you,'" he said. "For coming."

I flashed my teeth in a haphazard attempt to ease the tension I felt. "I will."

And thank you, Mr. García, for allowing me to show my face at your dead daughter's funeral.

The Garcías were good people. But even seeing them in this broken state, I was angry at them for the way they'd treated their daughter. I know I'm hardly one to talk about hurting Hadley after how things ended between us. But they should have known better.

Hadley hated driving. She hated the angry drivers and confusing roads. Whenever her parents had her drive anywhere, even if it was just to school or to the grocery store, she'd beg them to drive her instead.

"You just need more practice," they'd reply. "Stop being so afraid all the time."

I couldn't help but think that the same conversation had taken place before she grabbed the keys that day. After over a year of driving, she was still afraid of the road, but they'd written her fears off as a simple lack of practice. Was practice going to stop the other car from colliding with hers? Was practice going to make the ambulance arrive at the scene faster? Was practice going to bring her back?

Now I was mad at the other driver. A confused elderly woman who'd had her license taken away. A hazard who shouldn't have been driving in the first place.

Of the two people involved in the accident, who was it that walked away with only a scratch on her forehead? The girl who had goals, dreams, and a future? The one who was just months away from graduating high school? From getting to the point that we all waited for? No. It was the ninety-something-year-old woman who didn't even have much longer to live.

I flinched when someone touched my shoulder. My father had approached me from behind.

"Parker," he said. "Are you ready to come sit with us? They're about to start the service."

I nodded.

I took a deep breath, trying to calm my racing thoughts, and sat next to my father. I watched as others shuffled to their seats until I recognized someone sitting just a few rows ahead of me. Kenzie Bennett was Hadley's best friend. Her blonde hair, which she usually pulled up in a ponytail, fell down in loose curls.

Before I had a chance to look away, she turned her head and locked eyes with me. Her eyes were red, and all I could think about was what she probably thought about me. She probably wondered why I was there, thinking I shouldn't have been. She hated me. She hated me the way all girls hate their best friends' ex-boyfriends.

After a few seconds, she looked away, hunching down and resting her face in her hands. I felt bad for her. I didn't think of how she'd be feeling after the loss of her best friend. Up until this point, I didn't think of her at all.

"Good morning," the priest announced over the podium. "We are gathered here today to commemorate the life of Hadley García ..."

Some guy with a Lincoln Cross Country hoodie sat in front of me. And I thought about how Hadley never got into sports. She was more of the sit-on-the-bleachers-writing-poetry type. That was what I loved about her, I think. She'd say some of the most profound, most beautiful things, and you couldn't help but sit there in awe, trying to wrap your mind around them.

"The righteous perish, and no one takes it to heart; the devout are taken away, and no one understands that ..."

It just wasn't fair. Death happened every day; I knew that. But not like this. It wasn't supposed to happen like this. Old people died, but that was to be expected. You live your life and do your thing, and people miss you when you're gone, but it's all right: you had your chance. You had all those years to do something with your life, but now it's someone else's turn.

But what pissed me off the most was the knowledge that a lot of the time people don't—a lot of people don't ever do anything particularly helpful or worthwhile with their lives. There were people who thoughtlessly breathed air, worked mindless 9 to 5 jobs, yelled at fast-food workers, and got to live to be ninety, leaving nothing for this world but a carbon footprint. Then there were people like Hadley: bright, kind, passionate. People who had the potential to truly contribute something to this godforsaken planet, and who died at age seventeen because of something completely stupid and unnecessary like a car accident.

"Blessed are those who mourn, for they will be comforted ..."

People kept talking about God, but if there was really a god, why would he take her? Why would he let so many abusers, terrorists, and serial killers live but so suddenly take out someone innocent who actually cared about the people around her?

I looked around at all the people who came to see Hadley for the last time. Did they know I didn't belong here? I was her ex-boyfriend. She wouldn't have wanted me here.

"As in Adam all die, even so in Christ ..."

Hadley was gone now. She was really gone now. She wasn't coming back. She was gone. She was dead. It wasn't fair. It wasn't right. Why did we need to commemorate her? Why couldn't she just be here? Where was she now? I just wanted to talk to her.

The last time I talked to her was about three weeks ago. She passed me in the halls and said "Hi." I said "Hi" back, but I swear I didn't know. I didn't know it was the last time I'd ever talk to her. If I did, I would have said something else like, "I'm sorry" or "You still have a beautiful smile." I couldn't believe she was really gone. She couldn't be gone so soon.

"Flesh shall perish together, and man shall turn ..."

But you can't get time back. You can't get people back. When they're gone, they're gone, and that's it. That's it. I screwed up. I never got to make sure things were okay, and now I would never be able to. She was gone.

"Our tears are wiped away. Unite us together again in one family to sing Your praise forever and ever. Amen."

My mom rubbed my back as the congregation began to sing.

Broken away from my thoughts, I kept my eyes on the back of the pew in front of me. I hadn't realized how intensely I'd been staring at it.

"Are you ready to head to the burial?" Dad chimed in.

I shook my head, eyes still on the pew. "No."

"Okay," Mom replied. "Do you want to wait and—"

"I don't want to go."

"You don't want to go?"

"No."

"Okay," she said softly. "You don't have to go."

Chapter

Two

I followed a cobblestone path, twisting through a grove of trees at night. The trees met each other at the top like shadow people holding hands, and I couldn't make out anything more than five feet in front of me—except for a dim light ahead that grew brighter the closer I got to it. Pretty soon, the trees became more spread apart, and I realized that the light was sunlight. I was in a secret-garden-looking place, and it was daytime. The cobblestone path led to a well, and sitting on the edge of the well was a girl in a long, flowy white dress. Her dark brown hair was long and wavy, with a white daisy poking out above her ear.

When I realized who she was, I ran to her. "Hadley!"

She looked at me, her brown eyes full of light. "Parker!"

"So, you are alive! Where were you?"

She repeated, "Parker."

"Hadley? Can you hear me?"

"Parker," she said again.

"Parker," my fourteen-year-old brother, Chase, said, waking me from my dream and bringing me back to my dark bedroom. I hadn't seen him since before my parents and I left for the funeral.

I sat up and rubbed my eyes. My body ached. "What?"

"Mom made soup and wanted me to bring you some since you slept through dinner." He pushed the bowl he was holding with both hands out to me. His curly brown hair, which was slightly longer and lighter than mine, fell in his face. I wondered if he'd move it away when his hands were freed.

I sat up straighter, taking the bowl. "Oh. Thanks."

From outside the door, I heard, "Is he awake?" Then, my mom entered the room, bringing the light from the hallway in with her. "Oh, Parker, sweetie."

Chase, seeing that his presence was no longer absolutely necessary, left the room, probably returning to his own.

Mom sat at the foot of my bed, holding a spoon out to me. "Here. I saw that your brother forgot this, and I didn't want you to burn your face trying to drink from the bowl or something."

I snorted half-heartedly and took the spoon from her. The savory smell of homemade chicken noodle soup summoned hunger pains in my stomach. I couldn't remember the last time I ate. "Thanks." I probably looked like a starving animal thrusting spoonfuls of noodles into my mouth, broth escaping and dribbling down my chin.

She watched me eat for a moment, then said, "I'm always amazed at your ability to sleep for so long."

I wiped my face with the back of my wrist. "Yeah, well, I haven't really slept at all this week." Putting the bowl of soup on my nightstand, I asked, "What time is it?"

"Almost eight."

"And it's—"

"Saturday."

I groaned and picked up my phone. Checking the lock

screen, I saw that she was right. And that Mallory and a few of my friends had also been trying to get a hold of me.

Mom rubbed my shin. "Parker, how are you feeling?"

"Stiff," I said, stretching my arms above my head.

She half smiled, exhaling through her nose. "No, I mean … how do you feel *emotionally*? You've hardly said a word since we got home from the funeral."

"Fine, I guess."

"Why don't we talk about it?" she pressed. "I think you might feel better if we talk about it."

"Annette," my dad said from the hallway, "don't make him talk about it."

She flipped her head back. "Where did you come from?"

Dad looked guilty, like he'd been caught doing something he wasn't supposed to. "I was just passing by."

"Oh, well," she said, waving him away, "we don't need you right now. Thanks, dear." She turned back to me. "Parker—"

Dad sighed, flipping the light on and coming in. "Seriously, honey, leave him alone. He doesn't want to talk about it."

She looked at me. "Parker, baby, do you want to talk about it?"

"Um." I squinted at my dad. "No?"

She sighed. "Parker, please. You're hurting, and we want to be there for you. You've got to talk to us though."

I offered a smile. "I'm fine, Mom. Really. I'm just tired."

"Okay, well …" She reached for and squeezed my hand. "You know I'm here for you." Then, she stood up and made her way to the door.

"Thanks."

When she was gone, Dad took her place on my bed. "It's a lot to have to process."

I raised my eyebrows. "Yeah."

"She was a very sweet girl. A good person." He paused. "It's horrible the way life screws us over. I truly believe that only the good die young."

Only the good die young. If it cost your life, what was the point of being good?

When he realized I wasn't going to say anything, he stood up. "Well, Parker, your mom's right. We're here for you. Just let us know what we can do."

"Okay," I said. "I will."

He smiled one last time and left.

I grabbed my phone. Mallory was probably losing her mind, so I called her first.

"Parker!" she said, skipping "Hello." "Thank God. Why haven't you answered any of my calls?"

"I was sleeping," I said.

"For an entire day?"

"Pretty much."

"Oh. Well, are you okay? Are you sick?"

I sighed. "No, just tired."

"Okay," she said slowly. "How was it?"

The funeral. "It was good," I said. "Depressing, but what can you expect?"

"Right." She paused. "Well, did you talk to her parents? Did they like the wreath? We were told her favorite color was purple, so we did that. We wanted to make it special for them."

I rolled my eyes. Because the wreath the student council made was going to be the most pressing topic at Hadley's funeral. But I knew Mallory only asked because she cared. She spent hours working on it after school so the Garcías would know how loved their daughter was at Lincoln. "Um, yeah. They loved it." In actuality, I had no idea.

"That's good. I'm glad. Do you want me to come over?"

"No," I said. "I'll be fine. But thank you."

"Of course," she said. "What about tomorrow?"

"Probably not, Mallory. I'm sorry."

"Don't worry about it." I could hear her soft, reassuring smile through her tone. "Well, I guess I'll see you on Monday."

"See you on Monday."

At school, everything looked so normal. Groups of kids laughed and talked. Teachers patrolled the halls. People smiled and waved as they passed each other. Even the ones I'd seen at the funeral looked unaffected. It didn't feel right. Didn't they know Hadley was gone? How were things supposed to go back to normal so soon, not even a week after she died?

As I approached my locker, Gage waved at me. "Hey, man. Are you feeling better?"

"Yeah," I lied.

"How was the funeral?"

"It was good. Weird, I guess."

"I wish I could have been there," he said. "From what I heard, Mr. Godfrey is the only teacher who didn't reschedule his tests that day. I seriously don't know what's wrong with that guy."

"Yeah."

After a moment of silence, he said, "Well, I'm supposed to talk to Mrs. Clem before class starts, but let's talk later, okay?"

And that basically set the tone for every conversation I had the honor to partake in for the rest of the day. "Hey, Parker!" "How was your weekend?" "Oh yeah. I heard about that." "Sucks." By lunchtime, I couldn't stand it anymore. I couldn't talk to another person. I couldn't look at anyone. I took my lunch to my car and picked at it until a text from an unknown number grabbed my attention.

It read, *Parker, this is Hadley's mom, Carrie. Would you be able to stop by our house after 6 today?*

My face felt hot, and a million thoughts swirled around in my head. How did she get my number? Was this a joke? A confrontation?

In my hand, the phone suddenly weighed fifty pounds, but, before I could stop myself, I replied, *Yes.*

Chapter

Three

"Parker," Hadley's mom greeted, opening the door. "Come in!" She had her auburn hair curled and a full face of makeup, but it wasn't enough to hide the dark circles under her blue eyes.

Inside, the kitchen was spotless. Every dish I assumed they had was hidden in the cabinets, with only a single blender on the counter showing that people actually lived there. The granite tile shined. Hadley had mentioned once that her mom used deep cleaning as a coping mechanism. Judging by the lack of dust or clutter anywhere, I could tell Mrs. García was hurting.

The cheerfulness in her voice transported me instantly to the first day I'd met her. She had tried so hard to make a good first impression. Carrie García had always been one to worry about appearances. Unfortunately for her, though, there was nothing she could do about the sadness that glistened in her tired eyes.

"So, Parker," she said, leading me into the living room where her husband sat on the couch. "What have you been up to? What's new?"

I was afraid to sit down and risk messing up the perfectly aligned couch pillows. "Nothing much," I said. "Just school."

Something in her eyes made me realize how insensitive it was to refer to school as *nothing much*. For someone who had just lost their daughter during her senior year, going to school must have meant everything.

As quickly as it had disappeared, her cheeriness returned. "Well, that's great." She glanced at her husband. "You know Manuel."

Hadley's dad stood up. He didn't look angry like I expected him to, for some reason. Like at the funeral just days ago, he looked sad. He held his hand out to me. "Parker, how are you doing?"

"I'm doing good." I shook his hand. "And you?"

He half smiled. "Eh."

Looking at the Garcías now, I could see Hadley in both of them. She had Mr. García's dark eyebrows, dark eyelashes, and soft brown eyes. She had Mrs. García's high cheekbones and upturned nose. She was a merger of them both, but still completely her own. I remembered that, even with all her shyness and insecurities, Hadley had been beautiful.

Mr. García cleared his throat. "Parker, we invited you over because we were going through Hadley's stuff and found something in her room."

As if Mrs. García could see my mind furiously searching for what this had to do with me, she elaborated, "A box of letters."

"A box of letters?"

"Yeah," she drew out slowly. She nodded at Mr. García. "Can you—?"

He stood. "Oh yes." To me, he said, "I'll be right back."

He retreated to another room, leaving Mrs. García and I to sit in awkward silence. With my mind coming up blank on possible small talk, I focused my attention on the entertainment center. Spotless.

When Manuel returned, he held a white box that had a flowery black design. He sat back down and pulled the black cover off, revealing a thick stack of paper with Hadley's handwriting sprawled on top.

Mrs. García said, "We found it in the back of her closet. We thought there might be something—anything—in here that might bring her closer to us. But most of these letters are addressed to you—after the first few she wrote to the dog. But I think we took those ones out." She handed me the box. "Anyway, we didn't read more than a few because we didn't want to invade your privacy—or hers."

I stared at the box like it was a dead animal they had placed in my hands.

"If there are any for us that we missed, will you please tell us?"

Still dumbfounded, I asked, "You want me to read them?"

She smiled. "Yes. We want you to have them."

"You want me to have them?" The animal may as well have sprouted extra legs and stood up.

She nodded as if it should be obvious at this point.

I handed it back to her. "No, I can't. I couldn't."

"Please," she said, refusing to take it. "They're yours. It would mean so much to us." She looked me directly in the eyes. "And I know it would mean so much to Hadley. I think she'd want her words to be read."

"But," I protested, unable to find the rest of my argument. Hadley and I broke up, like, a year-and-a-half ago. Whatever was in here couldn't be good, and I just couldn't see how she'd want me to read something she'd kept hidden this whole time. I tried to find the words to protest again, but then I saw the pleading in Mr. García's eyes.

"Please, Parker," he said. "Just take them. Let us know if there is anything for us—if we missed any."

My mouth was dry. And nothing would come out except, "Okay. I will."

Chapter

Four

She'd want her words to be read. She'd want her words to be read. She'd want her words to be read.

But by *me?* By her ex? I couldn't imagine the incriminating things she'd probably written in those letters. And what if her words weren't incriminating? What if, instead, they were kind? Wouldn't that make things worse? And why did it matter if she wanted her words to be read or not? She was gone. She wouldn't know.

She was gone.

But I didn't want to fight with her parents, and I didn't want to throw them away, so I took them home.

After that, I didn't touch them. And I tried my best not to look at the box, although it sat on my dresser, staring at me like a haunted doll.

On Friday, I sat at the kitchen counter, shifting my attention between my math textbook and notebook page while my mom stirred boiling spaghetti on the stove.

Stopping mid-stir, she turned to face me. "Hey, Parker. Do you know where the tape measure is? I told your father I'd look for it when I came back inside and forgot."

"Oh." I put my pencil down and pushed a clump of hair away from my forehead. "I think it's in my room, actually. Do you want me to grab it?"

"No, you do your homework, and I'll go find it." She placed the wooden spoon over the top of the saucepan. "Can you just keep an eye on this and make sure it doesn't boil over?"

I stuck my thumb up in response and returned my attention to my homework.

A few minutes into me struggling with calculus, not keeping an eye on the pasta, Chase bounded into the kitchen. "Is dinner ready? Where's Mom?"

I closed the textbook and rubbed my temples. I'd barely made my way through half the problems, but it still felt like too many. "Good question." I remembered leaving the tape measure on my nightstand, so it shouldn't have been taking her this long to find it.

I turned the stove off, strained the pasta, then headed to my room.

Inside, my mom sat on my bed, a black-and-white box in her lap and a stack of paper in her hands. My stomach dropped when I realized what it was. "Mom! What are you doing?"

Jumping a little, she thrust the paper back into the box and slammed the lid on top. "Parker! I didn't see you there." Bringing her hand to her heart, she said, "You scared me."

I walked in and ripped the box away from her. "Why were you looking at this?"

"Well," she said, standing up, "it didn't look like something you owned. So, I was curious." She hesitated for a moment, then looked at me, cocking her head. "Who's Dakota?"

"I don't know. What are you talking about?"

"At the top of the letter—it says, 'Dear Dakota.'"

So, they didn't take those letters out after all. "It's probably her dog or something."

"And these were written by ..."

"Hadley."

"And why do you have the letters that Hadley wrote to her dog?"

I ran my free hand through my hair. "I guess some of them are for me. Or, like, most of them."

"You guess? Have you not read them?"

I put the box back on top of my dresser. "No."

"Seriously? You've had these for two years and haven't read any of them?"

"No. Mom. I've had them for five days. The Garcías gave them to me on Monday."

Her eyes lit up. "Wait. So, Hadley wrote you all these letters, and she was just holding on to them this whole time?"

"I guess."

"And you haven't read them yet?"

"Yes, Mom, I think we've established that I haven't read them yet."

She pointed at me. "Drop the tone. Why haven't you read them?"

"I just don't want to."

"Why?"

I sighed. "You remember how things were with her. There were a lot of things she didn't say." During our relationship,

Hadley went through phases where she'd be moody for no reason. When she was mad at me, I got the silent treatment until she felt better. It was annoying knowing she was mad at me for reasons I didn't know, but part of me was also grateful for it. Would I want to know the negative things she was thinking? I cocked my head toward the dresser. "Those are probably the things."

"I understand." She took a step closer. "But, Parker, you have to read them." Putting her hand on my shoulder, she added, "They might give you the closure you need."

I shrugged her hand off. "Closure? How is reading a bunch of letters Hadley wrote when she was *alive* going to give me closure? If anything, it's just gonna make things worse. She's gone." I clenched my fist, then unclenched it. "I don't really need another reminder of that."

"Oh, Parker. You should at least read the first few. If the Garcías gave these to you, they must be important."

"Or," I said, "maybe they also don't need a reminder that Hadley will never write anything again and wanted someone else to deal with it."

"Baby, I don't think that's why they gave them to you."

"Whatever," I said. "I really don't want to talk about this anymore. Did you find the tape measure?"

"Parker—"

I pushed past her and grabbed it off the nightstand. "Oh, here it is." I handed it to her. "Bye, Mom."

"Parker."

"I'll come down for dinner in a few minutes."

She sighed, putting her hands up in surrender. "Fine."

I closed the door after she exited and pushed my back up against it.

I took a deep breath.

Important.

Closure.

What closure did I need anyway? Everything that had happened between us was in the past. There were no old wounds. There were no unanswered questions. It was in the past. And I was the one who ended it, so if there was any closure to be had, I wasn't the one who needed to have it. And her death didn't change anything. I was at peace before, and I was at peace now. Everything was fine.

But Mrs. García's words came to mind. *She'd want her words to be read.* I never understood doing favors for dead people. But I'd also never had someone so close to me die before. Did I owe it to her?

I looked at the box. I almost had the fake lacy pattern memorized by now. I mean, I saw it every time I closed my eyes, along with the headline of that stupid newspaper and the wetness of Mr. García's eyes and Hadley's face when I passed her in the hall a few weeks ago.

The letters weren't going away—no matter how much I wanted them to. I couldn't pretend I never knew about them. I couldn't go on, living my life in peace, putting this behind me. They were here and they were real, and they were sitting on my dresser, waiting to be read.

She'd want her words to be read.

It was stupid. This was stupid. But before I could get my body to know what my brain did, I grabbed the box, put it on my bed, then sat down next to it. I held my breath as I slid off the lid and took out the first letter.

Tuesday, April 28

Dear Dakota,

Hey buddy, it's been a while, hasn't it? You may be wondering why I'm writing to you. Well, I was talking to my neighbor Mrs. Mortensen today. It was actually my first time ever really talking to her. I was just going for a walk and she called me over while she was weeding her garden. I thought it was kind of weird, but I have a hard time telling people "no," so I went over to her. Turns out, she's actually really nice.

I don't know why I started talking about this with her, but I told her that I felt kind of lonely sometimes. I felt really stupid after saying it, but she seemed to really understand. Her husband died a few years ago and her kids live in another state, so she definitely knows what it's like to feel alone. She told me it helped to write letters to someone, even if you never send them. I guess she writes to her husband sometimes. It sounded really weird, but tonight's been kind of rough, so I thought I'd try it. I immediately thought of you because I remember telling you everything back when you were still alive. You were such a good boy. I miss you.

So ... where do I even begin? I'm in 8th grade now. Daniel's at college and Reagan's a junior in high school. Life is just weird. Time is weird. It just keeps passing and I'm honestly terrified. I'm going to be in high school next year. My heart gets so heavy when I think about it. I'm not ready to grow up.

Sorry, I kind of trailed off there. Dakota, I don't have a lot of friends. I don't think anyone likes me. I feel really invisible at school. I also feel invisible at home. Maybe it's because no one's really been home to see me. Dad's been crazy busy since he took over the HVAC company and doesn't come home until late. And Mom had to pick up a second job to keep up with expenses since Dad's company's been struggling, so I almost never see her. But at least they're not fighting. You probably remember how they used to fight a lot.

My siblings obviously are also never home. But even in the rare moments when everyone is home, I still feel like an afterthought. Whenever Daniel visits, of course he gets all the attention because he left for college three hours away and everybody misses him. And, like, how can you not pay attention to Reagan? She's perfect. This year, she's taking 3 AP classes and she gets all A's. Her cross-country team made it to state and that's all anyone can talk about around here. I know it's wrong to feel this way, but I just feel so bad, so left out.

Mom and Dad try to talk to me when they're here sometimes, but I think they get bored or disappointed or something. I'm not exciting. I'm not in college. I don't play sports. I get good grades, but compared to Reagan, it isn't enough. I don't ever feel like enough. Well, Dakota, thanks for sticking around to read this long and depressing letter. I hope everything is going well for you in Doggy Heaven.

Love,
Hadley

I put the letter back on top of the stack and replaced the lid, my heart threatening to beat out of my chest. I hadn't been this acquainted with Hadley's thoughts since we broke up. And now she was dead.

It was too much.

Chapter

Five

Again, I dreamt of Hadley.

She wore a long white dress, and her hair fell onto her bare shoulders in curls. In the space we stood, there were no walls. The room was composed of shadows. Fog wrapped around her bare feet as she made her way toward me.

"Parker," she said.

I looked at my hands. They were gray.

"Parker, look me in the eyes."

I wanted to, but I couldn't. I could see the foggy, shadowy floor through my gray hands. My skin became increasingly transparent. Was I fading away?

"Parker, look at me."

"I can't." My hands were gone, and I couldn't see my legs at all.

She laughed, but it was a horrible sound—like a screeching animal. "Just look at me."

I did.

She was beaming.

"I'm disappearing, too," she said, her voice returning to

normal. Then, she reached her hand out to me. Just when her fingers were about to touch my forearm, I woke up.

It took me several seconds to register that I was in my own room.

Dim gray light seeped through the blinds, and the time on the alarm clock looked blurry to me, but I could already tell it was too early to be awake. Saturdays during offseason were strictly reserved for sleeping in late.

I rolled over, slamming my pillow on top of my head. I closed my eyes. I quieted my thoughts. I tried to fall back to sleep.

It wasn't going to happen.

Sighing, I moved the pillow back into place under my head, then rolled over and stared at my dresser until that stupid black-and-white box came into focus. I'd heard stories about people who kept Ouija boards in their rooms. After a while, things got freaky, and they'd start having nightmares about dying and demons and crap like that. Not that I believed Hadley's box would be demonic, but it had to be haunted, right?

I'd felt haunted since the funeral, though, so maybe it was just me.

Peeling the sheets off the top half of my body, I sat up. My neck was stiff and my head throbbed. My shirt clung to my chest with sweat.

I couldn't imagine why the Garcías would want me to read Hadley's letters so badly, especially when they weren't willing to do it themselves. It felt like a massive violation of privacy, even if she would never know about it. She was writing to her dead dog about how *lonely* she was. The fact that it was in eighth grade made it worse, considering I didn't even meet her until tenth grade. How much more did I have to read until it became relevant to me? I'd considered skipping the Dakota parts, but, like Hadley, her mom's words haunted me.

She'd want her words to be read.

Did that mean *all* her words needed to be read?

I kicked the rest of the sheets off me until they lay in a pile at the foot of my bed. Then, I hopped out and threw on a jacket and a pair of sweats before creeping out into the hall. My family didn't usually take their mission of sleeping in on the weekends as seriously as I did, but even they were asleep at this time. In the kitchen, I peered into the fridge for a solid two minutes before settling on a granola bar from the pantry.

Granola bar in hand, I reentered my room. There it was, waiting for me like an ugly dog.

I sighed and grabbed the box, setting it down across from me on my desk. Maybe the letters were important. Maybe there was something in there that I needed to read.

I took the lid off and put the letter I read yesterday on the bottom of the stack before taking the next one out.

Thursday, May 21

Dear Dakota,

I know it's been a while since I've written to you. Writing to you makes me feel better, but it also makes me feel sad. It doesn't make sense to me, but Reagan calls it catharsis (I didn't tell her about our letters. We were talking about something else). But, anyway, I want to tell you about what happened.

So in English, we were put into groups to do an assigned project. I got put with three people: Kenzie Bennett, Jackson Devictoria, and Catherine something (I feel bad. I have no idea what her last name is). As we were working together, I got to know Kenzie a little bit better. She's so nice! And not even the fake kind of nice. She's actually just really nice.

It's been weeks since we turned in our project, but today she texted and invited me to go to the movies with her and her friends on Saturday. I've never been invited anywhere before. And I don't want to say anything too soon, but I think I might actually have a friend. I'm so excited right now! I know normal people hang out and go to the movies with classmates all the time, but I don't. And it just means so much to me.

I'll let you know how it goes,
Hadley

Reading this one didn't make me feel as bad as the one I read yesterday, so I pulled out the next one.

Wednesday, September 2
Dear Dakota,

You wouldn't believe the day I had. I honestly feel like I'm walking on air; it was so good. Today was my first day of high school. Kenzie (we're pretty much best friends now!) came to my house last night and we painted our nails, watched a movie, and talked about how we were finally going to be freshmen. My dad only came into my room to shush us once, but even when we were silent, we still couldn't sleep. We were both so excited.

Then, today, we rode the bus there together. It wasn't

until I was there, with students filling the halls, that I realized just how big high school is. And the guys are so tall! I'm sure they could've trampled me and never even noticed.

My teachers are nice. All the students seemed to have their own people, and were so involved in their own things. My locker is super nice. I can't wait to go to my classes. Ugh, I wish I could tell you every little detail, but I have to get started on homework. Yeah ... that's the one thing I don't love about high school.

Anyway, I'll tell you this: I am so excited. I'm going to do things differently than how I did them in middle school. And I'm not going to be afraid. I'll finally get to find myself. I'll get to be somebody. I'm ready for every opportunity that will come my way. I just can't believe it. I'm finally in high school. I'm here. I made it.

Sorry, this letter is completely scattered. I just can't help it. I'm in high school now!

Til next time,
Hadley

It was as if someone had shot me in the chest. Hadley would never get to finish the adventure she'd been so excited to begin. And maybe it was funny, in a way. Hadley loved the idea of high school so much that she would be frozen there, in time, forever. Hadley would never know what it was like to finish high school. She would only know what it was like to start.

The thought made me catch my breath, and suddenly, the room felt so small. It was like the walls were closing in. They threatened to suffocate me.

I couldn't do this anymore. I had to get out of my room.

In the kitchen, I held my breath as I slid my car keys from the key hanger on the wall, adjacent to the back door. I slipped through the door, holding it as it closed so it wouldn't make any noise.

Then, I took a deep breath, letting the crisp October air fill my lungs. It was freaking cold, but I didn't care today. It'd been months since I allowed myself to go for a drive with no destination, so I was going to enjoy it, despite the tugging threat of winter approaching. Nothing compared to the feeling I had when I got to be alone, putting miles on my car and blasting the radio with the windows down.

In the car, I tried to let myself melt into the music even though the tightening in my chest increased with each note. I passed house after house until the houses started growing farther apart. Now, I was no longer in the suburbs but turning onto the highway past my school.

I'd driven to Hadley's house the day I got my driver's license. She was so excited, and although I was trying desperately to act cool, I was, too. With our favorite band, Golden Suns, blasting through the speakers, we drove through the neighborhoods around her house and then ended up on this very highway. Man, she looked gorgeous with the wind running through her hair, the backdrop of city lights and endless black sky filling the window behind her.

"Why do you keep looking at me like that?" she had asked.

My cheeks burned, but I grinned to recover and hoped she didn't notice. I shook my head. "No reason."

She slapped the console, pretending to be angry. At this point, she still had her shy tendencies but was slowly coming out of her shell. I loved it. "No, seriously! Do I have something on my face?" She pulled the visor down and scanned her face in the mirror, the small light invading the calm darkness of the car.

I'd chuckled, pushing the visor back up with my hand. "No, Hadley, there's nothing on your face."

She looked at me, her brown eyes so innocent and wide. "What is it, then?"

"You're just beautiful."

Her shoulders had relaxed. "Oh."

Oh.

I let the memory fade, cursing myself for allowing it to burn in my mind in the first place. The ghost of her memory sat in my passenger seat, but it had no business being there. She'd never sit there again. And while I'd known this already—ever since I broke up with her that day—there was this painful ache in my chest that accompanied the realization that this time, it was permanent. Knowing we'd never ride together again before was okay. It was the simple acknowledgment of life's tendency to pull people apart, but now it was the acknowledgment of death's innate ability to keep them apart. And death was so much stricter. This time, there were no more maybes, what-ifs, or perhapses. This time, Hadley was gone forever.

My fuel gauge indicated I had about a quarter tank of gas left, so I pulled off and parked at one of the pumps at the nearest gas station. After my gas tank was full, I went into the store to buy an energy drink and noticed Kenzie Bennett at the fridge in the back. I pretended not to see her, grabbing my drink when she had her back turned. Funny that she was showing up now after I had spent my morning reading about her.

At the front counter, I handed the curly-haired cashier a ten-dollar bill.

She handed me my change. "Would you like a receipt?"

"Parker?"

I froze at the sound of Kenzie's voice. In all the time Hadley and I had been together, Kenzie and I had never actually talked that much, so it felt weird hearing her say my name now.

I flipped around. "Oh, hey, Kenzie."

"Would you like a receipt?" the cashier repeated, taking on an irritable tone.

"Uh, no, thanks."

While Kenzie paid for her juice, I took my opportunity to slip out the doors. Unfortunately, that was as far as I got. "Hey, Parker. Wait up," Kenzie called.

When I turned and looked her in the eyes, she looked less confident.

"Um, hey," she said, standing up a bit taller. "So, um, I saw you at the funeral."

I nodded. "Yeah, I saw you there, too."

She nodded, too, but slowly. "Well, it was cool that you went."

"Thanks," I said. "It was cool that you went, too."

This clearly was not the answer she was expecting. "Yeah, well, thanks. I guess."

"Well, I'll see you around," I said, forcing a smile.

She didn't smile back. "Yeah."

Chapter

Six

                              Thursday, November 5

Dear Dakota,

    I don't think I know how to function on my own. When I spend time by myself, my chest aches. I feel broken, like I'm worthless and unneeded in this world. This feeling hits me the hardest around midnight when I'm trying to sleep.

    When this happens, I usually open the blinds and stare out my window. It's amazing to watch my quiet town transform into a sea of glowing city lights and cars zipping by. I can't help but wonder why there are cars on the road. I wonder who the drivers are—where they're going. And even more so, I wish I could be with them. I wish I could escape my lonely room and go somewhere where I know I won't be feeling empty the next morning. I want to feel like I matter because, right now, all I feel is emptiness and I'm not sure why.

    Most of the time, I only feel this when I'm alone. When

I'm with my friends, I find myself laughing and loving life. That is until those random moments creep in, where I feel like I'm there, but not really there. It's like I suddenly find the weight of the world on my shoulders and I feel like an imposter, like I don't deserve to be there. It's a new feeling. Maybe I'm just not used to having such solid friends.

See, Kenzie and I started sitting with a bunch of girls Kenzie met from drama. They're super funny and we've already started making plans to go to basketball games and stomps together. I went to some of the football games with Kenzie, back when school started and they were pretty fun. It's nice to feel like you're a part of something. I really like those moments where I can have fun with my friends and not really worry or get lost in my thoughts.

Between everyone's busy schedules, I've been trying to busy myself with plans and hanging out (which included hanging out for my birthday a few days ago, so that was fun). Everyone's got something going on in their lives, except for me, so it's really hard. Maybe I should take Reagan's advice and try to do a club or something. But, honestly, Dakota, the thought of forcing myself to be social with a bunch of people I don't know is the one thing that sounds worse than being alone. As much as I hate being alone.

Well, that's all I have for you tonight,
Hadley

Since seeing Kenzie a week and a half ago, I'd read just one of the letters. Maybe I should have read one on Hadley's birthday as a tribute to her. I mean, it was just the other day. But I couldn't bring myself to do it. And I wondered how many of the letters would just be Hadley telling her dead dog about how sad she'd been when she was younger. Although I didn't know her at the time and had no reason to, part of me felt guilty for it. I think it's normal for kids that age to feel alone and broken. Hell, I didn't know a single fourteen-year-old who didn't feel that way. But still, I wondered. Did she carry the feeling with her this whole time?

After school, I came home to find my mom leaning against the kitchen counter, shuffling through a stack of mail.

"What are you doing home so early?" I asked.

She glanced at me, then put the stack down. "Oh, they offered me a few hours off since I worked overtime last week for closing." She shrugged. "I was out of stuff to do today anyway, so I took it."

"Gotcha."

"Oh," she said, slapping her hand on the counter. "There's some mail for you." She cocked her head in the direction of a glossy postcard sitting on the counter about a foot away. "UNO."

I raised my eyebrows. "UNO."

University of Northern Oregon.

"I'm not gonna say anything, Parker."

"Cool."

"I did want to talk about something else though." She waited until I met her eyes before she asked, "How are you doing?"

"I'm doing fine."

"It's been three weeks," she said—as if I needed a reminder—"since Hadley ..." She trailed off before finishing her sentence.

Since Hadley what, *Mom? Died?* "Yeah?"

"And I'm worried about you. You haven't really been yourself. You've seemed down. And I got a notice from your school the other day. You've had some tardies?"

"Okay, so maybe I slept in a few times," I said. "I've just been tired lately. But I'll set another alarm."

She snorted. "I'm not worried about that. I mean, I am. School is important. But I'm more worried about you. Hadley's death ... of course it would affect you. And I don't want you to feel like you're going through this alone."

"I appreciate that, Mom. But you don't need to worry. This isn't ..." I sighed. "This isn't about Hadley's death. I mean, it's sad she's gone, but she hasn't been in my life for over a year. I have no reason to ..." This time, I was the one to trail off. No reason to *what*? Feel exactly how I was feeling now? How pathetic was that? "I've just been tired. I swear, that's it."

"I have a hard time believing that."

"Well, I don't know what to tell you."

"Have you been reading her letters?"

I felt sobered at the mention of the letters. I think I stood up taller. "I have been, actually."

"Are they helping at all?" Her eyes lit up. I'd be a jerk to disappoint her.

So, I smiled. "Yeah. They've been helping a lot."

She smiled back. "Good." After studying me for a few seconds, she looked down and hit the counter once more. "Well, I won't press anymore, but if there's anything I can do, *please* let me know, okay?"

"Okay," I said. "I will."

She left and I took my turn to lean against the counter. Maybe I lied a little bit. But I couldn't tell her the truth. My mom always got so worked up about everything. If I said even the smallest thing was wrong, she'd never leave me alone. She'd never sleep. She'd never chill. And her constant worry always did more harm than good, so it was better to just not give her anything extra to worry about.

I reached out to the UNO brochure and slid it to myself. It had a picture of their campus with the words *Apply Today!* scrawled in yellow at the top.

I shook my head.

You knew my mom was really worried when she had an opportunity to lecture me about the University of Northern Oregon and chose not to. The University of Northern Oregon was my dream school. And I think, under different circumstances, I would have been thrilled to see that they were sending *me* junk mail. It was, like, tangible proof that they wanted me, that I could get in.

Of course, my plans changed once Mallory and I had started talking about college. Her dream school was Aldrich University, and it was imperative she went there because of the pre-dental program it had. The thought of losing her once college began killed me, so I thought about it. And thought about it. And thought about it. After a while, it started to make sense. Aldrich was closer than UNO and it had a good pre-med program. I wouldn't have to break up with Mallory, and we wouldn't have to try the whole long-distance thing. It was perfect.

Except my parents totally freaked when I told them at dinner a few months ago.

"What about UNO?" my mom had asked. "That's your dream."

"Well," I said. "Aldrich is a really good school, too. It's a better school, actually. And the pre-med program—"

"What's the real reason you don't want to go to the

University of Northern Oregon?" Dad interrupted, his fork making a *clink* sound when he laid it down on the plate.

"I—huh?"

He had taken on his sensible and level-headed dad persona. "Well, Park, you haven't applied to either school yet, and it's logical to apply to multiple anyway." He'd raised his hands. "But you've talked about UNO since you were a kid. You mean to tell us that you just … *changed* your mind? I mean, it happens, but not with you. At least, not with things like this. What's up?"

"Well, Mallory—"

Mom shot Dad a look. "Mallory."

Needless to say, they weren't very happy that I was basing my college plans on my high school girlfriend. Especially since I "have a new girlfriend every six months." That one stung. And it wasn't true. I'd been with Mallory for a year at that point, and it didn't feel like she was going away any time soon. But I ended up appeasing them by promising that, when the time came, I would apply to both schools. And one or two backups.

Now, holding the UNO brochure in my hand, the memory felt like it took place a lifetime ago. This was the first piece of mail I'd gotten from a college since Hadley's funeral. Before then, I'd gotten several. Not from UNO, but there were brochures from Texas Christian University, Northern Arizona, even Aldrich. And each time I got something from *anywhere*, my mom got so excited. I was pretty sure she kept the brochures to put in a scrapbook or something. And I wouldn't tell her, but I got a little excited, too. The thought of moving out and making a life for myself, whether that happened to be at the University of Northern Oregon, Aldrich University, or anywhere, really, was exhilarating.

Now, it was terrifying. I'd been set on Aldrich for so long, but what if it was the wrong decision? All it took was one wrong decision to screw up your entire life—or end it. Now was the time to fill out applications and decide for sure where my future was going to take place, and Aldrich didn't feel right. But UNO didn't feel right either. Nothing felt right. And what if it didn't matter anyway?

I put the brochure down.

I didn't feel at all ready to make this kind of decision. Not when the promise of a future was beginning to feel so flimsy in the first place.

The next day at lunch, our usual table was empty when Gage and I arrived.

"So," I began as Gage pulled out his Black Panther lunchbox. I stopped talking so I could silently laugh to myself. One, because his uncle looked just like Chadwick Boseman, and the idea of carrying a lunchbox with what looked like your uncle's face on it was hilarious. Two, because most high school seniors wouldn't be caught dead sporting a superhero lunchbox in the first place.

Gage, however, didn't have the confidence of most high school seniors. He had more. And his self-assurance and likeability allowed him to get away with basically anything. As his best friend, though, I felt I had a duty to keep him in check.

But, then again, after about two hundred times, maybe it was better to keep my mouth shut.

Gage paused his overly intricate process of taking out the contents of his lunchbox to give me the side-eye. "Yes?"

"Um." I shook my head in an effort to focus on my original thought. "Have you applied to Princeton yet?"

While I'd been talking, he picked up the apple from his lunch and took a bite. With apple juice spilling from his mouth and chunks threatening to fall out, he ever so gracefully responded with a muffled, "Yeah."

"Have you applied to any other schools?" I asked.

He swallowed the apple chunks and shrugged. "Yeah, but I don't really care about those."

"What if you don't get into Princeton?"

He glared at me. "I'm gonna get in."

"Yeah, but how can you be sure?"

"I've made sure my whole life. I've got a 3.98 unweighted GPA, 1600 on the SAT—because you know I've taken it five times—I'm on the varsity lacrosse team, student council, leadership for NHS. I exceed my community service hours almost every month. I've perfected my essays. There's no way I'm not getting in."

This was all true. Gage had worked hard for Princeton his entire life—or at least as long as I'd known him. He stayed true to himself, only doing the things he wanted to do, but he's always made sure to excel in all those things.

The one thing that had originally surprised me, though, was the student council thing. As vocal as he was about his passions, Gage never expressed an interest in student council. But with my dating Mallory came all of Mallory's student council friends, and with Mallory's student council friends came, "Oh! I've always wanted to do StudCo!" from Gage.

Mallory was actually thrilled at the idea of Gage joining. They'd been wanting someone new to run for treasurer, and Gage's campaign slogan *No one sits alone* attracted loners and popular kids alike. It also helped that people naturally gravitated toward him because of his open and friendly personality.

"Fair," I said. "What if you get in—sorry, *when* you get in and *when* you attend, what if you realize it's not for you?"

"Come again?"

"Like, what if it's not everything you thought it would be and you end up stuck?"

He studied me. "We're not talking about me, are we?"

"Well—"

"Hello, boys!" Mallory greeted, walking up to the table with a tray of food. Her long auburn hair was wavy today, with two pigtails at the top. It looked cute and preppy—just like her. Her friends Brittany and Sarah followed close behind.

I stood up to let Mallory kiss me on the cheek. "Hey, babe." Then, I turned my attention back to Gage.

As the girls sat down, he advised, "Just focus on the things you are sure about and you'll find your way. Like lacrosse."

Lacrosse. After everything that had happened lately, lacrosse was the last thing on my mind.

"What are you guys talking about?" Mallory asked, running her fingers along my shoulder the way she knew I loved.

"Oh," Gage said, waving her off. "Just guy stuff."

"Gross," she said. "So, we're all going to the basketball game this Friday?"

I squeezed her hand. "Mm, I don't think so."

"Why not?"

"I just don't feel like it this week," I said, rubbing my neck.

"Oh, come on, Parker," Mallory whined. "It's the first game of the season. You have to come."

"I don't know. I've got a lot of homework, and my mom needs help with this thing," I lied.

"I'm sure she has whatever *thing* it is under control." To Gage, she said, "Come on, Gage. Tell him he needs to come."

I looked to Gage. He'd been helpful so far. "Come on, man. You really should come," he said.

Okay, so that was the end of his helpfulness.

I looked at each individual at the table.

Brittany smiled like she didn't know what was going on. Sarah's smile was more sympathetic. Gage looked smug. And Mallory just waited expectedly.

Nobody offered an escape.

"Fine," I said, putting my hands up in surrender. "Fine, I'll go."

Chapter

Seven

After school on Friday, I went to Mallory's house to do homework while she read her Regency book. That's what it started out as, at least. We soon found ourselves on her couch, her legs wrapped around my waist and arms wrapped around my neck as we kissed. I tangled my hands in her hair, then slowly grazed them down her neck and down her back until—

She backed off and away to the cushion next over. Her hands flew up to fix her hair, straightening the pieces that typically ran along her part. "I'm glad you made time for me today."

I wiped my mouth and tried to hide my frustration at the interruption. "Why do you say it like that?"

"Like what?"

"Like I don't ever make time for you."

"Well," she said, twirling a strand of auburn hair around her finger and examining it, "you haven't really been lately." She looked at me. "You've seemed kind of distant, actually."

"Oh. I didn't realize."

"Don't get me wrong," she said. "I *love* that you're here.

Being alone with you is making my entire week. I just worry a little."

I looked into her eyes. Her midnight-blue eyes were one of the major reasons I fell for her. "I'm sorry. Things have just been really weird lately."

She smiled in a way that would've been reassuring. "Oh, I'm sure. It's senior year. There's a lot of pressure. A lot of decisions to make. It's stressful." She placed her hand on my thigh. "I'm just saying, don't freeze me out. I'm here for you."

"Right. Um, could I ask you a question?"

The fingers that were on my thigh now ran along my temple to my jawbone. Mallory's unabashed expressions of affection always made me melt. This time, I felt a weird mixture of love for her, and unease. "You know Hadley García?"

Her smile dropped. "Yeah?"

"I was just wondering … what did you think of her?"

"What did I think of her?"

"Yeah."

"Well, I didn't know her that well, but she seemed nice. It's awful that she's gone."

"That's it?" This wasn't the reason I brought Hadley up. It was supposed to be a segue into the real thing when I told her about the letters. But her answer was disappointing. There was so much more to Hadley than seeming nice. More to her than being gone.

"Well, yeah," she said. "What else is there to say?"

"I don't know. Something more substantial?"

"More substantial? Isn't it disrespectful to discuss the dead like this?"

"Well, it's not like she can hear us. No one else can hear us right now either."

"Okay," she said, her expression looking hesitant. "Well, to tell you the truth, I'm pretty sure she hated me because of you. As if I was the reason you two broke up or something. I feel like 'She seemed nice' is the most generous thing I could say about her, not knowing her that much. I feel bad that she's gone."

"I don't think she hated you," I mumbled, suddenly feeling guilty. "She wasn't like that."

"Well, that's great." She exhaled. "Can we stop talking about this now? It's making me uncomfortable."

"Can we talk about it later?" I felt stupid asking. Mallory and I didn't usually talk about heavy things, mainly due to the lack of heavy things happening during our time together. But I always knew that if anything ever came up, she'd be the first person I could go to. She was understanding like that.

"Maybe. I don't know." She stood up. "But I have to get to school and start setting up for the game, so I think you should go home. Sorry."

Driving home from Mallory's, I played our conversation in my head. It was probably unfair of me to spring Hadley onto her like I did, but I wanted to talk to somebody other than my mom about the letters. Maybe Mallory wasn't the one to go to. I don't know.

Since I ended up having more time Friday afternoon than I'd anticipated, I opened up a bag of Doritos and pulled out the black-and-white box.

Thursday, June 3

Dear Dakota,

It feels like 9th grade flew by. Sure, it was my first year of high school. It was my first year getting to actually do all the things I've dreamt about, since watching how exciting they seemed in movies (ie. football and basketball games, pep rallies, drooling over older boys ... I still didn't go to any dances, though. The thought of asking someone terrified me, and, of course, I never got asked by anyone.), but it all passed by like a dream-like blur. I've been so insecure the whole year, and I wish I could change that. In fact, I'm going to change that! I hate hating myself and, after doing it for so many years, I feel like it's time to just not anymore, you know? But at the same time, it's hard.

Like, there are these girls. I share a couple of classes with them, as they are honor students, and, well, I take honors classes. But the thing is: they don't make me feel good about myself. I know they look down on me. And it was really confusing to me because these are the nice girls. These two girls are popular, gorgeous, smart, involved, and nice. Or I thought so, at least. I mean, they've never come out and said anything blatantly rude to me, but ever since I got put next to them at the beginning of second semester, I feel like they just hate me for whatever reason. Be it my clothes which aren't as expensive as the ones their doctor parents buy for them, or the way my face looks, or how dumb I guess they think I am in class, I'm just not sure. But whenever we have to talk for group projects, they look at each other like they're speaking in code. It's the simplest, quickest glance, but I can tell they're referring to me. And I can tell it isn't good.

What did I ever do to them?

I just hate feeling like I'm on the outside.

Dakota, I want better self-esteem. Next year, I want

people to look at me and think good things. I want them to admire my confidence. I want to surprise them and make them feel bad for the way they've judged me. I don't want to waste another year hating myself. Because now freshman year is over, and I have nothing to show for it.

I never have anything important to say, but you listen to me anyway.

Thanks,
Hadley

                                   Friday, September 17

Dear Dakota,

My mom made me go to the homecoming parade tonight. Kenzie wasn't even going because she had a church thing, and Monica and Eliza never hang out with me unless Kenzie's there.

So that meant I'd be going alone.

And my mom didn't get how much I couldn't do that. Because I hardly did anything besides read and listen to music all summer, she'd decided I needed to go to this one, particular school function. I guess it was her way of trying to be involved in my life. But so she dropped me off at the front of the building and I walked to the bleachers and waited for the pep rally to start.

Can I just say this? Besides the dance and the football game (and, still, it's debatable), homecoming events are a waste of time for sophomores and juniors. For freshmen, everything is new, so you want to be a part of it. For seniors, it's a way to live through all the high school-y things one last time. But for sophomores and juniors, there really isn't anything new or nostalgic.

My mom didn't care for this explanation, either.

But standing in the bleachers, trying to blend in with the crowd of students next to me, I thought maybe I was wrong. Because, Dakota, tonight I experienced something new and it shook me. Well, I saw something new, I should say. Someone.

Wearing a black hoodie, he stood next to that kid from my government class, Gage. He was lean and had dark curly hair, carrying himself with confidence and humor.

As students flooded the courtyard, the boy continuously became lost and found from my vision. When he looked back at me, I was afraid he'd think I was weird for being at a function like this on my own, but the second time he looked back, he smiled.

He smiled at me.

I looked behind me to see if there was someone else, but there wasn't. Everyone was moving forward like one big wave, all lost in conversation with each other. No one was looking at him. No one, except me. And when I smiled back, his grin became wider.

I can't believe it. It's so stupid, I know. But these things don't happen to me. It's always Kenzie or Eliza or Monica who comes to lunch with some story about a handsome stranger picking them out against a crowd. But, this time, none of them were there. In fact, it felt like nobody who was there was actually there, like it was just me and him. The moment lasted forever, it seemed, until Gage said something and he looked away.

I didn't see him again. The moment was too good and I didn't want him to find out I really was there by myself, so, when the crowd dispersed to participate in the various activity stations set up around the courtyard, I called my mom to let her know it was over.

Now, I can't stop thinking about him. Who is he? Is he kind? Is he funny? If he's friends with Gage, I wouldn't doubt any of those things, but, still, I long to know for myself. I just don't know how I will be able to function until I see that smile again.

Well, I need to go to sleep now.

So much love,
Hadley

I put the letters away. It seemed that this was where I became relevant. Although, I didn't actually remember that night. At least, I didn't remember the Hadley part of it. If anyone asked me when, exactly, our story started, I wouldn't think it was that far back. But Hadley was always good at noticing things other people didn't.

I nearly pulled out another letter until a text lit up my phone screen, revealing the time. Guess I didn't have as much extra time as I thought.

I grabbed my keys and drove to the basketball game. Cars filled the parking lot by the gym. It always amazed me how much school spirit Lincoln had. Inside, the hundreds of voices chatting created a humming sound. After checking my phone, I looked over the sea of people until I met eyes with Gage. He waved me over.

"Where's Mallory?" I asked.

"She's distributing T-shirts," he said. "I managed to get out of it, but she, Brittany, and Ben will be back later."

In the distance, I heard the classic *bum, bum, bum* of the drums—the marching band beginning the fight song. The Lincoln side of the crowd cheered about going and fighting and winning, and then erupted into a fit of screaming and clapping. Gage turned to me. "Dude, can you believe lacrosse starts in just a few months? I'm freaking stoked."

Leave it to Gage to choose the most inconvenient times to begin small talk—especially about a topic that weirdly made knots form in my stomach. "Yeah, it's exciting."

He clapped his hand on my shoulder. "Imagine, Parker. You, me, senior year, varsity. This is gonna be the best season of our lives." Taking his hand away, he said, "You know, I've actually been craving our Saturday morning practices lately. Which is weird because I love sleeping in."

The knots sunk deeper. Senior year. Varsity. Having to be an example to lowerclassmen. The daily commitment. People relying on me. My heart sped up. I knew lacrosse season was approaching, but I didn't think it would come so soon. And never had I imagined that I'd feel the way I did now when it came. It didn't make sense. I loved lacrosse. It was everything to me.

It was where I met Gage—youth lacrosse tryouts. We were both twelve. Back then, he was a skinny kid with an afro, and I was an equally skinny kid with a ridiculous buzzcut. While I wasn't shy, I didn't have any friends who wanted to do lacrosse with me. That meant I was at tryouts alone, standing around awkwardly.

Catching me by surprise, Gage had bounded up to me and stuck out his hand. While puberty, at that point, had my voice in that awkward, squeaky stage, Gage's was still super high. "Hey, I'm Gage. What's your name?"

I'd shaken his hand. What kind of sixth grader shook hands? "I'm Parker."

For the rest of tryouts, Gage and I had been inseparable. Then, after we realized we'd both made the team, we only got closer. Of course, Gage and I had a lot in common, like our sarcastic sense of humor and our disdain for a certain sports team in Seattle, qualifying us to be best friends, but our love for lacrosse was the strongest bond we shared. Doing it each year was never a question.

Until this year.

Senior year.

I couldn't do it. I wanted to, but I didn't have it in me. Scratch that—I didn't want to. I *wanted* to want to, but something felt off. Next week would be a month since Hadley's passing. Ever since her funeral, I struggled to sleep during the weeknights and would sleep all day during some weekends. What if things didn't change by the time lacrosse season started? How could I possibly be the person everybody expected me to be? "I actually don't think I'll be doing lacrosse this year."

The referee's whistle blew and everyone's eyes followed the ball with anxious anticipation, their nervousness expressed through grunts and *oohs*. But Gage didn't engage like he normally would have. Instead, he stared at me, as if we were the only two people in the world, having the only conversation that mattered. "You what?"

"I don't think I'm gonna do lacrosse," I repeated, louder, although I knew it wasn't my volume that he struggled with.

"Why not?"

"I just don't want to."

He looked at me like he was slowly realizing I belonged in a mental institution. "Parker, it's our *senior* year. This isn't the year you just up and decide you don't want to do lacrosse."

"Well …"

"Parker, six years. *Six years* of blood, sweat, tears, late nights, early mornings, working our butts off to make varsity, finally *making* varsity. And you're just gonna throw it all away the last year? The most important year?"

"It's not like it's the last year we'll ever be able to play," I countered.

"Together, it is."

"You don't know that."

"Um, hello? You should give me some of that crack you're smoking because, unless you plan on moving to New Jersey for the next four years, it kind of is."

"You're making a bigger deal out of this than it needs to be."

"Are you kidding me? Is this not a big deal to you? Because last time I checked, lacrosse was everything to us. Does it mean nothing to you anymore?"

"Gage, knock it off. Of course it doesn't mean nothing."

"Then, why don't you want to do it?"

"Because I just don't want to, okay?"

The referee blew his whistle again, and we watched as Player 23 dropped the ball and moved away from the hoop where he'd been standing.

When I returned my attention to Gage, his expression softened. "Parker, is everything okay?" He put his hand on my shoulder. "What's going on? Do you want to talk about it or something?"

I shrugged my shoulder, swinging his hand off. "Nothing's going on. I'm fine. Does there have to be a psychological reason for everything? I just don't want to. I don't want you to badger me. I just want to watch this stupid game that you wanted me to come to. Can we do that?"

"Yeah, of course. Whatever."

I watched the game with my arms crossed in silence. Maybe I should have just told him about the insomnia. Maybe he would have actually listened to me about Hadley and the letters. But maybe, like with Mallory, I'd end up just wasting my breath. He wouldn't get it. Nobody got it.

Within a minute, Mallory and her friends were joining us in the stands. "Wow," Mallory said, "the view is so much better from up here."

"Well," Ben, Mallory's tan-skinned, black-haired, and intimidatingly attractive student council friend, said, "it kind of helps that we're actually watching the game instead of handing out T-shirts behind it."

Mallory jokingly pointed her finger at him as if he was a genius. "You might be onto something there."

Gage turned to them. "You guys ran out of T-shirts already?"

"Yep," Mallory said, with one big nod.

Brittany, with her widened eyes, looked traumatized. "These students are ravenous."

"So, how's it going?" Mallory asked, shuffling closer to me.

"Good," I said dully. "I'm gonna go get some nachos. Does anybody want anything?"

"Um, okay," Mallory said. "Can you get me some cotton candy?"

"Ooh, same," Brittany chimed in, unaffected.

"Yup," I said, already squeezing my way past the row of students. The truth was that I couldn't care less about nachos or their stupid cotton candy. I just needed space.

Passing the concession stand, I made my way out the door and into the frigid November air.

I took a deep breath.

The city lights sparkled along the horizon, around a patch of black lake. I really missed watching the city lights. The activity always brought an air of simplicity, back when life actually felt simple. Now, with each blinking beam, I felt like I was being mocked. It was like they were laughing at me and the barely functioning mess I'd become.

I turned around, jumping when I realized I wasn't alone.

A blonde sat against the wall, hugging her knees against her chest. She met my eyes.

"Kenzie?" I asked.

"Hey, Parker." Her eyes were red.

I motioned to the spot on the ground next to her.

"Go ahead."

Taking my spot against the wall, I asked, "What are you doing out here? It's freezing."

She shrugged. "Had to get away."

"I don't blame you. It's pretty loud in there."

"Yeah."

For a few minutes, we both sat there, silent, watching the horizon.

I cleared my throat. "So, when I saw you a few weeks ago— at the gas station. That was weird. I'm sorry."

She waved me off. "You don't have to apologize. I get it."

Another minute of silence passed between us. I didn't know why talking to Kenzie felt so important at that moment, but it was. Something about two people looking into the valley at the same time felt strangely intimate. There was no way to know what was going on in the other person's mind, but it almost didn't matter because you were still looking at the same thing, sharing the same moment. In this instance, though, I felt like I did know one thing. "So, I bet I can guess why you're out here."

She looked at me curiously. "Go for it."

"You only came to the game tonight because your friends dragged you out of the house. You don't want to be here because you miss Hadley and being here reminds you of all the times you came with her and that reminds you of the fact that you'll never get to come to these things with her again. The thoughts and noise got to be too much, so you decided you're better off sitting out here, alone, in the freezing cold."

"How did you know?"

I shrugged, grabbing the aglet of my shoelace and shoving it backward through one of the holes in the flap. "I guess I can kind of relate."

She wiped her nose. "They don't get it. I know they miss her. They were her friends, too. But I was her *best friend*. I wish I could go out with them and enjoy the last high school things I'll ever be able to go to, but she took such a big piece of me when she left." She dropped her head, her forehead landing in her palm. "It's just not the same, and it's not fair. This is the first basketball game I've ever gone to without her." Her voice broke on "first." Tears slowly, and then quickly, began streaming down her face. She was quick to wipe them away with her jacket sleeve, but it did her no good. They kept coming. "I'm sorry. I'm so sorry."

A lump formed in my throat. "It's fine. Don't worry about it."

She sniffled as if she was beginning to compose herself. Then, she erupted in a fit of tears.

Powerlessness overcame me as I watched it all unfold. I'd never seen anyone get this worked up before, much less Kenzie Bennett. Was I supposed to hug her? Tell her it would be okay? "Kenzie," I said, "are you okay?"

Her words came out as gasps. "I'm. Fine." She buried her head in her arms. "I just. Miss her. So. Much."

I didn't feel close enough to Kenzie to touch her. It was weird. So, I inched closer and let my arm hover over her shoulders a moment before putting it back down in my lap. "I know, Kenzie. I know. It's okay."

She looked at me. Her blue eyes were wet and bloodshot. They made me think of a storm on the ocean. "This is so embarrassing."

With her face only inches from mine, I felt tempted to reach out and brush the stray hairs off her cheeks. Instead, I said, "You don't have to stay here, you know? You can go home if you want. You don't have to stay just to make your friends happy."

She took a shaky breath. "I can't leave. Monica's my ride."

Before I could stop myself, I said, "I can drive you home."

"No, you don't have to." She turned her head away from me.

I leaned my head against the wall. "To tell you the truth, I don't really want to be here either. Driving you home would give me a valid excuse to leave."

"Well, in that case …" She looked at me again. "I'm happy to help any way I can."

I snorted. "I'll be out here if you want to go tell your friends you're leaving."

She wiped her eyes with her fingers and stood up. "I really don't want them to see me like this, but I'll wait if you want to go tell your friends."

I stood up and glanced at the door. They probably wondered why I was taking so long. There had been only a few people waiting in line for concessions when I got there. Mallory and Brittany would miss their cotton candy, but they'd understand if I had to leave for a family emergency. Or something like that. "Nah, they'll be fine."

Chapter

Eight

I had honestly thought the craziest thing I'd be doing Friday night would be going to a basketball game I didn't want to go to. Now, here I was, abandoning my friends to drive Kenzie Bennett, the best friend of my dead ex-girlfriend, home.

Instead of speaking, Kenzie stared out the window like a dog worrying it wouldn't be able to see every single tree we passed.

I cleared my throat. "So, where do you live?"

"City center." She pointed forward. "Just keep following this road."

"Okay."

From my peripherals, I noticed her shift in her seat. "Thanks again for taking me home."

I glanced at her. Her tears must have washed away the small amount of makeup she'd been wearing. "Like I said: don't worry about it."

From there on out, the car remained silent, except for Kenzie quietly feeding me directions. I didn't mind it though.

Talking felt useless, so I kept my eyes forward, listening to the gentle hum of tires gliding over the road.

When I stopped at her house, she thanked me one more time, then ventured to her lit-up porch.

When I got home, I checked my phone, and it looked just like I thought it would: home screen filled with too many notifications, including texts that read: *I changed my mind about the cotton candy. Can I get nachos instead?* and *Hello?* and *Dude, where'd you go?* and *Parker, where are you?* and *Did you leave?* and *Parker???* Also, a few missed calls from Gage and Mallory both.

I copied and pasted, *Sorry, family emergency*, and sent it to both of them.

As heavy as both my eyes and brain felt, I couldn't resist opening the box.

Wednesday, September 29

Dear Parker,

That's what I found out your name was. I was walking to chemistry when Gage passed me.

"Yo, Parker!" he called.

I'd been walking with my eyes to the floor, as I normally do, but looked up in the direction his voice traveled.

You turned around, eyes lighting up at the sound of your name. "Oh, hey man," you replied. "What's up?"

Then you came and did that confusing handshake thing that guys do. I don't know; I don't understand it.

But there it was again: your smile.

You didn't see me, but if I was another girl, I think maybe I would have walked up to you. I would have said hi and asked you your name, pretending I didn't already hear it.

I would have acted confident, as if the possibility of my voice shaking or words coming out tangled didn't scare me. I would have asked you if you remembered me, the girl from the other night who you had picked out against a crowd. Who you had smiled at.

But I'm just me and I didn't do any of those things. Instead, I dropped my eyes back to the floor and finished my walk to chemistry, holding your name in my mind as if it were an heirloom in my hand.

Mark my words, though: I'm going to be that girl someday. I'm going to talk to you.

Until then,
Hadley

I rubbed my eyes and pulled out the next few. Reading her letters felt like reading a book. And I was not used to reading a lot of books in my free time.

Friday, October 8
Dear Parker,

We went to the football game tonight: Kenzie, Eliza, and me. You know, I'm not super sure how I feel about football games. I mean, it's nice to get out of the house and be with friends, while also showing school spirit or whatever, but I always felt like people did more pretending to enjoy them rather than actually enjoying them.

To be honest, I'm not sure why I went. I guess there's just something magical about Fridays. You go through the day, waiting for that final bell to ring. It's like the one saving grace you need. Teachers are more easygoing. Classmates talk to you more, it seems. And then, I don't know, you've got this energy bubbling inside of you. You just don't want it to end, so you say yes when Kenzie begs you to go to the game. Even though a nap calls your name. Even though you know the guys screaming behind you are going to give you a headache. Even though social situations freak you out.

But it wasn't too bad, I guess. I bought some popcorn and braved the cold, wrapping myself up in the blanket Eliza brought to share. Right on cue, I was starting to get a headache from the two freshmen beside me, who were screeching out of boredom. But, when I saw you, it didn't matter anymore. You were standing by Gage and a bunch of other guys I recognized but didn't really know. You wore a blue baseball cap, with your dark curls spilling out, watching the ball on the field like a cat watches a bird. You seemed genuinely invested in the game. So I was wrong. But, still, you weren't entranced by it, smiling and responding whenever someone spoke to you.

I felt my heart threaten to burst out of my chest. And this intense ache in the pit of my stomach. The sight of you would torture me all night. I just had to talk to you; it's all I wanted.

I needed to get away from the crowd so I could breathe fresh air I didn't have to share, so I excused myself, making my way to the outdoor restrooms. When I came out of the women's restroom, you were there, talking to one of the concession vendors nearby.

My heart skipped a beat.

And Parker, if I didn't already before, now I really believe in the magic of Fridays. It's gotta be real because during the time I stood there, frozen and staring at you like a total creep, you turned around and ... smiled ... at me.

"Hey," you said, nodding farewell to the vendor and walking toward me.

My mouth suddenly felt super dry. I couldn't believe it was really happening. "Um. Hey."

"What's your name?" you asked.

"Hadley," I replied.

"That's a pretty name." You smirked. "My name's Parker. It's nice to meet you."

My cheeks flushed at your compliment, immediately shifting my eyes to the floor in fear that you would see. Even without looking at you, I felt your gaze. I mumbled something similar, silently cursing myself for being the most awkward person alive.

You stood there, just a moment longer, before excusing yourself and walking away. "Well, I'll see you around!"

I'll see you around!!!

I know our conversation was brief, Parker, but I want you to know you made my night. This was the first football game where I didn't feel like another misfit lost in the crowd. Tonight, I felt seen. And of all people, it was you who made me feel seen. It feels unreal, but I just want it to happen again. I want to talk to you again.

And I really hope I didn't scare you off with my inability to form words. I just couldn't make myself talk, but I promise, the next time we speak—if there is a next time—I won't seem so scared.

warm regards,
Hadley

The memory made me smile. It was so simple back then. And I really liked talking to Hadley, too. I didn't know it meant so much to her. I just thought she was cute, even though—and especially because—she was so shy. I felt like there was something more to her, and I had to find out what it was.

Monday, October 25

Dear Parker,

Okay, so I'm confused. For some reason, you keep talking to me. I'm fine with it, but this is weird. Like, today at lunch, I was eating with Eliza and you came and just plopped down in the seat across from me.

"Is it okay if I sit here?" you asked. "I don't know where my friends went."

"Yeah," I replied, scared to make eye contact.

You nodded at Eliza and then leaned across the table. "So, Hadley, how are you?"

Eliza was staring at me. I couldn't see it, but I could feel it.

I smiled, gaining the courage this time to look you in the eyes. And, oh, they were pretty eyes. Brown. Just a few shades lighter than mine. "Pretty good. How about yourself?"

"Pretty good," you replied. "It's been a long day, though."

Eliza couldn't believe you were talking to me. I just knew it. I was the shy one. The one who never talked to boys. Especially cute ones. For some reason, this gave me confidence. "Oh, how so?" I asked, propping my elbows on the table.

That's when you began ranting about your math teacher and the ridiculous assignment she'd given you.

Then, just a few hours ago, Eliza called me. "How do you know Parker Everett?" she asked.

I shrugged, although she couldn't see. "I met him at a football game."

"Do you two talk a lot?"

At first, I thought she was interested because she was jealous, but now her voice sounded too accusatory to be just a little envious. It sounded like she knew something I didn't.

"Not really. Just in the halls sometimes."

"Does he always flirt with you like he did today?"

I felt myself blush. "Oh, he wasn't flirting with me."

"Uh, yeah. He was."

I felt so giddy. "You really think so?"

"I didn't tell you that to make you happy."

"Then why'd you tell me?" I felt like she was being really rude.

"I just wanted to know if he does that a lot."

"I guess so."

She sighed. "Do you like him?"

I felt that butterfly feeling in my stomach. Do I like you? The truth is, I kind of do. Being around you makes me happy and I can't stop thinking about you. But I don't like having someone pressure me into admitting my feelings. How was I supposed to admit them to Eliza when I had yet to admit them to myself? Besides, I don't even know you, really. It's a mystery as to why you keep talking to me.

All I know is that I like it.

And not because you're popular, or cool, or attractive, but because maybe, just maybe, I like you.

"I don't know," I finally told her.

"Well don't," was her cold, hard reply.

It made me angry. Like, who is she to tell me who I can and can't like? What I can and can't feel? "Why not?" I asked.

"If you knew him like I know him, then you'd understand."

"Well, how do you know him? Because from what I know about him, he's an amazing person. He's really nice and he likes talking to me. I don't know why that bugs you so much."

"He's just using you," she said.

"What do you mean?"

"He's a player. He's using you to look cool."

I snorted. "Don't you think if he were going to use someone to 'look cool,' he'd choose someone that would actually make him look cool?"

"Hadley, I don't really understand it, either, but I guess that's just what's happening."

Ouch. "You don't think he just likes talking to me?"

She sighed. "Hadley, don't get the wrong idea, okay? You're amazing. You're smart. You're really pretty. Parker's just not the type to see that."

"And how do you know this?" I felt like crying. I also felt stupid for wanting to cry over a boy I had just started talking to.

"Because we went out."

"You what?"

"Yep." She said something along the lines of, "I didn't tell anyone about it because it was during the summer. I met him at my cousin's summer kickoff party last year. I thought he was cute, so I asked for his number. We started texting. I found out he also went to Lincoln. We became a thing. I liked him a lot. But then August came and he told me he wanted to break up. He used this B.S. excuse that having a girlfriend during the school year would ruin his GPA, so his parents made him end it. Then, he had a different girlfriend by September. It really showed me what a jerk he is. He doesn't talk to me anymore."

I didn't know what to say. "I'm really sorry, Eliza."

"It's alright," she replied. "There are better guys anyway."

"I promise I won't go out with him," I told her. "I won't like him anymore."

"You can if you want," she said. "I'm just thinking of you. It's better you find out this way than get your heart broken."

"Thanks, Eliza," I said. "You're a good friend."

"I know," she replied before saying goodbye and hanging up.

Parker, I don't want to believe it. It's hard to believe that someone as nice and funny as you could be so awful. Then again, the idea that someone like you actually enjoys spending time with me is pretty illogical anyway.

I don't really know.

Sincerely,
Hadley.

I remembered Eliza. We'd dated the summer before ninth grade. She had short, dirty-blonde hair that landed just above her shoulders in waves and bangs that grazed her eyebrows. She had large hazel eyes and brown freckles that splattered her face and arms. She was pretty, but not the kind of pretty that you could see and appreciate from across the room. It was the kind of pretty you only noticed up close. It was the kind of pretty that caught you by surprise.

It was the kind of pretty that possessed me to give her my phone number when she was standing so close to me, drink in hand, by the bonfire that night. I wouldn't have taken a second look at her any other day. And to be completely honest, I was never as interested in her as she was in me. I think I was just bored the summer we were together. She always wanted to know where I was and who I was with. She was demanding. Bossy. When I'd realized my relationship with her was preventing me from going out with girls who would give me the space I asked for *and* that I enjoyed talking to, I knew I had to end it.

She clearly didn't take it well, and it was nice to see that she was still trying to sabotage my dating life a year and a half later.

Friday, November 12

Dear Parker,

Tonight's the last football game of the season. It's a home game and so my mom's going to drive me. I know you're going to be there. You don't miss those kinds of things.

And you know what, Parker? I'm tired of this. I'm tired of being afraid all the time. And I don't care what Eliza thinks. I don't even care what you think, so don't get the wrong idea. I'm not doing this to flatter you. I'm not doing this to prove myself to anyone. I'm doing this for me. I'm doing this because I'm tired of living in the shadows. I'm tired of putting my happiness in the hands of others, while I wait for my life to take me to some magical place where I feel content and secure.

It's not going to freaking happen.

So I'm just going to do this one brave thing just this one time and see where it takes me. Maybe I'll be completely humiliated and want to die. Maybe you'll feel the same way and things will actually work out for me for once. Or maybe, despite the outcome, I'll feel proud of myself for taking control of my own life. That's what I want more than anything.

So I'm just going to do it. I'm going to tell you how I feel about you tonight and then I guess we'll go from there.

Here goes nothing,
Hadley

Chapter

Nine

The Wednesday after Thanksgiving break, Gage and I found ourselves alone at the lunch table, waiting for the rest of our friend group to get there. Distracted by the bustle of the holidays, probably, Gage hadn't brought up the topic of lacrosse since the basketball game. And for that, I was grateful. It wasn't a for-sure decision not to do lacrosse, but there was also no increased desire *to* do it. I just didn't want to think about it at all.

"So, I gotta tell you something," he said, opening a plain red lunchbox this time.

I'd just shoved a handful of Doritos into my mouth when he said this, so it was full when I asked, "What's up?"

"I've decided to ask Kenzie Bennett to Winter Formal," he said nonchalantly, pulling out an apple.

I started coughing—Dorito debris spilling out as I reached for the water bottle in my backpack.

"You good, man?" Gage looked me up and down.

I took a big chug of water. "Um, yeah." I coughed once more for good measure. "Kenzie Bennett?"

"Yeah. I mean, I know it's a little weird, all things considered. But I just feel so bad for her. Can you imagine how hard it would be to lose your best friend senior year?"

The image of Kenzie crying the night of the basketball game flashed in my mind. "I can't imagine," I mumbled.

"Right? Like, that's just gotta suck. So, I figured it's the least I could do to make life a little more enjoyable. 'Cause our friend group's pretty fun." With the last sentence, he nudged my shoulder with his elbow.

"Yeah, it'll be fun." I chewed my Doritos slowly now, grabbing only one at a time. "But Winter Formal's not any time soon, though, right?"

He stared at me. "Winter Formal's in, like, two weeks."

"Are you serious?"

He nodded slowly like I was an idiot.

"Crap."

"So, I'm guessing you haven't asked Mallory yet."

"Nope," I said, popping the P at the end of the word.

"Ooh," he said, "boy, you better get on that before she flips."

I scrunched up the empty Dorito bag and shoved it onto my lunch tray. "No kidding."

                                          Saturday, November 13
Dear Parker,

Well, I did it. When Mom dropped me off in front of the school, I met up with Kenzie and we walked to the stadium together.

"Are you sure you still want to do this?" Kenzie asked, just before we made it to the gates.

I nodded. Just when I was finally able to calm the butterflies crashing around in my stomach, she had to bring it up again. "I am. I'm terrified, though."

She smiled wide. "Hadley, you're a legend. I could never do it." A few steps later, she asked, "So what is he like anyway? You haven't told me anything."

I smiled at the thought of you. "Well, he's been kind of quiet lately, but before that, he'd talk to me every time I saw him at school. He's really funny. Attractive. Smart. I just ... I feel happier when he's around. But, I didn't tell you this, but he had a thing with Eliza. They were dating actually."

She raised her eyebrows. "Oh."

"Yeah."

"Well, why did she never say anything about him?"

"She didn't say anything to me until I said I liked him."

Kenzie stroked her chin, taking a moment to think. "Well, then that's the first time she's ever said anything, as far as I know. It can't really mean that much to her." She paused again, this time, starting to speak with more enthusiasm. "I think you should go for it. No matter the outcome, I think it would be good for you. And you've got my support. One hundred percent."

I couldn't help but grin. I felt so lucky—so loved—to have a best friend like her. I was terrified, Parker, but knowing that I did have someone in my life to love me unconditionally gave me the courage I needed. "Thank you."

"You're welcome." We entered through the gate and she stopped again. "Now, you go talk to that boy and I'll save you a seat."

"Okay," I said. "See you in a minute."

"See you." She turned to leave, her ponytail swinging behind her.

And that's when I realized: I was alone.

It felt like my nerves were punching me in the abdomen, and suddenly the big zoo of teenagers that surrounded me was silenced.

I couldn't face you.

What would I say?

I hadn't rehearsed. I was all by myself. I wanted to throw up. I wanted to throw up so bad. Why did I think this was going to be a good idea? Seriously, what was I thinking?

But then I thought about those Friday nights when I went home, locked my door, and lay in bed. Those nights when I'd reflect on the day and feel nothing but disappointment because I didn't raise my hand when I knew the answer. Because I looked down whenever someone I wanted to talk to passed me in the hall. Because I had one life and I was wasting it by being so freaking scared all the time.

I want to be able to connect with people and get to know them without the fear of talking to them getting in the way. You know, Parker, I didn't do it for you. I did it for me because it's important to me and I need to start somewhere.

I might as well start by jumping off the high dive.

I gave myself the sixth pep talk of the day and I was ready. I was totally ready to talk to you.

But then I saw you on the bleachers, with all those guys, and fear flooded over me. Gage must have noticed because he smiled at me.

This gave me courage.

I waved at him. You turned around. When you registered it was me, you smiled and stood up. That made it easier.

"Hey," you said, walking up to me. "Are you looking for somewhere to sit?"

I shook my head. "Um, no," I said, pointing to the other direction. "My friends are saving me a spot actually. I was just ... walking by, I guess."

"Oh." You grinned. Uuuugggggghhhh. "Well, it's nice seeing you."

I smiled, trying to ignore the tsunami swirling inside me. "You too."

"Well, awesome. I think I'm gonna go back to them now." You didn't know what to say, I guess.

With your back to me, I hesitated, then took a deep breath. I was not gonna chicken out. "Wait. Parker."

You turned around. "Yeah?"

"This is weird," I said, "Really, really weird. But I was hoping to talk to you."

"Ah, that's not too weird." You took a step towards me and I truly wanted to die. Every step you took manifested such confidence and it only made me want to shrivel up even more. There was that and the fact that I suddenly felt two feet tall. "What's up?"

Deep breath. Seventh pep talk. Come on, Hadley. You can do this, I told myself. He's just a person. The worst he can say is no. The worst he can do is say he's not interested.

I opened my mouth and, instead of the eloquent confession I'd intended, word vomit spewed out. "Um. Well. I really like talking to you, Parker. And I don't know why you talk to me, but when you do ... I like it. And I'd like to keep talking to you. I'd like to get to know you more because I really like ... you."

I waited for the lightning to strike down and kill me right there. I waited for the laughter. I waited for the humiliation and the anger and the disbelief.

But it didn't come.

When I finally gained the courage to look at your face, I was shocked at what I saw. For the first time since I saw you at the pep rally, you didn't seem confident or completely sure of yourself or smooth.

You were caught off-guard. You were surprised. You probably weren't sure what to say next. Instead of looking collected, you looked how I felt every day. For the first time, I didn't see you as some mythical god who could only truly exist in my thoughts, but I saw you as human and I wasn't afraid.

"You ... do?"

I nodded swiftly, my heart beating fast. "Yeah, I do." I wanted to say something else, but there were no words. Part of me was terrified that if I didn't keep talking, I'd face rejection.

I don't like rejection.

"I don't know what to say." Was this when the rejection came?

I felt my confidence die a little. "That's okay," I said. "I just wanted to get that off my chest. You don't have to say anything."

I turned around and took a deep breath. I'd done it.

"Wait, Hadley," you said, taking your turn to call out.

I turned around.

"I like you, too."
And so that happened.

I'll keep you informed,
Hadley

The letter made me smile and then made me feel sick to my stomach. She thought so highly of me—ever since the beginning. And honestly, I didn't even realize I liked her so much until she'd said she liked me. At the time, I wasn't looking for a fling or a girlfriend or anything. But then, when she walked up to me and looked at me the way she did, something washed over me. After she'd turned around, it became obvious.

Chapter

Ten

The truth was that I didn't want to go to Winter Formal. Not this year.

But I knew it was a big deal to Mallory. Everything that happens senior year is a big deal just because it's the last time you get to do any of it. I used to feel that way about senior year, too. But it was different now. Since Gage brought it up the other day, I started to realize all the hints she'd been throwing my way. Sending me pictures of dresses she liked, talking about winter colors, sharing random details about when she'd be home and not doing student council things.

I'd just have to pretend that I knew what she was doing and that I didn't say anything because I had something planned and not because I was a complete idiot.

I needed supplies so, after school on Friday, I knocked on Chase's door.

"Don't come in," he warned through the door.

But I'm not one to follow directions, especially from my younger brother.

I opened the door. Fortunately, for both of us, he was sitting on his bed, just scrolling through his phone.

"Get out!" he said, thrusting his phone face-down onto the bed.

"Dude, chill. I just wanted to see if you want to come to Wal-Mart with me."

"No. Get out."

I leaned against the doorframe because I knew it bothered him. "Doesn't it suck being stuck at home all the time? I'm literally giving you a chance to leave. I don't get why you're not taking it."

He stood up and bounded toward me. "No offense, Parker, but I would rather be stuck at home than stuck in a car with some narcissist who can't bother to respect my privacy. Ever." He shoved me into the hallway and slammed the door.

"I'm not a narcissist!" I yelled through the new barrier between us.

Whatever.

I sighed.

Things didn't used to be this way with Chase. In fact, there was a time when we were best friends. I'd always been the cruel oldest, and he'd always been the whiny youngest, but when we were kids, these differences didn't matter that much. No fight or temporary favoritism from our parents could make us forget how much fun we had with each other.

There was one summer when we were treasure hunters. And we were serious about it, too. We'd wake up at seven in the morning—because successful archaeologists start early—and go out to the backyard to dig a hole. The hole had gotten to be pretty massive—probably like six feet wide and two feet deep. Of course, I'm sure I remembered it being a lot bigger than it actually was because the world just seemed that much bigger at nine years old. But Chase and I had been really proud of this stupid hole.

After we'd finished digging, we went treasure-hunting around the neighborhood, looking for cool finds in the cracks of the sidewalks and on the front lawns and in the bushes of our oblivious neighbors.

When we'd returned home with our backpack full of rocks and discarded action figures, two angry parents waited for us at the kitchen table.

"What is that in the backyard?" Mom had asked.

My first instinct had been to play dumb. "What do you mean, Mom?"

She'd glared at me. And whenever she gave me that look back then, I always feared laser beams would shoot through her eyes and penetrate my skin. "When I was in the backyard today, I tripped in a hole. It surprised me because I specifically recall telling two little boys that we were not to dig holes in the yard because people could get hurt if they didn't see them. Do you two know why there's a hole in the backyard?"

I glanced at my dad, who had offered no escape. He looked just as mad.

Then, I looked at Chase with his long, ratty hair and big brown eyes. The poor kid would have done anything for me. "I have no idea," I'd lied. "Chase must have done it."

Chase had looked up at me, his sparkling eyes full of shock.

Mom had looked at him, her expression softening only slightly. "Chase, is this true?"

Chase had looked at me again. Why was his older brother, whom he admired so much, lying about their adventure together? Of course, I hadn't thought twice about betraying my younger brother. I didn't want to get in trouble.

I remember Chase staring at the floor, his lip quivering. "Yes, Mommy."

"And Parker didn't help you do it at all?"

Just because I was disloyal, didn't mean he was. "No, Mommy."

"Okay, then," she'd decided. "You don't get dessert tonight. You know you're not supposed to be digging holes. You could get hurt, and I would be really upset with myself if that happened."

"Okay," he'd said before starting to cry.

Part of me had felt guilty that he had to take all the blame for something we both had done. But I'd also felt victorious for getting out of it. Slowly the guilty part took over the victorious part though.

That night after dinner, Mom had gotten out the chocolate ice cream. Chase was clearly upset, but he'd gone straight to his room when Mom ordered him to.

Mom didn't say anything when I'd decided to take my heaping bowl of ice cream and head up the stairs with it. Looking back, I was pretty sure Mom knew exactly what I was doing. She wasn't afraid to be the bad guy when she had to but felt strongly about Chase and me always having each other's backs.

I'd knocked on Chase's door. I could still hear him crying.

"Who is it?" he'd asked between sobs.

"It's Parker."

"What do you want?"

"I want to come in," I'd said.

"I don't care what you do," he replied stiffly.

I'd taken this as my invitation to come in. I'd hid the bowl of ice cream behind my back and shut the door behind me.

He asked, "Parker, why did you lie?"

"Because I didn't want to get in trouble."

"Well, now I am in trouble! And I don't get any ice cream." He had wiped his dripping nose with his pajama sleeve.

I moved my arm to reveal the bowl of melting ice cream I'd been holding. "Do you want to share mine with me?"

He beamed and, just like that, I had been forgiven.

Memories like that felt weird, and I tried to figure out at what point things changed between us. I think it all started around the time I entered high school. By then, I was too old to be regularly hanging out with an elementary school kid. But even after we'd become separated at the hip, Chase upheld his bubbly, unique personality.

He'd always been pretty shy, but that reversed once you got him out of his shell. He loved to make people laugh. He'd also tell ridiculously long-winded stories that never seemed to end linearly from where they'd started. He was obsessed with superheroes and then his obsession turned to anime. We all knew this because he never stopped talking about it. He was annoying but loveable. He was Chase.

But something changed this year. Instead of his annoying, loveable self, he was cold and closed-off.

It was weird, but I supposed that's just what happens with puberty in some kids.

After I finished taping the helium balloons (thirteen of them, spelling *WINTER FORMAL?*) to Mallory's concrete porch, I rang the doorbell and positioned myself in front of them, a bouquet of red roses in hand.

She gaped as soon as she saw me. "Parker, are you serious?"

I grinned. "Mallory Davis, will you go to Winter Formal with me?"

She squealed, running up and wrapping her arms around me. I had to stomp my foot down to prevent myself from falling backward. "Yes! Of course!"

When she pulled back, I moved a hair out of her face and kissed her. "Good."

"In all honesty," she said, "I almost thought you forgot about it."

"Psh," I said, kissing her once on the cheek. "I could never."

✉

On Monday, Mallory's friends Heather and Piper joined us at lunch, in addition to Brittany and Sarah and the other girl whose name I couldn't remember, despite her sitting with us often. Gage, the other guys, and I ate our lunch silently, zoning out into our separate worlds while the girls discussed shoes, makeup, dresses, and other dance-related things.

"Parker, do you have a royal blue tie?" Mallory's voice snapped me back to reality.

"I don't even know what color royal blue is."

She glared at me.

"But I could definitely find one," I quickly added.

"You think that color would look okay?" she asked.

"I don't know."

She sighed, then shot her friends an exasperated look. "Boys."

I was relieved to hear that, thinking I was free to go back to Zone-Out World.

I was wrong.

"Parker." Gage nudged me. "I gotta show you the flyers Coach had me make. I almost forgot." He reached into his backpack and pulled out a white sheet of paper that read, *Bring the Blue! Try Out for LAX on Wednesday, February 21.* "I know it's basic," he said. "But it's just a first draft."

I tensed up. "Looks good, man. Isn't it a little early to be making flyers though?"

"It's never too early to think about trying out for lacrosse," he said. "Speaking of"—I rolled my eyes. Here it came—"have you thought more about doing it this year?"

"Um, no. I haven't."

"Come on, Parker," he said, slamming his hands against the table. "It's *senior year*. You have to do it."

"I don't have to do it."

"But I want you to do it."

I studied him. A gleam in his eyes said he thought he'd won this time. "It's not gonna happen."

"Dude, come—"

I stood up. "I don't want to talk about this anymore."

Chapter

Eleven

Thursday, November 25

Dear Parker,

I keep that night in my mind. Every night before I fall asleep, I play it like a movie, going through each little thing. Your husky voice. The slight chill in the air. That twitch in the corner of your mouth when you smiled after you said it. Those four words.

"I like you, too."

I couldn't be happier.

But I also couldn't be more confused.

You sit with Eliza and me at lunch every day now. She hates it, but I don't really mind. You flirt with me a lot and you text me sometimes, but that's really it. Every moment that I get to see you is cherished, but this just isn't how I imagined my first relationship to be like. I mean, are we in a relationship? That's usually what happens when two people like each other, right? They get into a relationship.

Haha, I just realized I was writing that kind of fast. My hand hurts. Not as much as my head, though.
Ugh.

Well, I wish you were less confusing, but it's fine!
Hadley

                                        Monday, December 6
Dear Parker,
      My head is spinning. Today was the day. After school, you walked me to the bus as you usually do.
      "So, question for you," you said. "If you're sixteen, why don't you ever drive to school?"
      I felt my face flush. "Oh, I hate driving."
      "Really?" You didn't seem to believe me. "Why?"
      "It just scares me. Like, some people don't let you make left turns. You have to watch fifty things at once. Cars are coming up so fast from the other direction that you could collide with them just by turning the steering wheel even a little bit." My heart was beating faster at this point. "And, still the scariest thing about the whole process, somehow, is having my mom in the passenger seat."
      You laughed and were pretty soon laughing so hard that you were doubled over and we had to stop and wait for you to catch your breath. After you gained composure, you said, "I'm sorry. But my mom's the same way. That's why my dad teaches me now." You coughed. "But, um, that's rough. I'm sorry it's scary for you."

"It's fine."

"Have you thought about asking your dad to teach you? Maybe that would make it easier."

"That's even scarier than driving with my mom."

"Okay. Noted. Well, when I get my license, I'll drive you wherever you want."

My stomach twisted. You say things like this a lot. You talk about making plans, but then never do. I kept waiting for you to enlighten me on what we were and it just felt like it never came up. You'd talk about wanting to hang out all the time and then we never would. I couldn't take it anymore. And, being faster than my mind, I guess my mouth couldn't, either.

"Parker, what are we?"

What are we?

What ARE we?

That's the worst way I could have phrased it. I wanted to crawl under a rock, but I worked on making myself stand up tall while I waited for your response, instead.

You scrunched up your face. "What are we?"

"Yeah, like, what is this?"

You thought about your answer. I could tell because you were so careful about saying it. "Well, you're my girlfriend, right? And I'm your boyfriend."

Ah, the butterflies almost knocked me over this time. "Yeah, cool. That's it. That's what this is."

You laughed. "We don't really act like it, though, huh?"

"Yeah, not really."

"We'll fix that." You smiled at me.

So, that's it. Boyfriend. I have a boyfriend. You're my

boyfriend. I have a boyfriend and his name is Parker. My boyfriend, Parker.

Until next time, boyfriend.
Hadley

Hadley was so jittery and overthought everything. At the time, it was cute. I never thought about it as much as she did though. And the thought of being her boyfriend hadn't even occurred to me until she'd asked that day. Just like that time at the football game.

Tuesday, December 14
Dear Parker,
    Today we hung out for the first time outside of school. It's been hard getting together when neither of us can drive, but we made it work this time. I met you at the park next to Lincoln. Bare and green trees mingled with each other, bordering the damp sidewalks. We talked about school and our friends and our excitement for the holidays coming up. Then, the conversation got deeper. We talked about your family and my fears and the value of a moment.
    As we walked between the trees in the park, the distance between us gradually shrunk. You reached for my hand and I grabbed your fingers the only way I knew how.
    You laughed. "Have you held hands with a guy before?"
    I shook my head. "No ... this is my first time."
    You let go of my hand. "You do it like this." Then, you interlocked your fingers with mine. It was warm and sent electricity through my stomach.

For several minutes, we walked in silence. I couldn't think of anything to say, focusing on the way my hand felt in yours. Thinking of all those days I felt worthless, like no one would ever love me like this. I know it's far too soon to use a word like "love," and I can't say I love you. But I loved this. I loved holding your hand and feeling content with where I was and who I was with—not feeling invisible, not feeling unwanted. To me, it was love.

Love,
Hadley

                                        Friday, January 7
Dear Parker,

Ever since we got together, I've felt like waking up in a dream every day. I saw a quote the other day about falling in love. And I never thought I'd be able to relate to such a happy quote.

But, turns out, when some doors open, other doors close. Eliza started eating with her friends from band. I'm pretty sure she hates me. I think she hates you, too. But I can't tell you that. And you're probably part of the reason she hates me. But I definitely can't tell you that. I thought losing her would be hard, but I haven't really noticed. We were never really that close anyway. Also, we started eating with your friends and I've been loving that so much.

Honestly, I was terrified the first time we went to join their table. For the first few days being back from break, it had just been you and me at the old table (I always expected

Eliza to join us, but it didn't take too long to realize that wasn't going to happen anymore), so when you suggested it, I definitely wasn't prepared. I walked slightly behind you as you led the way there, grasping my hand with your fingers.

Boys have always scared me. Groups of boys are worse. But groups of boys who do sports? Kill me now.

When we got to the table, they all looked at us. It felt like a scene in a movie where everything goes in slow motion. Stopping mid-chew, they looked at me, assessed me. My mind raced. I wanted them to like me because they were your friends, but I've never been good at impressing people. My biggest fear wasn't that they wouldn't like me—I'm used to that—but that they wouldn't approve of me for you. To them, I wasn't Hadley as much as I was Parker's new girlfriend. If they didn't like me, I felt it could ruin everything.

"Hey guys," you said, taking a seat at the end. "We're sitting by you today."

One of the boys with dirty blond hair nodded toward me. "Is this the girl?"

"Yeah, this is Hadley," you said.

Then, Gage said, "Hadley's super awesome. You guys are gonna love her." He shot me a big smile and my apprehension melted away.

And, just like that, I was in. In with them. In with you.

Until next time,
Hadley

I smiled at the memory of Hadley meeting my friends. She

was one of the only girls I brought back to sit with them. It always felt a little weird, though, because she didn't talk to them very much. I guess she never got over the groups-of-boys-who-do-sports thing. But even so, it was nice. Nice having her there, nice getting to hang out with the guys during the school day.

Tuesday, January 11

Dear Parker,

I sang in the shower today.

I didn't realize I was doing it until I walked out of the bathroom and met my father, who smiled at me, in the hall.

"That was a lovely tune," he said. "A song on the radio, Hadley?"

"Oh. I don't know," I replied, feeling my cheeks flush.

He laughed, leaning his head back like he does. "Well, you've got a beautiful voice. I should walk by the bathroom door more often."

I laughed at the ridiculousness of it all. "Thanks, Dad."

He nodded once, continuing his route down the hall.

I just kind of stood in place, holding my crumpled, damp towel in my arms. The song that had been playing in my head was the same one I heard on the radio the other day.

I liked it because it reminded me of you.

To the boy who makes me sing in the shower,

Hadley

The next letter I pulled out was addressed to Kenzie. She was the first recipient I found who wasn't Dakota or me. My eyes began scanning the top of the letter until Mrs. García's words ran through my mind—the ones about respecting privacy. Did that apply to me, though? Maybe she just meant that they, as parents, should respect their daughter's privacy? And it wasn't like I wasn't totally invading *Hadley's* privacy, either. And *also*, I was curious.

I paused for a second longer before sighing. If my privacy mattered to the Garcías, then I should probably care about Kenzie's. I moved it to somewhere in the middle of the stack before I got tempted again to keep reading.

Saturday, January 22

Dear Parker,

To celebrate the fact that I finally got my license, I drove to your house! And I hated every minute of it. Even with the maps app, I got so lost. I'd be lying if I said I didn't pull over in a random neighborhood and cry out of frustration.

After I was able to compose myself and make it so my voice would work without shaking, I called you. From there, you directed me to your place over the phone. You're really good with directions.

By the time I knocked on your door, my legs were shaking and I felt like an absolute mess. What's worse is that your mom was the one who opened the door.

She smiled after looking me over. "You must be Hadley!"

My mouth felt like it weighed a hundred pounds, but I tried my best to bend it into a smile. "Yeah."

She looked at me a second longer. Then, flung the door open. "Oh, I'm sorry. Please! Come in. Parker was just plugging his phone in to charge. He should be down soon."

"Hey!" you said, stumbling into the entryway.

Your mom nodded. "And there he is."

"We're gonna head up to my room," you told her.

"That's fine," she said. "Just make sure you keep the door open."

"Will do!" To me, you said, "Let's go, Hadley."

As you led me up the stairs, I couldn't help but notice the way the inside of the house looked. My mom was super into modern, clean decor and it didn't look half as chaotic as yours. Chaotic in a fun way, of course. All your walls were white, but there were splashes of color in random places, like the reddish-brown hardwood floors, yellow curtains, and blue furniture. Pictures of you and your brother were hung up all over and the living room and kitchen weren't super messy, but not super clean, either. My mom always made sure that the house was spotless, especially if she knew we were having people over. After being in your house for just five minutes, she'd complain that the colors were giving her a headache and start rearranging the assorted pillows on your couch.

I thought it was perfect, though. It felt like the perfect place to make a second home.

Your room, unlike the rest of the house, definitely looked like a boy's bedroom. You had some band posters hung up and two lacrosse sticks making an X just above your bed. Across from the bed was a brown desk with a laptop and next to that was a black dresser, with a flatscreen TV above it. Like the downstairs, it wasn't clean but it wasn't too messy, either.

You plopped onto the right corner of your bed.

Like an idiot, I just stood there by the door until you patted the spot next to you.

"You want me to sit on your bed?" I asked.

You cocked your head, smiling. "Yeah?"

"Okay," I squeaked, awkwardly making my way over. Ugh, Parker, I know it was weird, but this was my first time going to a boy's house ever. And I didn't think during my first visit, they'd invite me into their room and ask me to sit with them on their bed. And I didn't expect the boy to be you, okay? It was just weird.

Nothing really weird happened, though. At least, at first. We just talked. Somehow we got onto the topic of our futures and you asked me what I wanted to do with my life.

"Be a writer," I replied almost instantly.

All of a sudden, I realized just how close you were to me now, with your thigh pushing into mine. "Really? Why?"

I felt my face heat up. Part of me worried you'd tell me it was a silly dream, like my parents often did. "I love to write," I said. "I love the idea that someone's thoughts on paper can actually change people. I love that it can change the world."

"And you want to change the world?"

The question caught me off-guard. Of course I do. "Well, who doesn't?"

"A lot of people," you said, making space between us. I silently cursed myself for asking. "There are so many people who just don't care."

I laughed. "I don't think I'm wired to not care."

You leaned in again. "I really like that about you."

I turned my head to look at you, my face mere inches from yours. "Really?"

You leaned in closer, the corners of your mouth tipping up. "Yeah."

Everything that happened from that point on was in slow motion. Your eyes flickered from my eyes to my lips to my eyes again. Then, you moved closer until they were out of focus. Your top lip touched my bottom one and I became hyper aware of my mouth. I remembered the first time we held hands and how you'd asked me if it was my first time because I was doing it wrong. I was afraid you'd say something about this, but you didn't. Instead, you parted your lips while I kept mine locked. Then, I caught onto your movements, opened my mouth a little, and followed your lead. Warmth flowed throughout my body and it almost felt like electricity surged where we touched.

You pulled away and looked at me. Then, you kissed me once more on the lips and then on the forehead. "So what kinds of things do you like to write?"

I swear, my head was full of those squiggly lines from the cartoons. "Um, poetry. Mostly. Short stories, sometimes." I didn't tell you about these letters. Of course, that would be weird. But that's where I practice most of my writing.

You smirked. "That's cute."

"What do you want to be?" It felt weird, continuing our conversation. All I could think about was your lips on mine. I secretly wished we could go back to that, but you were so cool. You were so interested in me.

"A doctor," you said, eyes lighting up. "Like my dad. I'm gonna go to the University of Northern Oregon for my bachelor's and then to medical school."

"It sounds like you've got it all figured out," I said.

"Yeah, I've been thinking about it since I was a kid."

I couldn't help but smile at that.

Before I left, we saw your mom in the kitchen again. She stood by the doorway and asked me questions about what I like to do, how school's going, and what my family is like. I don't know if you know this, but you have her eyes and nose. It's really cute, actually. And, the fact that she gave birth to my favorite person in the world aside, I really like her. She's so warm and funny and I felt like she really cared about me, even though we'd just met.

"So has Parker met your parents yet?" she asked.

You stood on the other side of the kitchen, scrubbing the skin of a red apple on your shirt. "I haven't, actually," you said.

"Oh, well that will be fun when you do," your mom said.

Right. So meeting my parents. Because that's something you do when you're in a relationship with someone. I mean, I got to meet yours—at least one of them.

I guess I should probably start by telling my parents I'm in a relationship.

Hadley

I put the letters away when I realized what time it was. I needed to start getting ready for the day.

I was in deep now. Reading Hadley's letters had become the secret I kept. It was funny because each one she wrote and addressed to me was a secret of her own—a secret I was never actually supposed to know.

It started to get lonely—being the only person, besides my mom and Hadley's parents, who knew about these letters. The burden of being the only one who actually knew what they said was starting to feel a little heavy.

I wasn't used to keeping things from Gage or Mallory, but Gage wouldn't understand, and Mallory didn't want to understand. Everyone expected me to be over what happened by now. But how was I supposed to do that when these personal testaments—that Hadley once was a living, breathing person on this earth—still belonged to me?

There was one person who could possibly understand. She was going on a date with my best friend tonight.

"So, have you decided where we're going to eat?" I asked Gage over speaker phone, squirting toothpaste onto my toothbrush. Mallory had been grilling me about it all week, worried that we'd miss out if we didn't make reservations soon. I told her it was a surprise and that Gage and I had it under control. Here it was, Saturday morning, and we didn't have it under control in the slightest. But that's part of the fun.

"I'm thinking Italian."

I brought the toothbrush to my mouth and began brushing furiously, not bothering to stop when I said, "Sweet. Sounds good to me."

"Are you brushing your teeth?"

"Yeah."

"Well, stop. You know I hate when you do that on the phone."

"Can't," I said before spitting foam into the sink. "I've got a busy day today. Don't have a second to waste."

"Okay, well, whatever. You finish brushing your nasty teeth, and I'll see you later tonight."

"Yes, sir."

The hours before a school dance were always chaotic, and I made it worse for myself by reading the letters when I first woke up. But it was fine. I'd just have to double my speed now.

I rinsed my toothbrush, made a protein shake, finished getting ready, did chores, ran errands for my mom, cleaned the car, picked up the corsage … et cetera, et cetera. I got home with just enough time to change into a tux and fix up my hair. I decided to slick my curly hair back for the occasion. I knew Mallory thought it was sexy.

After that, I drove to Gage's house to pick him up first, since Mallory made it clear she'd need extra time to get ready.

Gage didn't live super far from me in his redbrick house with the perfect lawn. Over the years, it had become a second home to me, and I always felt like breathing a sigh of relief when I drove up to it. After I'd been waiting in front for a few minutes, Gage walked out in a black evening suit and light blue tie.

I rolled my window down and whistled. "Damn. Lookin' hot, man. Can you be my date, instead?"

He grinned, sticking his hands on his hips and saying, "Honey, I'm out of your league." He climbed into the backseat and shut the door. "Okay, so I looked up Kenzie's address this morning, and I'm pretty sure I've got the directions memorized. Make a right at the stop sign."

"I know," I said without thinking.

"You know?" From the rearview mirror, he raised an eyebrow. "Oh, duh. Hadley."

I nodded. Yes, Hadley. Kind of.

Kenzie's house looked different during the day—more like where you'd find your typical suburban family. The blue house had a white door, with trees blocking the two shuttered windows a little bit. A few minutes after Gage disappeared into the house, he came out walking side by side with Kenzie Bennett.

My jaw dropped.

The Kenzie I'd watched walk into that house a month ago, with slumped shoulders and tear-stained cheeks, was not the same Kenzie who walked out. No, this one was radiant. Gorgeous. Her silky blonde hair curled into some sort of updo on the crown of her head, and she wore a feathery blue dress—similar to what I'd imagine Cinderella wearing to prom. She was smiling as she talked to Gage and walked with her head held high. As she got closer to the car, I noticed her sparkly blue eyeshadow and charcoal eyelashes.

I looked down when I realized they'd be able to see my gawking as close as they were now. Gage opened the door and Kenzie slid in, filling the back with her skirt.

"Um, hi, Kenzie." What was I doing?

"Hey, Parker," she said softly.

Gage gave me a look through the rearview mirror. It was like, *I hope you don't make this weird for me.*

As I backed out of the driveway and drove to Mallory's, I restrained myself from staring at Kenzie through the rearview mirror. It was more difficult than I'd be willing to admit. Why couldn't I just act normal?

When I rang Mallory's doorbell, her mom answered. "Parker!" She gasped, her hand flying to her chest. "Look at you! You look so handsome. Come in, come in."

As usual, the inside of the house was clean, with low light falling on the gray walls and brown furniture.

"Jer," she called in the direction of Mallory's dad, who sat on his loveseat in the living room, eyes glued to a tablet. "Look at Parker. Doesn't he look handsome?"

He looked me up and down. "You clean up good, son."

"Thanks." I stood awkwardly and, as always, worried the Davises would call me out on it. Like Mallory, they always knew what to say and how to act. I was pretty sure they could read minds, too. And as well as we got along, I worried they secretly thought I wasn't good enough for their daughter. She was the most perfect girl I'd ever been with. How could anyone be good enough for her? "Um, where's Mallory?"

"Upstairs getting ready. You know how she is. Everything's gotta be perfect." She motioned to the couch beside Mallory's dad. "You can take a seat though."

I thanked her and took my seat near Jerry, who went back to staring at his tablet. Mallory's mom, Susan, ventured into the kitchen, leaving me in silence. It wasn't for a terribly long time, though, because Mallory emerged from the top of the stairs a few minutes later. She wore a sparkling *royal blue* dress that showed off her shoulders, hugged her curves, and stopped just above her ankles. Her hair fell down in tight ringlets, and she beamed when she saw me.

"You look gorgeous," I said, standing up. Her dad didn't say anything, but I knew he was thinking the same thing by the way he smiled at her.

"Thank you." She made her way over to me and touched my chest. "So do you."

"Wait! I need pictures before you two leave," Susan called, running in from the kitchen with her phone.

Mallory widened her eyes at me, like she was annoyed at the suggestion, but still smiled with her teeth. She turned to her mom. "Okay, but we need to be fast. We've got dinner reservations."

She shot me a look to confirm, and I nodded.

Jerry laughed, standing up. "Don't doubt your mother. You know she's the queen of speed." He looked at his wife and winked. "Just make sure you don't take 'em so fast that they come out blurry."

After Susan made us pose in the living room for almost ten minutes, Mallory said, "Okay, okay. We gotta go now." She kissed her mom on the cheek and hugged her dad. "I'll see you guys later."

"Now, wait a minute," Jerry said as Mallory grabbed her gray coat off the rack by the door. "What's your curfew?"

She paused and smiled, knowing she'd pass the test. "Midnight."

"Good." He looked at me. "And what time will she be home?"

"Eleven-thirty," I replied.

He chuckled. "Very good. You kids have fun."

"Thanks," I said, opening the door for Mallory.

When we were outside, Mallory asked, "Okay, so do you actually have a restaurant you're taking us to, or did you just tell me it's a surprise because you and Gage don't know?"

I touched my chest. "My girlfriend has no faith in me. Of course we have a restaurant. How does Italian Tonight sound?"

"Italian Tonight? That's perfect!" She narrowed her eyes, dropping the smile. "How long ago did you make this little decision of yours?"

"Three hours ago." She opened her mouth, but before she could freak out, I said, "But I've made reservations. They had one spot left."

She clamped her mouth shut before opening it again. "Okay, Parker. I won't say anything. But I'm glad you were able to get a spot."

I rolled my eyes, then opened her door for her. When she saw Gage and Kenzie in the back, she said, "Oh no. I didn't know you two were back there. I hope we didn't keep you waiting too long."

I slid into the driver's side. "Oh, Mallory, it was an eternity. I almost panicked because I forgot to crack the window open for Gage to breathe."

I looked back and noticed Kenzie smiling to herself while Gage shook his head. "Don't listen to him, Mallory. We weren't waiting for too long at all. You look lovely, by the way."

"Thank you, Gage. You look really nice, too." She turned her gaze to Kenzie and smiled but didn't say anything.

When we walked into the restaurant, just about every table was filled with families, couples, and kids from school. I silently thanked the party that canceled, knowing we'd be kicked to the streets had we tried to come in without a reservation.

The young cashier smiled at us. "Hello. Welcome to Italian Tonight. Do you have a reservation?"

"Yes." I leaned against the desk. "Parker Everett."

She skimmed the record book on the desk with her lips pursed. "Ah, yes. Parker Everett. I see you right here." She picked up four menus. "Will you all please follow me?"

Together, we followed her through the maze of tables, the sounds of clinking silverware and soft orchestra music wafting through the air. She set the menus in their places next to the silverware napkins as we slid into our respective sides of the booth.

"My name's Rhonda. I'll be your server tonight. Can I get you anything to drink?"

I was the only one who asked for something other than water.

She scribbled into her memo pad. "Excellent. I'll be right back with those."

The way we were positioned had Mallory sitting beside me with Kenzie directly in front of me. It made staring at her even more impossible to avoid. Still, I tried my best. Whenever Gage or Mallory spoke, I stared at them like my life depended on it. When Kenzie spoke, I looked down at my plate.

When we were finishing our food, Gage made some joke, and Kenzie threw her head back laughing. Her light blue eyes sparkled, and her freckles jumped out against her flushed skin. She stopped laughing when we locked eyes.

She looked down, and the heat of Mallory's gaze fell upon me.

Gage, the one person I wasn't afraid of right now, didn't notice. "So, Kenzie," he said, "how long have you been playing soccer?"

"Just about ten years." She grinned. "I love it."

Gage leaned back. "Ten years? That's wild!" The way he talked to other people was always interesting to watch. Especially now, in his formal attire, he looked like a businessman, carefully gauging the people he spoke to and saying exactly what he needed to make himself seem competent but friendly.

"Yeah," she said. "And you play lacrosse, don't you? How long have you been doing that?"

"Not as long as you've been playing soccer," he said, "but since I was twelve."

"That's still really cool."

He nodded in my direction. "That's how me and this one met."

At Gage's cue, Kenzie looked in my direction, and we held eye contact for a second before she turned her head and I looked down.

"Cool," she muttered.

There was a moment of silence before Gage looked at his phone and cleared his throat. "Well, we can officially be fashionably late, now. You guys want to get going?"

"Yeah," Mallory said, her flat voice filling me with anxiety. "Let's do that."

Besides the bass from the radio, the car ride to school was completely silent.

When we got to the school, Gage hopped out and opened the door for Kenzie. As they made their way in, I tried to follow them, but Mallory grabbed my arm.

"What?" I asked.

"I need to talk to you," she said, pulling me around the building. "Alone."

When we were out of earshot of Kenzie and Gage, I asked, "Is everything okay?"

She looked at me as if the answer was obvious. "No. You've been staring at Gage's date all night."

"No, I haven't."

"Okay, so you're lying to me now?"

I shifted my feet. "No. I mean." I sighed. "Well, she was sitting right across from me at dinner. I would have had to force myself not to look at her. Which would have been weird." As epically as I'd failed at it, I did try and force myself not to look at Kenzie. And it was weird.

She huffed. I had a point. "So, then it's not going to happen the rest of the night?"

I reached for her hands. She kept them away from me at first but eventually allowed me to hold them. "Of course it isn't. Mallory, you're the only girl I want to look at."

She met my eyes. Hers sparkled with hurt. After a moment, the hurt faded. "Okay, I believe you. I'm sorry."

"Don't worry about it," I said, trying not to show the guilt I felt. "Let's go in, shall we?" I offered my arm out to her.

She linked her arm with mine. "Okay."

As we walked through the doors, Mallory said, "Wow. They did a good job."

She wasn't kidding. Placed around the commons area were bare trees with patches of cotton beneath them to look like snow. White Christmas lights and snowflakes wrapped around the stairs and covered the DJ's stereo system and tables. White curtains hung over the window like they wanted you to forget that you were inside a high school.

After the girl at the door ripped our tickets, we found Gage and Kenzie, who were already dancing to the booming music. From that point forward, there was no more drama with Mallory. We just had fun as our bodies melted into the music. I watched as Kenzie fully emerged from her shell, swinging her arms and jumping as she danced. I let myself notice this, then returned my attention to my girlfriend, where it belonged.

That was until "Party In The U.S.A." by Miley Cyrus came on.

"Dang," I said to the group. "This is a classic."

Whiteness replaced the jubilance on Kenzie's face. She pointed behind her, at nothing in particular. "I'm gonna ..."

Without finishing her sentence, she turned around, almost running out the door.

"What's her problem?" Mallory asked.

I shrugged. But I had an idea.

Gage pointed toward her, then looked at us. "I should probably check on her, right?"

"That would be the gentlemanly thing to do," Mallory replied.

"Right," he said. "Okay, I'll be right back."

Mallory gave me a quizzical look, to which I just shrugged again.

Gage returned a minute later, while the song was still playing. "She said she wants to be alone."

Mallory snorted. "I don't blame her. This song makes me want to be alone, too—tearing my eardrums out." She looked around. "I wonder who chose this playlist."

By the time the song was over, I was the only one from our group on the dance floor.

"Where'd Gage and Mallory go?" Kenzie asked, returning out of nowhere.

"Oh, um, Gage went to get some water, and Mallory went to talk to some of her friends."

"Oh. Okay."

A few moments of uncomfortable silence passed between us before I got the nerve to ask, "Are you …"

"Kenzie!" Gage said, returning with two plastic cups. "I thought you'd be back soon, so I got you some water."

She smiled, taking one of the cups. "Oh, thanks, Gage. That was thoughtful of you."

He looked at me. "Where's Mallory?"

"She saw Ben and them and wanted to say 'Hi.'"

Eventually, Mallory returned, and the four of us resumed dancing and acting like normal. But it didn't feel normal. For a different reason now, trying not to watch Kenzie was harder than ever.

After the dance ended, I dropped Kenzie off, then Gage, then ended up parked in front of Mallory's house, kissing her goodnight.

I pulled out my phone and checked the time. *11:29 p.m.*

"Your dad's gonna be so proud of me," I said.

"My dad's already proud of you."

I shook my head. "Nah, he knows you're too good for me."

She didn't deny it. "Ah, just wait 'til we both get into Aldrich. He'll be beaming."

Aldrich struck me. Another reminder. It was coming up. I kissed her again. "Thanks for such a wonderful night, Mallory."

She smiled. "I love you, Parker Everett."

"I love you, too," I said automatically. "Mallory Davis."

I drove home, guided by the sparkling city lights poking through the trees on the horizon. Mallory and Gage seemed so happy. I wanted to feel that, too. I wanted to feel young and alive while relishing in these last moments I'd have with them in high school. But tonight, all I felt was emptiness. And I didn't know why.

When I returned home, all the lights were off. Everyone was probably asleep, except for Chase, who I knew was hiding away in his room, messing around on his laptop.

I unbuttoned the top buttons of my shirt, then loosened my tie and tossed it onto the couch. After trudging to the fridge, I poured myself a glass of milk and sat on a barstool at the counter. Any attempt to fall asleep tonight would be in vain. I took a sip of the cold, creamy liquid and sighed. Something inside me itched to read the next letter, but I knew it would only magnify that empty feeling. Why did I have to feel this way? What was missing? Was it Hadley?

I didn't want to be with her again. But I wanted her to be here. She should have been here. And when I read her letters, it was almost like she was. And it was like she was happy—nothing like the girl she became before I left her. Maybe that's what I worried about—meeting that girl again through the letters. I couldn't do it. But I couldn't not do it. Hadley's story had to be told. Her words had to be read. But I couldn't keep doing it alone. That's the one thing I knew for sure.

Abandoning my freshly poured glass of milk, I rushed to my room and exchanged my jacket, shirt, and slacks for a lacrosse hoodie and black sweats.

I grabbed my keys, started the car, and drove off without even stopping to think about what I was doing. Forget that it was past midnight. Forget that this would likely ruin my relationship with Mallory if she found out. I didn't care. At least, not at that moment. I just drove and drove and drove until I found myself parked on the side of the road in front of Kenzie Bennett's house.

Chapter

Twelve

I stepped out of the car and made my way to Kenzie's front porch. This was stupid. This was so stupid. There was no valid reason for me to pull up to her house in the middle of the night.

But I had to talk to her.

And there was no other way to contact her—not unless I wanted to ask Gage for her number. Would that be more suspicious than pulling up to her house in the middle of the night? Even just trying to find her online, I knew, would give me enough time to realize how much I should just leave this alone.

Now, I stood in front of her door, fist just inches away from making contact.

I took a deep breath. *I can't do this.*

I turned around to leave.

But it was too late. A dog barked from the other side of the door.

Her parents would probably call the cops if they caught

me standing outside. How was I supposed to explain that one? I looked around, figuring my best bet would be to just walk away. Maybe I could get back to my car before anybody saw me.

Then, before I had a chance to step off the porch, the door opened. "Parker?"

I flipped around. Kenzie's dark makeup was still intact, but she wore blue pajamas with rubber ducks all over them and her hair was loose, falling down in uneven kinks and curls.

I scratched my head. "Hey, Kenzie. What's up?"

"What's up?" She cocked her head. "What's up is that it's after midnight and you're at my house, making my dogs bark while my family is sleeping." She gestured toward me. "What's up with you?"

"Not much," I said, kicking a pebble with my shoe. "In fact, I was just leaving. So, I'll see you at school." I turned around.

"Parker, wait."

I turned back around to face her.

"What are you doing here?" she asked.

"Well, I … I got home and I just … I felt … I needed to see you. Talk to you, I guess." I ran my hand through my hair. "It's really stupid."

"I don't understand." She stared at me as if she was trying to decipher a puzzle.

"I have these letters."

"Letters?"

"Yeah, letters. From Hadley."

If I didn't have her full attention before, I definitely did now. Her mouth hung open as if she wanted to say something but couldn't find the right words. She glanced behind her. The dogs weren't barking anymore, but one was sniffing under the door and growling. She looked back at me, then pointed toward the road. "Can we talk in your car?"

I glanced at my car. "Yeah. Of course."

Once we were tucked away in the privacy of my blue Toyota Corolla, she asked, "So, letters from Hadley?"

That's why I drove all this way to talk to her, wasn't it? Because I wanted to tell her about the secret I'd been keeping? Because she was the only person I thought could understand? Now, I couldn't say. I looked at the girl sitting in my passenger seat and regretted even bringing it up. "Uh, yeah."

She waited for me to continue.

It was too late to take it back. I'd made my bed, and now I had to lie in it. "Yeah, so when Hadley was alive, she wrote all these letters. From, like, eighth grade to ... I don't even know how long ago. And a few days after the funeral, her parents gave them to me."

"Why'd they give them to you?"

"Well, most of them were addressed to me."

"Okay, so you're telling me about Hadley's letters to you because ...?"

"Well," I said, rubbing my steering wheel, "I don't think they were written *to* me, exactly. They're like diary entries, but in the form of letters addressed to different people. Me, mostly."

"So, you have Hadley's diary entries?" She leaned forward in her seat. "But you haven't read them, right?"

"I mean, I have been ... reading them."

"Unbelievable." She paused for a moment, cautiously adding, "What do they say?"

"That's private." I wasn't sure why I felt guarded all of a sudden.

She scoffed. "Well, yeah, I'm sure she thought that, too, when she was writing them."

"Well."

"So, were any of them addressed to me?"

I thought of the letter I saw for Kenzie, tucked away somewhere in the middle of the stack. "No, not really."

"Then my original question still stands. Why are you telling me about this?"

She was giving me this. I could lie. I could end the conversation. I could get out of this and go home and forget that I ever drove to her house in the middle of the night. I could even forget her—if I really tried.

Instead, I opted for the truth. "I haven't told anybody about them," I admitted. "But it's killing me. Keeping them to myself. And after tonight, I just thought if I could tell anyone, it would be you. You know, because you knew Hadley like I did. Better, even."

She took a moment, I assumed, to process this. "They must be pretty heavy."

"Well, it's just … yeah. It's like she's here again. But she's not and I just …"

She waited for me to continue, but I didn't. I didn't know what to say.

Finally, she sighed, staring at the glove box. "You want to know why I left during the dance?" She turned her head to face me.

"Why?"

"'Party In The U.S.A.' was our song." She shook her head, the smallest hint of a smile creeping onto her face. "You know, Hadley wasn't the most outgoing person. There were a lot of things she wanted to do but didn't because she was afraid. At least, that's how it was at the beginning of our friendship. She actually grew a ton." Her smile faded. "But anyway, a group of us went to a dance in, like, eighth or ninth grade, and Hadley was afraid to dance.

"For the whole first part of the night, we tried to get her to join us, but she just stood against the wall with her arms crossed, shaking her head. Then, suddenly, 'Party In The U.S.A.' starts playing, and I decided I couldn't stand it anymore. I started dancing like a complete *idiot*, like, flailing my arms around and kicking, you know." Kenzie snorted. "She was laughing so hard at me, so I grabbed her arm, dragged her into the circle, and forced her to dance with us. And she actually did, like she didn't care if anyone was watching anymore. After that, she wasn't really afraid to dance as long as I was there with her." What looked like pain flashed in her eyes—just briefly. "And that's how it became, like, our 'friendship song.' Whenever we hung out, just the two of us, we'd play it and dance to it, or sing. Whenever one of us was sad or having a bad day, the other would send it to them. It was like our way of letting each other know that everything would be okay." She sighed. "Just seeing the link was enough to make me feel better.

"But when it came on tonight," she said, her voice faltering as if the memory pained her, "it made me realize that we were never going to be able to do any of that again. She would have screamed the second she heard the intro playing at the formal, but she couldn't. She wasn't there. And I thought maybe it was like her way of telling me, from beyond the grave, that I would be okay without her." She paused a moment before adding, "And that made me realize even more that I'm not. I'm not okay at all. But I don't have any other choice but to pretend." Silent tears followed her last word.

The air in the car felt heavy. Seeing Kenzie like this, I realized that I didn't know her at all. Even when Hadley and I were dating, I didn't know her. She was always busy doing her own thing, and Hadley and I only hung out one-on-one most of the time anyway.

But from what Hadley told me about her and what I saw at school, Kenzie had her life together. She was known for being one of the best soccer players at Lincoln. She was in AP and honors classes. She was friendly. She was liked. She never crumbled in front of people—even after Hadley's death. But here she was again, crumbling. Crumbling in front of me, the last person I'm sure she wanted to talk to.

I felt the urge to hold her, but I couldn't, of course, so I said, "Wow. I'm sorry."

She shook her head. "I know. Everyone is. No one can imagine what I'm going through. That's what they say, at least. Or they say I'm so strong or that Hadley's in a better place or that I'll feel okay someday. But it's all just words."

I leaned my head back against my seat and laughed—an ironic kind of laugh. "I get it."

I felt her eyes on me. "I guess you've also been struggling more than you let on."

I wasn't sure if it was supposed to be a question or a statement, but I answered, "Yeah. I know it probably sounds cheap, coming from me, but I miss her. A lot. I wish she was still here."

"Me too," she said, wiping her eyes. "So, these letters—do they help at all?"

I thought about this for a moment, then said, "Yeah. They're a little hard to read, but they also make me feel close to her."

"Can I read them?"

I looked at her. Her eyes looked gray under the shadows cast by my car blocking the streetlamp. "Yeah."

She smiled. "Thank you. And thank you for coming tonight. Even if it is in the middle of the night. I think I needed this."

I smiled back at her. "Me, too."

Chapter

Thirteen

The Monday after a dance, especially if it was a big one, always felt weird. Everyone walked around like they had some kind of social hangover. The walls became naked as the student council took down the posters—making the Christmas trees they left up at the main entrance look even more pathetic and out of place. Some groups buzzed while stories of first kisses were exchanged. Other individuals sulked around after realizing the person they'd been *so* excited to go out with was *actually* a loser, and now they were stuck sitting next to them in chemistry for the rest of the semester.

I took my history textbook out of my locker. Dances never really affected me. Been to a million of them. No, the way I felt now had little to do with what happened at the dance and a lot more to do with what happened after. The part nobody knew about.

Well, almost nobody.

"Parker," Kenzie said, approaching my locker.

I looked around, scanning the faces of students in the hall to make sure none of them belonged to Mallory. When I saw that we were good, I said, "Hey, Kenzie. What's up?"

"Nothing. I just was thinking a lot about the other night."

Did she have to be so loud? "Yeah?"

"Yeah. And we didn't really talk about it, but when can I read the letters?"

Saturday night. The letters.

Can I read them?

Yeah.

There was no way I could let her read them. They were so private. And I hardly knew her. I didn't even know everything they had to say.

But I had promised.

What did I get myself into?

"Oh, yeah. Um, about that—I don't really think that's a great idea," I said, scratching my head.

"You don't want me to read them anymore?"

"Well ..."

She waited for me to finish, but I didn't. "You're not serious." She paused again, clearly waiting for me to say something.

I didn't.

"You've got to be kidding me. Why would you come to my house and tell me that my best friend, who you know I miss *excruciatingly*, left something behind and that I could see it and then just be like, 'Oh, actually, never mind'? What's wrong with you?"

I wasn't prepared for her to get this upset. Hopefully, nobody could hear her. No one needed to know I was at her house. "Kenzie, shh. Calm down."

"Did you just *shush* me?" Obviously, this was the wrong thing to say.

I looked around me. The coast was still clear as far as Mallory was concerned, and everyone else looked involved in their own conversations. But still. I lowered my voice. "Listen, I just … I'm not ready to give them up. I haven't finished reading them, and it's not that I don't trust you, but I'm not ready to part with them yet."

"Then, why would you tell me about them in the first place?"

"I don't know."

She sighed, looking away. Then, she returned her attention to me. "Well, what if we read them together, then?"

"Read them together?" I was not prepared for *that*.

"Yeah. You said reading them alone was killing you, so we can read them together."

"Ah, I don't know—"

"Parker, please. You have no idea how much this would mean to me. I haven't been able to stop thinking about it since you brought it up the other night. I miss her so much. I *need* this."

I wanted to protest again, but something stopped me. Honestly, the idea of reading them with her sounded nice. No one understood what I'd been going through the past two months. They didn't know Hadley like I did. But Kenzie did.

"Okay," I said. "We can do that. But we can't read them at my house." I didn't want anyone to get suspicious. I knew my mom wouldn't think anything of it, but I could see her thoughtlessly saying something to Mallory—who definitely would.

"Okay, well, we can't meet at my house either. My parents are renovating right now. But we could meet somewhere public to read them. Like the library or something."

"No," I said—probably too quickly. "That won't work either."

"Why not?"

"It just won't."

"So, if not the library, then—"

"Nowhere. It can't be anywhere public," I said. "They're too private." Someone from school would be bound to see us if we hung out somewhere in town.

"Okay." She stood there a moment, hand on her chin and lips pursed. Then, her eyes lit up. "Oh, you know what? If you don't mind driving a little bit, my family has a lake house we don't really use in the winter. I've been going up more recently to do homework and stuff. We could meet there."

A lake house? "I think that would work."

"Awesome. Are you doing anything Friday? The night before Christmas Eve?"

My parents didn't have any plans, and Mallory would be out of town for almost all of Christmas break. "No, I am not."

"Do you want to ride together?"

"No. Um, I'll just meet you there if that's okay."

She unslung her backpack from her shoulder and dug in it until her hands resurfaced with a notebook and pen. She scribbled something on the paper, then ripped it away and held it out to me. "This is the address." She paused, then pulled the paper back to write something else. "And my number, in case you have any questions."

I took the paper and shoved it in my pocket. "What time?"

She looked at the ceiling as if her schedule was written there, then said, "Be there at seven."

"Seven," I noted. "Sounds good."

With that, she gave me a brisk nod, flipped around, and headed down the hallway as if our conversation had never actually happened in the first place.

✉

I took a deep breath as I lifted the box of letters off my dresser. What had only belonged to Hadley and I would now belong to Kenzie, in a way. Was I ready for it? I didn't know. Nevertheless, I shielded the box under my jacket to protect it from the rain, which was now coming down hard, as I left the house that Friday night.

In the car, I turned the stereo up to muffle the raindrops bouncing off the windshield, the GPS voice occasionally cutting in to give me directions. Out of the city, I turned onto a winding, evergreen tree-bordered road and arrived at the address Kenzie gave me, twenty-six minutes after departure. Mist covered the mountains, which guarded the property like walls of a gothic snow globe. Through the fog, a small, cabin-style lake house sat at a lower elevation than the lot Kenzie had told me to park at. Behind the house was a dock hovering over a vast black lake.

After parking my car on the asphalt parking pad, I walked down the wooden stairs to the house, which had a dim yellow light pouring out through the windows. I pulled my black hood over my head, zipping Hadley's box under my jacket once again. The trees grew taller as I took each step down.

I slid my hood off once I made it onto the porch, the awning a haven from the rain. Within a few seconds of my banging on the door, it swung open to reveal a damp Kenzie.

Instead of saying hello, I asked, "Did you just get here?"

She squeezed the ends of her wet hair. "How can you tell?"

I laughed, making my way in through the door before she stopped me.

"Take off your shoes," she ordered.

"*Take off your shoes—*"

She glared at me. "Please," she said, finishing my implied sentence. "Please take off your shoes. Thank you."

I complied, not breaking eye contact the entire time I untied my shoelaces, and slipped my sopping black Converse off my feet, placing them neatly beside the exterior doorframe.

She stared at me. "You're a lot more obnoxious than I thought you were."

"That's usually the case," I said. "May I come in, now?"

Ignoring me, she walked away from the door and to the fireplace where a small fire burned. Then, she opened the doors of the fireplace and poked the logs with a fire iron. I came in after wringing my jacket over the porch and hanging it on a hook by the door.

"So, is it okay with your parents that I'm here?" I asked.

"I didn't ask."

"Oh."

She hung the fire iron up and shut the glass doors of the fireplace. "They won't care though. This has kind of been my hideout since Hadley died, and they know it. They don't really ask questions."

"That's kind of nice," I said. "To have a hideout."

"As far as running away from your problems goes." She glanced at the box I held in my hands. "So, that's it?"

I tapped the top of it with my index finger. "Yeah."

She stared at it for a moment before standing up. "You're probably as cold as I am. You can come sit by the fireplace if you want."

"Okay," I said, accepting her invitation.

"Do you want some hot chocolate?"

"Sure. That'd be awesome."

She pursed her lips into a soft smile. "Okay. Wait right here."

While she bustled in the kitchen, I stared at the box sitting next to me by the fireplace. No turning back now.

She returned with two mugs. She handed me the one that had *It's too early for people* written on it in cursive. "So, you want to get started now?"

I took one last look at the box, then shifted my gaze to her. "Yeah." I set my hot chocolate down and handed the box to her. "I read a lot of the ones on top already."

"Okay. Thanks." She took the box from me, lifted the lid off, and pulled off the top letter. "This feels so weird," she said, inspecting it. "This is definitely her handwriting."

For the next while, she read each letter carefully. I felt on edge as she alternated between smiling, nodding, and gritting her teeth, so I tried to distract myself by taking inventory of the lake house's interior as I listened to the rain pounding against the roof. There were cheesy plaques on the wall about camping and fishing. There were also family pictures with several little blond kids in them. I wondered if they were Kenzie's cousins or something. There were too many of them to belong to just one family unit. Adjacent to the fireplace and sharing a wall with the front door was a brown couch with pillows that didn't fit a particular theme. Nothing inside the small, closed-off living room fit a particular theme—unless it was supposed to be the aesthetic interpretation of the Cabin Family meets Fifty Shades of Brown.

I glanced down as she pulled one out that said *Sunday, January 23* at the top.

"Wait," I said. "I don't think I've read that one yet."

"Oh," she said. "Do you want to read it together, then?"

I swallowed. "Yeah. Yeah, we can do that."

"Okay." She began reading aloud.

Sunday, January 23

Dear Parker,

When I told my parents we were dating, my mom was super excited. She insisted on meeting you. In fact, she got upset when she found out that I met your mom before you met mine. The look on her face made me feel really bad. In my defense, though, I didn't expect her to react the way she did. I actually expected her to react a lot more like my father did, who didn't even try to hide the fact that he wasn't pleased.

"You're too young," he said.

"She's sixteen!" my mom said in defense.

He glared at her. "Sixteen is too young."

"But Daniel had a girlfriend when he was like fourteen," I protested. "Remember? Rebeckah?"

"I'm pretty sure he was older than that. Probably seventeen," Dad said.

"So, I can have a boyfriend when I'm seventeen?" I asked.

"No."

"Manuel," Mom said. "Come on, this is exciting for Hadley. She actually has a boyfriend."

I wasn't sure if she was implying she didn't think I could get one, but I'll take it.

Dad threw his hands up in the air. "Fine. But I need to meet this boy. To see if I approve."

"Oh," I said, suddenly losing my courage.

"That's a great idea," Mom said.

But I did not think so.

"When are you going to bring him over?" Dad asked me.

"I don't know," I said. "When do you want me to?"

"How about Saturday?" Mom asked.

So, that was that.

Until Saturday,

Hadley

Kenzie shot me a look and I gestured to the letter box. She pulled out the next one and read.

Saturday, January 29

Dear Parker,

It's Saturday. The day you and my parents met.

Around five o'clock, I was lying on my freshly made bed and talking on the phone with Kenzie when I heard a knock on the front door.

"I have to go," I told her.

"Okay," she replied. "Make sure you tell me everything."

Kenzie paused. "Oh, I remember this." I felt my face go hot at the realization that there were probably a lot of things she remembered that Hadley told her about me.

"I will," I said.

"I'm serious," she pressed. "Don't you dare leave out a single detail."

I laughed. "Okay, okay. I have to go now."

I didn't tell Kenzie that I was nervous about the whole thing. Earlier this morning, my dad started going off again about how I'm too young to date and how he was going to ask you a bunch of questions to make sure you were "appropriate" or whatever. I wasn't sure if he actually would. He's usually pretty quiet around my friends. But I've never had a boyfriend before. I had no idea how he would be. To be honest, I didn't realize he cared that much about my life to care about who I was dating. He always cared about who Daniel was dating because he and Daniel were so close. And Reagan was too perfect to worry about dating anyone in high school. Maybe now that my siblings are both too busy with work and college to ever visit, Dad has more time to focus on what I'm doing. When he's not busy with work, that is.

By the time I exited my room, you were already standing in the doorway, my mom right next to you. Seeing you just made me so happy, like my apprehension nearly melted away. You were wearing jeans and a blue flannel shirt. Nothing too fancy, but I could tell you made an effort to dress up. You took this seriously.

Mom looked at me, then back at you, then at me again. "Hadley, he's here!"

I made my way over.

"Parker, right?" Mom said to you. "It's good to meet you. I have dinner in the dining room if you want to make your way over."

You took your hands out of your front pockets. "Okay. Thanks. It's good to meet you, too." As she walked away, you turned to me. "Hey Hadley."

As if it were instinct, my hands flew to my head immediately to smooth down my frizzy waves. I smiled. "Hi, Parker. How are you?"

"Pretty good. How 'bout yourself?"

"Pretty good," I said.

At the table, we sat across from each other. You seemed perfectly content, confident like you always are. I, on the other hand, was losing my mind again. The more I thought of you meeting my father, the harder it got to breathe. I felt like my childhood asthma would come springing up on me at the thought.

When Dad came inside from gardening, he walked straight from the backdoor to the garage, carefully slipping the muddy gloves off his hands. Then, he walked right past the table and headed to the sink, where he carefully began washing the dirt from the crevices of his hands and nails. "Dinner smells amazing, Carrie," he told my mom.

We usually don't eat so early in the afternoon (well, we never really eat together. Period.) unless Mom is cooking pot roast and we are having guests over that she's trying to impress. I love that—that my mom was trying to impress you. My biggest concern was impressing my dad, though.

"Thank you," she said, lifting the lid off the slow cooker in response. "Pot roast."

He dried his hands on the towel that hung from the cabinet door under the sink. "Oh, I can tell. Believe me." Then, he glanced at us. I saw it! Still, he flipped his head faster than the time it took to see us, trying to be subtle, nonchalant. "Would you like help setting the table?"

At this inquisition, you stood up.

Dad glanced at you again in his peripherals, but looked away when Mom said, "Oh, no. Parker, you're our guest. You can go ahead and sit down and we'll take care of it."

"Are you sure, Mrs. Garcia? It's no problem at all."

"Yes," she replied cheerfully, "Hadley doesn't have friends over to eat that often, so I want to be the one to make things comfortable for you."

I internally groaned. What'd she have to tell you that for?

You slowly sat back down in your seat and smiled at me.

Working around us, Dad meticulously placed the plates, cups, and silverware on the table—the way the foods teacher at school taught us. The Right Way. Still, he refused to look at you, and I think you noticed because you raised your eyebrow at me.

Oh, how I hoped he didn't see that.

I just shook my head, praying that you'd get the message, "Just go with it. He's testing you." And then I prayed that this whole awkward charade could be over already. It didn't make anything easier.

Just as he was finishing, Mom came in with a plate of sliced-up pot roast. She placed it in the middle, beside the creamed corn and mashed potatoes. "Okay," she said, taking her oven mitts off. "It's ready."

Slowly, Dad reached across the table, stabbing one of the slices of meat with his fork. He placed it on his plate and began to cut it with a knife. He finally looked over while you were sipping from your glass of ice water. "So, Parker."

You coughed, then hurried to wipe your face with a napkin. "Um, yes, sir?"

"Do you have a job?" Dad asked.

"No, sir. I don't work since I'm on the lacrosse team."

"Lacrosse? You must not have time for schoolwork, then."

"Oh, no. I still make time for homework."

"What are your grades?"

"Manuel!" Mom scolded. "Parker didn't come here so you could interrogate him. He's our guest."

He didn't really acknowledge her. To you, he said, "My apologies, Parker. But grades are important to you, no?"

"Oh, of course," you said. "Grades are my number one priority. That's why I don't work during the school year."

"Then, why do you want to date my daughter?" Dad asked. "Will being in a relationship not distract you from school?"

In that moment, I wanted to die.

You looked scared, but I think you handled it well. You said, "No, sir. Hadley's not a distraction at all. She motivates me, actually." You looked at me as you said the next part. "And I want to date your daughter because she means a lot to me. I think she's incredibly intelligent, thoughtful, kind, and beautiful." You turned to my dad again. "I don't want to be a distraction because I know school is important, and I know you care about her school because you care about her but she is also important to me. I promise to treat her in a way you'd approve. And I would be grateful if you would allow me to keep seeing her."

The room froze. You remained still as a board, calmer than I ever could be in your place, but I could tell you sat in nervous anticipation, just like my mom and me.

My father kept a straight face as he said, "Well, as long as you are not a bad influence, then I think that's wonderful."

I was flabbergasted. But I also felt so much adoration

for you in that moment. I can't believe you got my dad to approve. And, also, I didn't realize how important it was to him that I was treated well. You're the reason I got to learn that. Thank you.

You mean a lot to me too,
Hadley

Kenzie smiled, shaking her head. "Oh, Manuel García. What an interesting man."

I shuddered at the memory. "He terrified me."

She laughed. "He scared me, too, when I first met him. But now that I know him better, I think he's one of the coolest people I've ever met."

I didn't say anything because I still wasn't sure how I felt about Hadley's parents. I'm sure they wanted her to be treated well, but I remembered all the nights Hadley cried to me about them ignoring her or pushing her too hard.

After a moment, Kenzie said, "That was a pretty nice response you gave him."

I shrugged. "Yeah."

"Did you mean it?"

I thought for a moment. If you fail to keep a promise, does that mean you made it in vain? Did it compromise the sincerity you felt at the time you made it? "Yeah, I did. At the time."

She nodded, looking down.

"I know it's probably hard to believe, with the way things ended. But Hadley meant a lot to me. Even after we broke up, she meant a lot to me." I sighed. "You know, I always kind of figured you hated me for what happened."

She was quiet for a moment before admitting, "I did hate you."

"Oh."

"I mean, Hadley is—was—my best friend. You were her first love. You broke her heart."

"I know."

She studied me, the fire's reflection billowing in her eyes. Then, she shook her head. "But it's in the past."

I couldn't look at her anymore. "Believe me, I wish I would have done things differently."

She hesitated, like she wanted to say something different but settled on, "That's good."

A cloud of tension formed in the room, and I was eager to make it dissipate. "Is it just me, or is it weird the way she wrote these? I feel like they're written like a story."

"I'm not surprised at all. Hadley read a ton of books. It was actually her dream to be a writer, so she tried to write everything like it was a book. Like, even when she told me stories over text, she'd add descriptions and dialogue tags." She smiled to herself. "I can see her writing these on her bed, looking up the right words to use on her phone."

"I can't believe how unfair it is," I said. "She'll never get to be a writer like she wanted."

"Yeah." She took a sip of her hot chocolate, then said, "Thanks again for letting me read these. I know you felt weird about it."

"No, I was being stupid. It's nice to share them with somebody."

"Well, thanks." She pulled out her phone. "It's getting kind of late, and it doesn't look like the rain is going to let up any time soon. I better get back home before my parents freak out."

On cue, I stood. "Yeah, same."

She stood, too. "Next week, same time?"

I felt weirdly excited about the idea of doing this again. I grinned at her. "Yeah, let's do it."

Chapter

Fourteen

As per tradition, I ate Christmas Eve breakfast at Gage's house. Over pancakes, Gage's mom asked me about lacrosse. My fork dropped, and I struggled to swallow the fluffy chunk of pancake I'd just shoved in my mouth. Gage told his mom everything, so I knew the question wasn't actually as innocent as it sounded coming from her.

After I swallowed, I cleared my throat. "I'm actually not doing it this year."

"Oh, really? Why is that?" She contorted her face to look surprised.

I sighed. I really liked Gage's mom and would never want to offend her, so I was careful to hide my irritation. Across the table, Gage was cutting his pancake stack so carefully, you'd think he was performing surgery on it. "I just want to focus on school."

"Oh, but it's senior year," she said. "Don't you think you'll regret not playing this season?"

The eyes of Gage's mother, father, and two younger brothers stuck to me as I formulated a response. I just said, "No. I've played for six years, and that time has meant a lot to me. This year, I'm not doing it."

She looked slightly taken aback but quickly transitioned to a smile. "Well, Parker, as long as you are doing what is best for you, then we're rooting for you."

Once everybody had finished eating and we'd cleared off the table, I followed Gage outside to the front porch.

"Why?" I asked him.

He raised an eyebrow. "Why what?"

"Why did you let your mom put me on the spot like that? I know you already told her I'm not doing lacrosse this year."

"You didn't tell me you weren't doing it. You said you weren't sure."

"I also said I didn't want to talk about it anymore."

"And I haven't brought it up."

"Then, how convenient that was for you."

He put his hands up in defense. "It's not like I put her up to it."

"Sure."

Gage hesitated a moment, then said, "Parker, I just don't get it. You know, I know"—he motioned to the door—"*she* knows you're not skipping out to focus on school. What's the real reason?"

"I don't have a reason," I said. "I just don't want to do it."

"That's crap and you know it. Parker, what's going on?"

"I don't need to explain myself to you." I didn't want to snap, but frustration welled up inside me. I wasn't sure I could keep it in. "Why can't you just accept that?"

"Because I know you," he said. "You would never just quit on something this important. Lacrosse is your life."

I turned away from him and toward the street. The overcast sky made Gage's ribbon-wrapped mailboxes and reindeer lawn ornaments look stupid. They didn't belong. They were trying too hard. Just let the sky be gray. Let the street look gloomy. "Lacrosse is not my life," I said.

He sighed. "I don't know how to say this. I mean, I've been wanting to say something, but … I don't know. You haven't been yourself, man. Like, there are moments when you feel like … *Parker*. But the moments don't stick around too long. I'm afraid that if I say anything, they won't happen anymore at all."

"I'm sorry that I'm not the *Parker* you think you know."

"It's not like that. I'm just worried about you, man." He put his hand on my shoulder. "Things have been off since Hadley G—"

I turned around to face him. "This isn't about Hadley." Because how stupid would that be? My best friend feels like he needs to have an intervention with me because my personality has changed or whatever. Over a girl I dumped a year and a half ago. A girl whose heart I broke. What right did I have to be *not myself*? To be *off*? To have someone *worry about me*? I didn't worry about her. And she's not part of my life anymore. So how stupid would that be?

"Okay," he said carefully, "but it's about something. Do you want to talk about it?"

I didn't want to talk about it. Gage wouldn't understand. Mallory didn't understand. Nobody understood. "I don't want to talk about anything."

"You're my best friend, Parker. I want to help."

"I don't want your help." What could he do? Other than make me feel worse.

"Then, what do you want me to do?"

Nothing. "I want you to leave me alone. I don't want to see you anymore. I don't want to talk to you. Just leave me alone."

Hurt brewed in his dark eyes as he took a step back. "You don't mean that."

"I do," I said. "I'm tired of you pestering me about lacrosse. I'm tired of you pretending to care."

"I'm not pretending to care. It's not about lacrosse."

"Whatever; I don't care. I'm done." I looked him in the eyes. "I don't want to deal with you anymore." I realized how harsh it sounded coming out, but I couldn't *stop* it.

"Fine," he said. "If that's what you want, then have a nice life, I guess."

The next day was Christmas. Some families, like Gage's, would go to church or read from the Bible or something to celebrate. Since my family wasn't religious, we never did any of that. But we always had Christmas dinner, where my mom would make salads and pies, and my dad would smoke a ham. We ate at the dining room table, just the four of us. The set up this year wasn't different, although the atmosphere was. For whatever reason, I felt like it'd be a great time to tell my family I wouldn't be doing lacrosse this year. They shot each other a look before returning their attention to me.

"Why not?" Mom asked.

"I just want to focus on school," I lied, "and finish the year strong."

"But lacrosse hasn't ever hindered school before. Why are you worried about it now?"

I shrugged. "I'm just not feeling it now."

"But—"

Dad cut her off. "You're an adult now, Parker." Mom glared

at him, but he continued. "You're old enough to make your own decisions. Just don't make any that you'll regret."

I nodded. Weird how my own family could make less of a deal about it than Gage. Goes to show how unimportant it was after all. Gage wasn't worried about me. He was worried about the team.

With Dad marking the conversation as over, Chase took the opportunity to cut himself another slice of banana cream pie. He did so with a dopey smile on his face.

"You seem pretty happy today," Dad said to him.

Mom looked at Chase and gaped as if she didn't realize it until now. "Yeah, you do. Any good news, Chase?"

He shook his head, trying not to smile but failing. "Nothing new. I'm just normal."

"It's a girl, isn't it?" Dad squinted at him.

Chase's face erupted in a deep blush, and he looked down.

Dad smiled at Mom. "It's a girl."

As planned, Kenzie and I met up at the lake house the following Friday, where we found ourselves sitting on that brown couch, the box of letters between us. The lack of rain today made the exterior of the house look less creepy but the interior of it much quieter.

Tuesday, February 15

Dear Parker,

I love you. When you speak, your melodic voice draws me into you and your deep brown eyes trap me there. You know, I've had brown eyes my entire life. Everyone in my family has brown eyes, except my mom. I've always wished I could have her pretty, blue eyes. But, alas, I'm surrounded by brown. And, until I met you, I never thought they were beautiful. Brown is just brown. It's so funny to me now because, when I'm looking into your brown eyes, it's like they're the most beautiful things I've ever seen.

Hadley

"You are bright red," Kenzie accused.

I turned away from her. "I am not."

She laughed. "You totally are."

I grabbed the pillow next to me on the couch where we were sitting and threw it at her. "I am not. Take it back."

She dodged the pillow, then looked at me with mouth agape, the corners turning up. "Did you just throw a pillow at me?"

My sudden casualness with Kenzie surprised me, too, especially after the week I'd had. Even today sucked, and I was not in the mood to leave my house, but something changed as soon as I saw her. She seemed happy to see me. Something about it made me forget everything I was irritated about. "I did, actually. What are you going to do about it?"

She glared at me, still trying not to smile. "Oh, just you wait, Parker Everett. Just you wait."

I raised my eyebrows. "Should I be scared?"

"Definitely."

I laughed, taking the pillow from her and putting it back in the corner of the couch. "You seem pretty happy today."

"I am. Something about the holidays does that for me. It

feels good to spend time with family and do the things we did when I was a kid. It's nice to just forget about everything else."

"I wish I felt the same," I said. "The holidays sucked this year."

"I'm sorry to hear that."

"Thanks. Yesterday was my birthday."

"Oh. Well, happy birthday."

"Thanks. It sucked."

"I'm sorry—"

"All I could think about is how I'm running out of time," I said. "I need to make decisions about my future. I need to figure out what I'm going to do with my life. Everything that is familiar and comfortable has a time limit now. And I can't really bring myself to do anything about it." I didn't know why I was telling her all these things. It was so personal, but she just sat there, listening, and I didn't want to stop talking. I couldn't. "Then I felt guilty because I got to turn eighteen, and there are so many people who won't ever get that."

"Like Hadley," she said.

"Like Hadley."

She looked down for several moments, playing with the yarn tufts on the pillow in her lap. "I don't blame you," she said. "Life doesn't really feel real for me anymore. Some days, I feel like I'm walking around in a nightmare, just waiting to wake up. Other days, I feel like I died when she did, but I just keep living—keep walking around in some purgatory or something, half alive. Waiting for God to assign me to heaven or hell. It doesn't feel right to think of the future when you realize it's not even certain you're going to get one anymore. Because Hadley didn't, you know?"

All I could do was stare at her, this enigmatic girl, hunched over in a purple T-shirt, her hair pulled back in her signature ponytail. I wanted to scream or jump up or hug her because she nailed it. She managed to put exactly what I'd been feeling for months now into words, when nobody else, including me, could. "Exactly," I said. "That's exactly how I feel."

She looked at me and offered the slightest smile.

Chapter

Fifteen

Monday, March 28

Dear Parker,

I can't stand it anymore. Honestly. I walk to chemistry with my head down. I hate the way these girls make me feel. I always looked up to them. They're both so gorgeous. They're smart. They get good grades. All the guys like them. They do student council and National Honor Society. They're friends with the teachers. They're always smiling.

And, yet, they make me feel terrible about myself.

I can't understand how someone who is supposed to be perfect in every way could possibly drag another person down to immense insecurity without even feeling bad about it. It makes no sense to me.

If this was any other time in my life, I would have thought the problem was me. Maybe I deserved it. Maybe I really am stupid and incapable like they think and I don't deserve the kindness and friendliness they show to everyone else.

But, no, Parker. I can't stand to think that way anymore. Because I know you would have hated what they were saying. And because you think I'm beautiful. You think I'm smart. No, you don't just think I'm smart. You think I'm intelligent which is way more important than being smart.

Being smart is about getting good grades. It's about knowing the right things to say and making yourself look good in front of other people. That's what smart is.

But intelligence is different. Being intelligent is about knowing—actually knowing. It's about understanding. It's the word for when someone can have a deep conversation and understand that the universe is much vaster than the small town she lives in. It's an appreciation for others.

It's the greatest compliment I have ever received.

I wish they understood that.

Love,
Hadley

The morning that school started back up, Gage texted, *Hey, man I'm sorry for pushing the lacrosse thing. Are we good now?* I didn't respond, and when lunch came, we made eye contact from across the cafeteria. I was the first to look away.

My phone vibrated in my pocket with his response: *Guess not.* Then, he sat at the old table with our lacrosse buddies instead of our usual spot with Mallory and the student council. Whatever. If he wanted to shun me for not playing a stupid sport, then fine by me.

From that point forward, he didn't acknowledge me when I

passed him in the halls. In fact, no one from the team did. Did I give them the chance to as I passed them with my head down?

Not important.

On Wednesday, I ran into Kenzie on the way to my locker.

"Oh, hey," she said. "How are you?"

I grinned. "I'm doing pretty good. I feel like the break was too short, but it's fine. How are you?"

"I'm doing pretty good. I feel the same way though." She laughed. "But it's good that I ran into you because I need to talk to you about …"

In my peripheral vision, Mallory made her way over from the end of the hall. Instantly, my mind took me back to the night of Winter Formal. She'd definitely think something was up if she saw Kenzie and me talking.

Kenzie was still in the middle of her sentence when I walked past her and called, "Mallory! Hey, babe!"

Mallory met me in the middle and grinned. "Hey, Parker." After a quick peck on the cheek, she launched into a rant about her upcoming English assignment. As we walked to class, I glanced back at Kenzie, who watched me like she was an old dog who had just been dropped off in the woods and I was her departing owner. I'd have to explain to her later. Surely she'd understand.

At Mallory's house later that day, I leaned over my calculus homework, sitting next to her on the couch. "This is pointless."

"No, it's not," she said. "Just keep working on it. You'll get it."

I leaned my head on her like a little kid. "I don't wanna do it anymore."

She glared at me. "It's a good thing you're cute." Then, on the coffee table in front of the couch, her phone pinged.

I sat up. "Who is it?"

She opened the phone to read the text, then set it back down. "Oh, it's just Kaylee. She's texting me about this girl from history."

"Oh, really? What girl?"

Mallory shook her head. "I don't know her name. She's so weird though. She sits right in front of Kaylee and is always chewing on her pencil. Never talks to anyone. Just sits there and chews on her pencil." She laughed. "It's pretty gross."

"What did Kaylee say about her?" I felt a lump form in my throat.

"She was just ranting. We have history tomorrow, and the thought of it is making her skin crawl." Her phone pinged again, and she showed me the screen this time. It was a picture of a beaver chewing on a log. She laughed. "Yup. Spot on."

I didn't laugh. "Has she actually done anything to you?"

"The girl?"

"Yeah."

"No, but it's pretty distracting. Not to mention super gross."

"You do this a lot," I muttered.

"Do what?"

"Talk about people like this. She didn't even do anything to you. She could be really nice for all you know, but you and Kaylee are making fun of her behind her back."

"It's not like we're making fun of her to her face."

"Yeah, but it's still wrong. You don't know how it makes her feel. She can probably tell that you don't like her."

"Are you being serious right now? You, of all people, are

going to lecture me on being a good person. Have you ever heard the way *you* talk about people?"

Her words struck me—I didn't think I had a problem with it. "Well, I shouldn't do it either."

"Yeah. Well, maybe you should work on that before you ride up to me on your high horse, giving decency lessons."

"Mallory—"

"Listen, Parker. You don't feel like working on your homework, and I don't feel like helping you, so you should probably leave now."

"Are you seriously mad at me right now?"

"I'm just done for the night. I'll see you at school."

I waited for her to change her mind, but she just started scrolling on her phone. So, I picked up my things and left. Surely some space would be good, and she wouldn't be mad anymore by tomorrow. But I couldn't stop thinking about her accusation. Did I really make fun of people as much as she made it seem? Was she just saying that?

Chapter

Sixteen

It snowed the next morning. Snow didn't grace Copperton very often, so it always caught us by surprise.

"I'm not kidding, Parker," Mom said, standing in the kitchen, her car keys in one hand and coffee in the other. "Promise you'll be safe driving today, or I'm gonna take your keys and make you ride the bus."

I grabbed my keys from the key hook. "Do you really think a bus full of loud teenagers is safer than my driving?"

"Parker, promise me."

"Fine. I promise I will be safe driving to school," I said in a slow, exaggerated manner.

She shook her head. "You're gonna be the death of me, kid."

"But I won't be the death of *me*. And you can count on that." I swung the door open, letting the cold in. "See you later, Mom."

On the other side of the door, my words echoed back to me. For a moment, I'd forgotten the gravity that came with driving—that came with life. It was stupid. It was stupid to act so nonchalant about it.

I took a deep breath and surveyed the world outside. The reality of today's weather was disappointing. The lawns, trees, and houses were dusted by a light layer of snow and the black road shined with water. Snowflakes fell and melted on the windshield sparingly. By the time I made it to school, the snow had all but ceased.

Since I'd left early today, I was able to slide into one of the closer spots in the south parking lot. It was nice since I usually had to park a lot farther from the building with my screwed-up sleep schedule leaving me exhausted and running late most mornings. Parking evenly between the two lines, I turned my headlights off and shut off the ignition. Just moments later, a Dodge Ram pulled in beside me.

Kenzie was the driver.

She turned her head, locked eyes with me, and then averted her eyes, grabbing her backpack from the backseat. Before I had time to unbuckle my seatbelt, she was out the door. Eyes forward and ponytail swinging behind her, she sped across the street to the building.

I hopped out and followed her. "Kenzie!" I called. After my calves started to burn from speed walking, I gave up and jogged to her. "Kenzie!"

She didn't look back, but I knew she heard me at this point, as I wasn't far behind now.

"Kenzie." When I was close enough, I reached out and grabbed her wrist.

She twisted out of my grip. "What do you want, Parker?"

"Are you okay?"

"I'm fine." Without looking at me, she reached for the school door.

I followed her into the little space before the second door to the hallway. "Then, why are you ignoring me?"

She met my eyes this time. "Well, since you don't want to be seen talking to me, I figured I'd make it easier for you and just not talk to you at all."

"Are you talking about yesterday? That's different. I just didn't want Mallory to see." I glanced down the hallway to make sure Mallory wouldn't see now, even though I knew she rarely came to this part of the school.

Kenzie followed my gaze before turning her attention back to me. "Why? We weren't doing anything wrong."

"I know." I scratched the back of my neck. "I just don't want her to get the wrong idea."

"Well, doesn't she know what we've been doing? About the letters?"

"No, I can't tell her about it."

She looked confused now. "Why not?"

"I don't want to cause any strain on our relationship."

"Why would telling her you're reading letters from Hadley with me cause strain on your relationship?"

"You wouldn't understand."

She glared at me. "You're right. I wouldn't understand how you could have so little trust in your relationship that telling your girlfriend something as simple as this would cause strain on it." She opened the second door. "Good luck to you both as you work through your issues."

I put my arm out in front of her and shut the door. "Kenzie, please. I don't want to stop hanging out with you. I need you. You're the only person I feel like I can talk to. Your friends who don't get it? That's Mallory, but times a hundred. Hadley wasn't a friend to her. She was her boyfriend's ex." I sighed. "I love Mallory. I don't want to lose her. But she just doesn't understand, and I can't make her."

She dropped her hand from the door and studied me.

After a moment, she said, "It still doesn't make sense to me."

"It doesn't have to." I put my hand on her shoulder. "Just please say you'll give me another chance. Please."

She stared at my hand—long enough for me to wonder if touching her was too inappropriate for the situation. She sighed. "Okay, fine."

I took my hand away. "Thank you, Kenzie. Really. And I'm really sorry I walked away while we were talking. That was really screwed up of me."

"It was."

"But we're good?"

"Yeah, fine. Whatever."

"Thanks," I said. "And you're okay if we just keep the whole Hadley thing between us?"

She looked at the bottom of the door for a moment, then looked back at me and nodded. "Yeah."

Chapter

Seventeen

Dear Parker,

    I know you're busy, but I still feel so low when you take hours to text me back. You're so gorgeous and intelligent and funny and everyone can see how much better you are than me. That's what scares me the most. You are my whole world, but you could leave me at any moment for someone prettier than me, fitter than me, smarter than me, funnier than me … the list goes on. Now, my heart hurts.

    Please don't leave me. I don't know what I would do without you.

Love,
Hadley

Kenzie put the letter down after reading it. "I remember

this." We sat in the living room of her lake house, where we'd decided to make reading Hadley's letters together an every-Friday night kind of thing. Having it on a Friday required a little creativity on my part to keep Mallory from being suspicious, but it was the only day that regularly worked for Kenzie.

I felt my face heat up. "She told you about this?"

Kenzie nodded. "Yeah. I mean, she didn't tell me a lot while you guys were dating, but she told me about this. She was worried this was the beginning of the end."

The beginning of the end.

Wednesday, April 13

Dear Parker,

It hasn't gotten any better. Most of the time, Brittany and Mallory act like I'm not even there. They just do everything without me, even though I kind of need to be graded on our labs, too.

Kenzie paused to look at me and my blood ran cold. Brittany and Mallory—*my* Mallory—were the girls in chemistry who made Hadley feel bad about herself. My first instinct was to defend her. *Mallory isn't like that.* But just last week, she kicked me out of her house because I called her out on gossiping about that pencil girl. *Mallory is like that. She's always been like that.* I guess it never bothered me before.

I gave Kenzie a *go on* motion with my hand and she continued.

So I've just gotten used to standing on the side while they do their thing. Then, today, out of nowhere, Mallory was like, "Um, Hallie. I know you like to be in your own little world, or whatever, but we really need that beaker." First of all, Hallie? Second of all, I'm only "in [my] own little world or whatever" because, whenever I try to say anything, they either ignore me or act like I'm stupid. I honestly can't stand it. I hate being in their group.

But that's not the point of this letter, Parker.

The point is to let you know that you make me forget about them. I don't ever tell you this because it would sound absolutely ridiculous, but when I'm riding in the passenger seat of your car, I feel like somebody. It's terrifying to say out loud or to even write down, but I can't help it anymore. I'm in love with you. I'm insanely, stupidly, so, so, so in love with you. To be in love is such a weird feeling, you know? It's like I'm able to fly. Just thinking about it makes me so happy. When I think of what we were, what we are, and what we can be, I get so excited, Parker. Just being around you makes me so happy.

The mean girls don't go away, but they don't exist when I'm with you. When I'm with you, the world is big and beautiful and right. For the first time in so long, it feels like such a wonderful place to live.

Thank you,
Hadley

Before Kenzie could say anything, I pulled out the next letter and handed it to her. It was only going to get worse from here, but I didn't want to talk about it. I couldn't.

Saturday, April 23

Dear Parker,

I love sunsets. I love the way the blue sky transforms into misty patches of red, pink, purple, and orange. The designs in the sky vary each night, but the sunsets remain constant, giving us something to rely on, even though we never know what to expect. I love the way they look from the passenger seat of your car. I love the way you look, gripping your steering wheel tightly enough to control the vehicle, but loosely enough to reveal your carefree outlook on life.

Sunsets are made for connection. I think that any two souls watching the same sunset and listening to the same music in the background will automatically fall in love—whether platonically or romantically—simply because of the ambiance it creates. I know that's not why I've fallen in love with you, but these evening drives merge my soul with yours in a way that has to be unique.

I want to watch sunsets with you for the rest of my life,
Hadley

Monday, May 2

Dear Parker,

Why aren't you responding to my calls?

I know you're busy and I don't have to know where you are every second of the day, but, even when we're together, it feels like you're not really there. When we're apart, it feels like you're not answering my calls because you're somewhere doing something better. When we're together, it feels like you wish you were somewhere doing something better. Did I do something wrong? Do you not like me anymore? Is there someone else? Are you going to break up with me?

At least, here, I can pretend that you're actually reading this,
    Hadley

Chapter

Eighteen

Trying to do my calculus homework alone at the kitchen table, I gave up and put the pencil down. My mind had been reeling since reading letters with Kenzie a few days ago. She didn't make me talk about it—the fact that *my* girlfriend was her best friend's tormentor. At first, I was grateful. Maybe, as shocked as she was, she'd decided to spare me the excruciating conversation. But then, maybe she wasn't shocked at all. Maybe she knew this whole time.

The thought made me sick to my stomach. Because *I* hadn't known. I didn't think Hadley ever talked about it. Maybe she did, but could I be blamed for not connecting the dots? For not listening?

Probably.

But it wasn't that simple back then. Everything I did felt justified. It felt right.

When I first met Mallory, it had been a little over a month before the end of sophomore year. Hadley and I had still been together. After lacrosse practice one day, Gage and I were starving so we'd driven a couple blocks from school to JP's, a fifties-looking burger joint that served the biggest burgers we could afford. I always got the same thing: a cheeseburger, a chocolate shake, and medium fries. Gage knew this, so he ordered while I found a table for us.

I picked one in the middle, straight across from the neon orange jukebox. Waiting for Gage to return with the food, I'd been scrolling through my phone. After that bored me, I studied the yellowing tiles on the black-and-white checkerboard floor. Once I couldn't stand that anymore, I looked up and noticed a group of girls at one of the booths by the windows. I'd seen them before when I came to sit down, but now one of them—a radiant girl with auburn hair—was staring at me.

I felt myself blush. It wasn't something that happened often, but at the moment, it felt like a natural response to the kind of attention I was receiving from this particular girl.

Mallory Davis.

I smiled—awkwardly, I'm sure—and raised my hand in a small wave.

This, in turn, had made her blush. She quickly recovered, then smiled back, swirling a strand of hair around her finger.

Our eye contact broke when Gage returned with a tray of shakes, burgers, and fries. Sitting in the chair across from me, he blocked my view of Mallory. "The service here is crap," he grumbled. "If they're gonna be so freaking slow, they could at least give you a number. But no. You have to stand there and wait for it."

"You whine too much."

"Listen, I've been playing lacrosse for the last two hours. The last thing I want to do is stand in some barely-above-fast-food quality diner for two more. Besides, I don't see you getting the food. Ever."

I'd craned my neck—just barely—to steal another glance at Mallory, who was back to engaging with her friends. "Fine. I'll get the food next time."

"No, you won't."

I stole one of his fries and shoved it in my mouth. "You're right."

After we finished eating, Gage excused himself to go to the bathroom. Then, the group of girls stood up, and my heart palpitated.

They made their way to the door, but Mallory stopped at my table. "Hey." She'd pointed back to where they'd been sitting previously. "So, I kind of noticed you staring at me back there."

I shook my head. "No, no. I was not staring at you. You were staring at me."

She giggled. "You look familiar. What school do you go to?"

"Lincoln."

Her eyes lit up. They were blue. Like the midnight sky. "No way! So do I."

"Yeah, I know," I'd said, leaning forward with a smile.

"Really?" She'd narrowed her eyes. "Do we have any classes together?"

"No," I said. "I don't think so. But you're on StudCo. I've seen you working at the events. I mean, you're kind of hard to miss."

"Compliments, right?"

"Oh, most definitely."

Someone behind me had caught her attention and she nodded at them. To me, she said, "I have to go, but it was nice talking to you." Then, she touched my forearm. "You should say 'Hi' if you see me at school."

I swallowed, the heat of her touch burning my arm like fire. "For sure."

She grinned, flipping her wavy hair behind her shoulder and walking away.

By the time Gage returned, that spot on my arm still tingled. It was all I could think about until I got home that night. Not what Gage was saying in the car. Not what was happening around us. And definitely not Hadley. All I thought about was Mallory and when I'd be able to see her again.

Chapter

Nineteen

Tuesday, May 10

Dear Parker,

Just tell me. Just tell me what's going on. I honestly can't handle the suspense. You used to call me every night. We used to talk for hours on end. We used to be so close. Now, you ignore me constantly. When you're with me, you can hardly sit still. It's like you're in a hurry to be somewhere else. Can't you tell that it's killing me?

Can you tell me what I did wrong? Do you not love me anymore? I used to think you were the only one who would never leave. And now I feel like I'm losing you.

Please, Parker. What's going on?

Hadley.

Saturday, May 21

Dear Parker,

It hurts so bad I could laugh. You called me last night. You told me it wasn't going to work. I knew it was too good to be true. I knew someone like you could never really love me. I feel so lost. I feel so dazed. But I guess I can't say I didn't see it coming. I just ... I wish I knew why.

Yours temporarily, I suppose,
Hadley

Tuesday, May 24

Dear Parker,

I know why now.

Mallory is why.

I mean, I suspected it might have something to do with another girl, but Mallory? Mallory, the girl everyone loves because she's mastered the art of faking being nice? Mallory who always gets whomever and whatever she wants? Mallory who makes chemistry a living hell for me every day?

Sorry my handwriting's so bad. I don't even know what to say. But enjoy your new girlfriend, I guess.

Hadley

After meeting Mallory at the diner nearly two years ago, I couldn't stop thinking about her. Her acquaintance felt like liberation.

When I'd seen her standing with a group of girls in front of the school library—just a few days after we met—I snuck up behind her. "Hi."

She flipped around. When she registered who I was, she'd smiled. "Why, hello there."

"When we met the other day, you told me to say 'Hi' if I saw you. So, I just wanted to make sure I did that."

"I almost thought you'd forgotten about me."

"Forget about you? How could anybody possibly do that?"

She hit my arm. "Stop it. You'll make me blush."

"I'm sure it's not the worst thing that could happen."

She'd laughed. "You know what? We should see each other again after school sometime. Maybe planned, this time."

"I'd like that." As soon as the words escaped from my mouth, Hadley's face flashed in my mind. "I just have to take care of something first."

I remembered the night I had called Hadley to break up with her. I'd been obsessing for days about how to do it and debating on whether I should even do it in the first place. I knew people talked about me and my tendency to end relationships quickly in favor of new ones. But the idea of staying with Hadley and trying to make it work seemed exhausting, especially with how moody and clingy she'd been toward the end. So, I told myself that I'd end it. And then I'd do everything I could to make it work with Mallory. Maybe I was repeating a cycle, but this would be the last time.

I'd always hated the breaking up part. Some girls took it okay; most girls didn't. It was always hard to tell which girl the current one was going to be. Even while it was happening, it was hard to tell which one Hadley was.

After I told her I wanted to break up, she was quiet for a long time. Her voice shook as she finally asked, "Why?"

"It's just not going to work," I replied. "I really like you," I said, "but this ... this is too much. I think we'd be happier apart."

"But I love you," she said, instantly placing herself into the not-okay category. "You make me happy. I don't think I can be happy without you."

"I'm sorry," I said.

I'm sorry.

"Parker, are you okay?" Kenzie asked, pulling me back to reality.

I blinked. "Yeah."

She put the box of letters on the coffee table and stood up. "Come on. Get up and put your shoes on."

"Why?"

She was already by the door now, slipping her boots on. "I think we've read enough letters for the night. Let's go out."

I stood up but didn't move past the couch. "Out? Out where?"

"A secret, fun place." She slid her coat on.

"I don't think that's a good idea."

"Of course it is. Now, come and get your shoes on."

While she went to the kitchen to grab a pitcher of water, I scanned my mind for ways I could protest. *I heard it might snow tonight. We haven't read that many letters; we should keep reading. I don't feel comfortable going to a secondary location with you since we just read about how I was a horrible boyfriend to Hadley; and also because you were mad at me last week and might take advantage of our time together to murder me or dump me on a dirt road, alone, to fend off wolves and deranged hitchhikers.*

When she returned to put out the fire, I almost told her the truth, but it was as if she'd read my mind. "If you're worried about someone from school seeing us, they won't. This place isn't anywhere near town, and I have never once seen anyone I know there."

When I realized any further attempts to change her mind were futile, I walked to the door and slid my shoes on.

Outside, the air was crisp, and clouds lined the sky like stretched-out pieces of cotton, creating a stripe over the full moon. I looked behind me at Kenzie, who was locking the front door. "So, what did you say this place was?"

She tested the doorknob, then slid the key into her pocket. "You ask too many questions."

In silence, we walked up the stairs to the pavement where her truck was parked. It made a clicking sound when she hit the *unlock* button on her key fob, and I got in through the passenger side.

She backed out and pulled onto the tree-lined highway, which seemed to wind into oblivion. The volume of her stereo turned up to reveal "my passenger seat" by youmeandtheothers, a song I'd listened to probably hundreds of times. I watched the trees pass by in a dark green blur as I sat back and dissolved into the music.

You're in the passenger seat
You're in the passenger seat
And the stars can't match the way you shine tonight
Yeah, you got them beat
You got them beat
In my passenger seat

When the song ended, "Polaroid" by Sara and the Sparks and then "Who We Are" by Chasing Signs played.

When I looked at her, she was gently tapping her fingers on the steering wheel. "I didn't think you were the kind of girl who listened to indie alternative."

She shot me a look, no longer tapping. "Oh yeah? What kind of girl did you think I was?"

"I don't know. The kind who listened to pop? Hadley almost

always listened to pop. The only band we could ever agree on was Golden Suns."

"That's interesting. Do you listen to all the same music your friends listen to?" she asked, raising her eyebrows.

"Of course," I said. Immediately, the thought of Gage's weird obsession with music from *Hamilton* popped into my mind. "Actually, I take that back."

She smiled smugly and returned her attention to the road. "Golden Suns, huh?"

I smiled at the flashes of pleasant memories the band name triggered. Summer concerts. Road trips. First kisses. I'd been listening to the band since I was twelve, so their music was there for a lot of the big things in my life. "Yeah."

"They kind of suck, you know?"

I whipped my head to look at her. "Come again?"

"They try too hard. Their lyrics don't make sense. The autotune is obvious. I could go on, honestly, but I'll spare you."

I huffed, scanning my mind for a comeback—something to say just to show her how wrong she was, but even if I came up with something good, my attempts would be futile. I learned years ago that you can't convert a hater. "Well, Hadley loved Golden Suns."

She snorted. "True, but there was a reason for that."

"Oh, yeah? And what was that?"

She raised an eyebrow.

"No! She listened to them for me?"

"I mean, she did like them, but she wouldn't have been nearly as obsessed with them if you weren't. She felt like they were your guys' thing, and she loved that. But even she agreed with me: they're extremely pretentious."

"They are not pretentious!"

"Oh please," she said, rolling her eyes. "They so are. And their fans are even worse."

"Stop talking." I covered my ears with my hands. "Stop talking right now."

"In your defense, though, there are worse things to be. At least you weren't one of those kids in middle school who, like, dyed their hair black and acted like they were so cool just because they listened to Billy Joel." She shook her head, smiling. "They acted like they were the only thirteen-year-olds who had ever heard of him."

There was a long pause.

Then, I muttered, "I never dyed my hair black."

She covered her mouth. "Oh my gosh, really? You were a Joeler?"

"A what?" I wrinkled my nose. "Can we talk about something else now?"

She threw her head back in laughter and returned her attention to the road.

Pretty soon, the trees turned to buildings, and we found ourselves in a town I didn't recognize. After a few minutes of passing grocery stores, gas stations, and other random businesses, she pulled into the parking lot of a building with a huge neon-yellow sign that read *3.14*.

She shut off the ignition. "You like pizza, right?"

I looked at her, wondering if it actually mattered, seeing as how we were already here. "Um, sure."

"Good."

Inside the low-lit building, the first thing that caught my eye was the redbrick wall with handwriting sprawled all over it. "You're allowed to write on the wall?"

"Yeah," she said. "They encourage it, actually. It adds to that aesthetic, downtown vibe they've got going on."

After we stared at the equally aesthetic menu on the wall for several minutes, I followed her to the cash register, where a twenty-something-year-old guy sporting gauges, long hair, and tattoos smiled at us. "Hey, hey, hey! Welcome to *3.14*," he greeted, pronouncing *3.14* as *pi*. "If you guys already know what you want, go ahead and spill. If not, might I suggest the Happy and High-Flyin' Hawaiian Calzone? It is positively superb."

Kenzie grinned, standing with the confidence of a girl who had ordered food here countless times before. "I'll have the Very Much in Your Face About It Veggie Pizza. Hold the mushrooms." She turned to me. "I always get that."

I raised an eyebrow. "If you always get that, then why'd you spend so much time looking at the menu?"

She flipped back to face the cashier, ponytail swinging. "It's good to know I have options."

The guy leaned toward us. "Kenz here is a wise woman. Knows what she wants as well as knowing it's not all there is. *3.14* is very blessed to have her continual patronage."

Kenzie chuckled, dropping the Miss Expert Customer persona. "Rick, you're my favorite."

After I'd ordered the Happy and whatever calzone (because, unlike Kenzie, I *didn't* know what I wanted—there were too many options), she led me up the stairs and to a table in the back. Bent license plates, posters of bands from various decades, and graffiti decorated the brick walls. "So, you have a usual *and* the employees know your name. How often do you eat here?"

"Sometimes my alone time in the lake house gets lonely, so I come here to keep myself sane," she said, placing her glass of water on the table.

I sat down. "I see."

She gestured to the room. It was completely empty, except

for a couple in their thirties and a family of tired-looking parents with two small kids. "Plus, this place is so great and barely gets any business. I feel like it's my duty to come and keep them running."

Somehow, it wasn't surprising to me that a pizza place masquerading as a downtown Portland joint in the middle of nowhere didn't get a lot of business. Instead of pointing that out, I took a sip of my Dr. Pepper, then toasted the glass in her direction. "That's very noble of you."

"Someone's gotta do it." Just then, the restaurant pager vibrated from the center of the table. She picked it up. "I'll be right back."

A few minutes later, she was back and placing the plate with the calzone in front of me. She sat down and, instead of eating her own food, stared at me.

"What?"

"Eat it," she commanded.

I stared at her as I cut off a piece and slowly brought it to my mouth. My eyes closed as my teeth sunk through a flaky crust into a cheesy and tomato-y explosion of savory ham and tangy pineapple. I swallowed. "Okay, wait. This is incredible."

"Right?"

I took another bite, closing my eyes again for the full experience. "How did you find out about this place?"

"My family comes to the lake house a lot during the summer. A few years back, we were driving around, trying to find somewhere to eat for lunch, and pizza was the only thing we could agree on." She took a bite of her pizza, closing her eyes and smiling as she swallowed. "I think I got more attached to *3.14* than anyone else in my family though. It's been my go-to ever since that day."

"Are you close to your family?" As soon as it came out, I realized how random, and perhaps too personal, it was.

Maybe she didn't think so, though, because she narrowed her eyes in thought. "Yeah," she replied. "There's a lot of us, so it gets crazy sometimes, but we have a lot of fun. I don't know what I'd do without them."

"How many siblings do you have?"

"Including me, there are six of us."

I coughed. "Six? Why on earth would your parents have six kids?" Hadn't they ever heard of birth control?

"Because I was the first one." She pretended to flip her hair with her hand. "Obviously."

"Okay."

"What about you? Are you close to your family?"

I had to take a second to think about this. Close is a relative term, and it was always hard to tell exactly what someone meant when they said it—especially someone who, I'd just found out, was a real-life member of the Brady Bunch. "Well, I only have one brother, and we used to be close, but, you know, life happens. You grow up, you grow apart."

"Yeah, I can understand that."

From the center of the room, a child wailed. "Don't pick the olives off my pizza! I hate that!"

The parents shushed the little boy and scolded the slightly older daughter, who was guilty of committing the olive robbery.

I gestured to them. "I bet they're pretty close."

"Probably." Kenzie laughed. "But things will get pretty tense if she keeps doing things he hates. Like olive stealing."

I took another bite of the calzone. If heaven was real, it would probably be made of this calzone. "What kinds of things do you hate?"

"What do you mean?"

"Like, what drives you crazy? What are your pet peeves?"

"My pet peeves?" She touched her cheek in thought. "I have way too many; I don't even know where to start."

"You sound like you have a lot of hate in your heart," I said, trying my best to keep a straight face.

"Oh yeah? And you're an angel?" she mocked. "I'm sure there are a billion things that drive you crazy."

"Nope. As far as pet peeves go, I only have one."

She leaned forward slightly, a glint of challenge in her eyes. "Oh yeah? What is it?"

"Okay, you gotta prepare yourself for this one."

"Okay." She leaned back and folded her arms. "I'm prepared."

"You know that 'Manic Monday' song?"

"By The Bangles?"

"Yep, that's the one. I hate that the radio never plays it on Mondays. It's always a Wednesday or a Saturday or something. It drives me insane. Like, why would you want to listen to a song about hating Mondays on a Saturday? It's like wearing days of the week underwear on the wrong days. Except it's worse because it's an oddly specific eighties song, and everyone's aware of when it's happening."

By the time I finished my tirade, I could tell she was trying not to laugh. "Hey, that's a good song."

I raised my hands in defense. "Sure. When it's played on the day of the week it's intended for."

"Okay, fair enough."

Our conversation shifted from songs played in the wrong contexts to other things, and I didn't realize we'd been talking for more than an hour until Rick approached and informed us it was closing time.

Kenzie stood. "Thanks, Rick."

"But before you go ..." He held out a Sharpie to her and cocked his head in my direction. "You've got a newbie here. Treat him right, Kenz."

She took the marker from him and smiled. "You got it."

After he left, I raised an eyebrow. "What's up?"

"You have to sign the wall," she said. "Rite of passage."

I took the marker from her. "I just write my name?"

She grabbed my wrist and led me to the wall. "You can write anything you want." She narrowed her eyes at me. "Just keep it appropriate."

I uncapped the marker and crouched down to an area that was fairly clean. "Oh, darn it. Now, I'm out of ideas."

"You're hilarious."

"And nobody from school comes here?"

"I haven't seen anyone."

"Cool." On the wall, I wrote today's date and *Kenzie and Parker were here.*

Chapter

Twenty

The next Wednesday at school, one of Gage's *TRY OUT FOR LAX* flyers greeted me at my locker. I ripped it off and crumpled it into the smallest ball I could form with one hand, then threw it to the ground and watched it bounce with the weight of the memory it carried. When I looked up, I locked eyes with Gage, who had suddenly appeared in the hallway, walking in my direction. He glanced at the paper ball, then put his hood over his head and swerved to create distance between us as he passed.

I opened my locker, using the door to hide my face. Why did I have to mess things up so badly? Gage was my best friend. Lacrosse was our thing.

The spring of freshman year, Coach had posted the lacrosse tryout results on the door of the guys' locker room. Gage and I were confident we'd make the team. We did every year. But nothing had prepared us for the tiny black words we'd see next to our names.

"Varsity," Gage had whispered.

"No way! What does mine say?" I'd shoved him out of the way and dragged my finger down the sheet until I found

"Everett, Parker." Nerves erupted in my stomach. "I made varsity, too."

The sea of guys waiting to find out if they, too, had made the team created a wave that pushed us to the back.

When we had found each other again, Gage squealed. "Dude, I can't believe we made varsity!"

"I know!" I shrieked in an equally high voice.

When a passing senior shot us a look, we both straightened our posture. "I mean," Gage said, lowering his voice, "it's chill."

"Yeah, yeah." Despite my best attempts, I couldn't wipe the grin off my face. "For sure."

That was one of the best seasons of my life, with Gage and I quickly earning comradery with the upperclassmen who were seasoned and skeptical of us bright-eyed kids. I'd never worked so hard in my life, coming home and knowing I'd exhausted every bit of energy at practice and at games. Every day, I fell asleep happy and woke up excited. This repeated for the next two years.

Now, it would just be Gage this year.

There was still time. Time to change my mind. Time to make things right with Gage and the rest of the team. Time to try out. But my chest tightened with the thought. The Parker who existed last year was gone now. So were his friends. It didn't matter anymore.

Oddly enough, the one place where I was starting to feel like there were things that mattered, where I didn't feel like a fragment of my former self one hundred percent of the time, was Kenzie Bennett's lake house. In a way, it had become a refuge each Friday night.

"Okay, but have you ever roasted Starbursts?" Kenzie asked, sitting a few feet away from me by the fireplace in the cabin living room. The fire crackled and filled the room with orange light and the sweet, smoky scent of burning wood.

"Starbursts?" I repeated.

She gaped. "You've never tried that? It's so good."

"Well, do you have any Starbursts here?"

After thinking a moment, her eyes lit up. "You know what? I think I do!" Then her expression fell. "Too bad it's raining outside."

"What does that have to do with anything?"

"Well, that's where our firepit is."

"Right," I said. "It's too bad we don't have access to a fire right now." I cocked my head toward the fireplace.

"What? We can't roast them in the fireplace."

"Why not?"

"Because … that's weird?"

"So, what you're saying is the only reason we shouldn't roast Starbursts over the fire right now is because it's weird?" I asked, squinting at her.

She squinted back at me in a squinting stare-off. Finally, she looked away. I had won. "Fine. I'll be right back," she said, standing. From the kitchen where she searched, cabinets slammed and silverware clinked.

In my pants pocket, my phone buzzed, pulling my attention back to the living room where I waited for her. A text from Mallory read, *Hey, what are you doing?* Before I could think of what to respond with, Kenzie returned with two short metal roasting sticks and an opened bag of Starbursts.

I exited my messages app and put the phone back in my pocket.

She handed me a stick. "If any melted Starbursts or fire end up anywhere they're not supposed to be, I will murder you and have a bill for my own funeral sent to your family when my parents murder me."

I laughed, taking the stick. "I hereby assume all responsibility."

"Good." She peeled off the wrapper of a red Starburst, stabbed the candy with the end of her stick, and held it over the fire. I followed suit with a yellow one until it bubbled. "They're ready," she said, pulling her stick out. "Make sure you wait for it to cool before you take it off. They get super hot."

"Noted." Once I'd managed to scrape most of the Starburst off the end of the skewer, I popped it into my mouth and the juicy lemon flavor exploded on my tastebuds.

She looked at me in anticipation. "Well?"

I swallowed. "The calzone and now this makes two out of two. I don't know how you do it, Bennett."

"I just have impeccable taste. You'll get there someday."

"I just hope I can attain your level of humility someday," I said.

She laughed. "Whatever. Here, roast some more and I'll start reading."

"Okay."

Monday, June 6

Dear Parker,

In chemistry, I used to text you. Now, I listen to Mallory and Brittany talk about you. I get to hear about your Friday night with Mallory. I get to hear about what a fantastic kisser you are. I get to hear about how hot and funny and amazing you are and it makes me sick to my stomach. Not sick like the general disgust at peers going on about their fleeting romantic affairs, but sick as in a sinking, emotionally debilitating pain deep within—the product of hurt and distrust swirling together like the winds of a tornado in my stomach.

The boy who saved me, taught me, and actually made me feel alive was a fraud. He lied about liking me, about being in love with me. Now he's sleeping with the enemy, so to speak.

Parker, if you ever listened to a single word I said, you'd know how I feel about Mallory. You'd know about how she treats me. You'd know everything.

And I used to think your knowledge of it would change everything.

But hearing her, now, describe the first pair of lips I ever kissed as soft and inviting makes me realize how much you betrayed me.

It makes me want to throw up.

And, to top it all off, my parents have started fighting again. I can't even talk to you about it. I guess I'm all the way back at square one.

From,
Hadley

A heavy silence fell over the room.

Kenzie then said, "Okay, I haven't said anything because you always look super uncomfortable whenever Mallory comes up, but I can't *not* say anything anymore. You knew how Mallory treated Hadley?"

I brought the skewer out of the fire. The starburst wasn't hot enough yet. "I didn't."

"But it says—"

"I know. And maybe she did talk about it, and I just wasn't listening, like she said. I just … she said a lot of things. She said a lot of negative things. After a while, I stopped listening. I know that's bad. It sounds bad."

When she didn't respond immediately, I wondered if I should explain myself more, but I refrained.

Eventually, she asked, very quietly, "Did you cheat on her?"

"Cheat on Hadley?" The words felt heavy coming out.

She nodded.

I cleared my throat. "No. No, I never cheated on her." I took a deep, shaky breath. "I ended things with her before I ever got together with Mallory. But, as you can probably tell, I checked out emotionally way before we actually broke up. I'd already met Mallory by then. She wasn't the reason I broke up with Hadley. She was more like an extra push."

I was too afraid to look at Kenzie. I hadn't intended to be so honest with her, and I didn't want to see the judgment in her eyes. It was none of her business. I never did anything wrong. That's what I tried to tell myself, at least. But there was always a part deep inside of me that thought, maybe, I shouldn't have ended things the way I did. Maybe I should have ended them sooner. Maybe I shouldn't have ended them at all. That part began surfacing the day she died. I tried to push it back down. Logically, I knew there was no right way to go about things. No matter what I did, there would be no winners. I knew that. But I'd hurt her. I was the first guy she'd opened her heart to, and I broke it. I caused pain to someone who was already in pain. Maybe that's what made it different. Maybe that's what made it wrong.

"I always thought you cheated on her."

"I'm a lot of things," I said, "but I'm not a cheater."

She looked at me for a long time, as if trying to figure out if I was lying or not. Finally, she said, "Okay."

Sunday, June 12

Dear Parker,

I always dreamt of my first summer having a boyfriend. I dreamt of holding his hand as we jumped barefoot and swimsuit-clad into the lake. I dreamt of lying beside him on a blanket as we watched fireworks take over the sky on the Fourth of July. I dreamt of staying up way too late every night, watching stupid movies and throwing popcorn at each other.

I didn't dream of being alone, like I was every summer, after being with the boy of my dreams. I didn't dream of being too heartbroken to even enjoy the things I normally did. Yet, here I am, two days into summer, writing a letter that you'll never read instead of talking to you. Sophomore year is behind me. Chemistry is behind me. The best year of my life is behind me. Funnily enough, though: you're not behind me. Not emotionally. I drag behind your memory like an old can tied to a bumper, watching and longing from a distance as the girl I hate the most enjoys the summer that was meant to be mine.

I hope it's great,
Hadley

The girl I hate the most. My girlfriend.

Friday, June 17

Dear Parker,

I'm just writing today to let you know I miss you. I miss your beautiful eyes. I miss your mom. And your dad. I miss Chase. I know I never got to know your family that well, but I miss them. I wish I could have gotten to know them better. I wish I could have gotten to know you better.

Hadley

Wednesday, June 29

Dear Parker,

I know how you feel about religion. You think it's a waste of time and a way for men to control other men. I get it. I mean ... maybe not in the way you do because you seem to get most things a little bit better than I do, but I can see your perspective. After all, the only time my Catholic father ever actually had us attend mass (and I was only eight at the time) was to keep Daniel in line when he was making stupid choices. I guess it worked out pretty well, though, as he managed to get into college and become friends with guys who waited until after high school to get their girlfriends pregnant.

Anyways, it's just funny to me because you hate church and that's exactly what Dr. Kenzie prescribed Monday night when I didn't want to get out of bed.

"Come to youth group with me tomorrow," she said over the phone. "It's so much fun. You'll love it."

I tried to think of an excuse I hadn't yet used. This wasn't the first time she's offered.

"You can't even think of an excuse," she said, reading my mind. "That's because you don't have one. At least not a good one."

"Kenzie," I groaned. "I appreciate the offer, but when I don't ever want to get out of bed or see another person again, I'm pretty sure forcing myself out of bed to go see people is a bit counterproductive."

"You've been moping over Parker for a month now. You need to get out and do something."

Her words felt like a knife. "This isn't about Parker. I don't care about him anymore."

Her judgmental, take-charge tone turned to understanding.

Kenzie looked pained as she read *judgmental.*

"Oh, Hadley. I know. I just hate seeing you like this, whatever the reason. Whether it's about Parker or not."

"Thanks."

"Okay, so I'll swing by your house around six forty-five."

"What? Kenzie, no."

"'Kay, see you tomorrow. I love you."

She hung up the phone.

Turns out it wasn't that bad, Parker. We got to her church and there were a bunch of kids sitting around in a circle on the floor. This man, Kenzie's pastor apparently, came running up to us. He shook my hand and introduced himself before inviting me to join the circle. There, we played these get-to-know-you games for like an hour before reading something from the Bible.

I've never read the Bible on my own and our weird family excursions to mass happened too long ago for me to really remember anything. But it was kinda nice. We read the story about the lost sheep. The pastor explained that the sheep are a metaphor for us. If just one of us goes missing, then Jesus would leave to find that one. I feel stupid for being touched by the story, but I couldn't help it. I feel so lost so often. It never occurred to me that someone would ever want to go to such great lengths to find me, as insignificant as I am.

Of course, I don't know if any of what we talked about was true, but I do know one thing that I didn't know before: despite what you said, religion isn't bad. It's just different.

But going back to the games we played before that:

There was this one game where the left column of people moved down the line and the right people stayed put. The goal was to get to know as many things about the other person as possible (like speed dating).

At one point, I found myself sitting next to this boy with ginger hair and sky-blue eyes. He immediately held his hand to me. "Hello. My name's Noah. What's yours?"

I'm pretty sure I blushed at the forward greeting, despite being fully aware of the forward nature of the game. I shook his hand. "Hadley."

He smiled, his pale eyes lighting up. "Hadley," he repeated, making me blush even more intensely. "So do you guys play these get-to-know-you games every week?"

"I actually wouldn't know," I admitted. "I'm just here with a friend. It's my first time ever coming."

"Oh!" I couldn't help but notice that when he spoke, his

whole body shook with enthusiasm, like a little kid. It was really cute. "Same, actually. I just moved here and my cousin invited me so I could get to know some kids at school and not be a total loner come September, you know?"

"I get that."

"Do you have another church that you go to?" he asked.

"No," I said to him, "I'm not really a religious person."

"Oh," he replied, "it's even cooler that you came tonight, then!"

Because I wasn't really sure how to respond, I asked, "Do you have another church you go to?"

He nodded. "Yeah! I go to The Church of Jesus Christ of Latter-day Saints." (I couldn't remember exactly what he said because it was a huge jumble of words, but I went home and googled a bunch of variations of what I thought he said and finally got to this. I'm, like, 98% sure it's right.) Leaning in slightly, he said, "And before you ask, I only have one mom."

I laughed. "I wasn't going to ask that."

He shrugged, flashing me his super adorable smile once more. "Well, you'd be surprised at how many people do."

"So, are you going to go to Lincoln, then?"

"I am! Are you?"

"Yeah," I said.

"Well, then junior year just got a whole lot better," he said. "By the way, Hadley, has anybody ever told you that your eyes are really pretty?"

By then, there was no hiding the blush. This kid had absolutely no shame. "It's kind of hilarious you're asking me that. Your eyes are so pretty; they're like the color of the sky. Mine are just brown."

His eyes widened in mock bewilderment. "Woah. I wouldn't ever repeat those words in front of the preacher guy over there. It's got to be some kind of sin to say 'just brown' when talking about eyes like those."

I scoffed. "You're just saying that."

"No, I try not to just say things. I like to be genuine."

So, Parker, I did not win that game. The only things I actually learned about Noah were that he went to a church with a long name, he would be going to the same school as me in the fall, and, for the five minutes that I spoke to him, he made me completely forget about you. I didn't feel unwanted or annoying. I didn't feel heartbroken. I felt comfortable. And I'm not used to feeling comfortable like that, especially with strangers.

Wishing you the best,
Hadley

Chapter

Twenty-One

As I stood in front of my locker, ten manicured nails clutched my shoulders from behind. "Guess who," Mallory breathed into my neck.

"Ben," I said, "we agreed we weren't gonna do this at school."

When I turned around, she swatted my shoulder. "That's not funny. And Ben wouldn't think it was funny either."

"I don't know. I think he would think it's pretty funny. I can ask him."

A deep blush covered her cheeks. "Don't you dare."

"Okay," I said. "You kiss me, and I won't say anything. Deal?"

She scoffed and quickly pecked my lips. "I have something for you."

"You do?" Without thinking about it, I brought my finger to my lips. I used to feel something whenever we kissed. Whatever it was, I hadn't felt it in a while. I wasn't sure why.

"Yeah." She took off her backpack, unzipped it, and revealed a teddy bear sporting a white T-shirt with *Parker* written in cursive on top of a red heart. "What do you think?"

"Babe." I took it from her as if it were a baby, like it would break if I dropped it. "I love it. What is this for?"

Her smile disappeared. "Seriously? It's Valentine's Day."

"Valentine's Day? That's not today." I pulled out my phone to check, and sure enough, the date was February 14. "Oh. Mallory, I'm so sorry. I completely spaced it." In fact, it wasn't even on my radar. Normally, I went all out for Valentine's Day. How did I miss this?

Her shoulders slumped. "That's okay. I know you've been busy."

I grasped her hands. "Babe, I promise I'm going to make it up to you."

"I know," she said, not sounding entirely convinced.

"I promise." I squeezed her hands a little bit tighter. "What are you doing after school? Let's do something tonight."

"I can't. I have a student council thing, and then I'm with my study group the rest of the night."

"Tomorrow?"

She shook her head. "I'm studying with this group the rest of the week, and I don't want to stay up late either. My test is on Friday, and I have to get a good grade." Her eyes lit up. "But Friday night, I'll be free. We can have a nice Valentine's dinner and then go to the basketball game. What do you think?"

I winced. "Ooh, Friday won't work. I'm gonna be busy."

"Right. Family night," she said, frowning. "Can't you get out of it for just one night?"

"I'm sorry," I said, remembering the lie I'd told her weeks ago about how my mom was implementing a weekly family night.

"But it's important to her since I'll be moving out soon. She's pretty strict about doing it every single week." I knew I shouldn't keep lying, but I was sure a white lie now would save our relationship in the long run. Mallory didn't like when I brought up Hadley, and reading Hadley's letters wouldn't last forever.

"Right. No, you should go if it's that important to her. I just miss you."

"Thank you for understanding." I kissed her on the cheek. "I miss you, too."

As Friday approached, I felt more and more guilty about lying to Mallory. It hadn't felt like a big deal before, but now I was lying to get out of *making up* for Valentine's Day. There were a few times I almost canceled on Kenzie, but I could never hit send on the texts I'd drafted to do so. It was like something inside me had to do our Friday thing. And when Friday rolled around and I got to see her, I realized that the thing inside me wasn't crazy. Just walking in through the door of the lake house made the apprehension melt off. It was the one time, during the whole week, when I felt like I could take off my mask. At least, partially.

Saturday, August 27

Dear Parker,

Summer is almost over and I'm not really sure how to face everybody at school. I've been used to my own darkness, except for forced conversations with my parents (and siblings when they've visited) and the occasional hang outs with Kenzie. Socially, I'm a mess.

Kenzie invited me to her youth group thing last week. I accepted because I'm desperate, I guess. When I got there, something was off, though.

I couldn't focus the entire time, not during pizza, music, talking, Bible study. All I could think about was how Noah wasn't there. I know. Noah! I don't even know him, unless you count what I learned during the few minutes we spent talking back in June. But still, I missed him. I didn't know why.

I asked Kenzie about him and she had no idea what I was talking about. There was no red-headed, blue-eyed boy from The Church of Jesus Christ of Latter-day Saints, who went to her church things. At least, not often enough for her to know him. And I guess that makes sense. He just said he came with his cousin. To make friends. He didn't plan on coming every time, just like I didn't. But why did it feel so personal that he wasn't there? I mean, yes, I haven't come since then, but he should be there.

Then, it hit me.

Noah was the only one who acted like he cared about me. I showed up that night and barely anybody talked to me, except for the people who had to because of the games. You could tell they didn't want to, though. They care about Kenzie, but I'm just her weird outsider friend. Why would they waste their time talking to me?

And then it hit me again.

Noah, I'm sure, is just like all of them. He showed interest in me, but that's only because he had to for the game. He was just better at faking than everyone else. I mean, how could I be so stupid? To think that he actually was interested in me? We didn't even talk outside of those five minutes. And here I am, dreaming about the next time we'll get to talk. Dreaming about seeing him at school.

It's stupid. I know that. But ... I don't know.

Hadley

The fire from the fireplace cast a golden light over Kenzie's face. As she pulled out the next letter, I couldn't help but notice how sad she looked.

Thursday, September 1

Dear Parker,

I've been thinking a lot and I've come to the conclusion that nobody cares. About me. I'm not Daniel or Reagan, so what reason do my parents have to care about me, other than having someone to criticize? Kenzie's my best friend, but she's too good for me. She's smart, pretty, athletic, and popular even. All I do is drag her down. I know she would be so much happier if she didn't have me around to worry about all the time.

And then, you, Parker.

You were all I ever wanted. I would walk to the ends of the earth to make you happy. But I guess I didn't do enough. And that's funny because you told me I was too much for you. I'm too much for everybody.

The one person I could be myself around left me for

somebody else. And I don't blame you, Parker. I would have done it too. Mallory is perfect. And I was never enough for anyone.

And I was too much for you.

All I've ever wanted was to be enough for someone.

But that's never going to happen.

And I'm tired of trying.

Hadley

She put the letter down and we looked at each other. "I think I know what's coming," she said. "I don't think I can read these ones."

Unlike Kenzie, I didn't know what was coming. It probably wasn't good. But I didn't want to end on this note. I took the box from her. "I can do it."

Sunday, September 4

Dear Parker,

I can't do it. I can't do it. I can't do it. I was thinking maybe things would get better once I had something consistent in my life again, but I really can't do it. I would rather die than go to school tomorrow.

Hadley

I mentally crossed my fingers as I pulled out the next one. It had to get better. I knew our breakup was hard on her, but I never thought it was something to be grieved throughout the entire summer and into the school year, too.

Tuesday, September 13

Dear Parker,

Do you remember Noah? Well, I saw him at school today and he actually remembered me.

I turned around after putting a book in my locker and, as if in a trance, locked eyes with a redhead in a blue, green, and white plaid shirt coming down the hall. He stared at me and my heart skipped a beat as soon as I realized who it was.

"Hadley!" he said, beating me to the greeting. "It's Hadley, right?"

"Yeah," I squeaked. "You remember me?"

"Of course I do." He grinned at me. "You were my first new friend in this town."

"Friend," my one brain cell repeated for me.

It seemed to have caught him off-guard. "Yeah. I'm sorry. Is it okay if I call you that? We're friends, right?"

I shook my head, pulling myself out of the weird daze I was in. "Yeah. Of course! I would love to be your friend."

He grinned, showing off slightly-crooked teeth. "Well, I should get going, but I hope I see you around."

I smiled, watching him walk away. "Yeah. I'll see you around."

It was a nice break from the darkness.

Hadley

Something clicked inside my brain. "Wait. Is this Noah Porter?" I was surprised at myself for even remembering his name. Noah had passed through Lincoln like the smallest blip on the radar. I was pretty sure he was only there for junior year. We had one class together. Social studies, I think. The only reason I noticed him was because he often wore a blue, green, and white plaid shirt. It was the same one I had in middle school that I'd spilled barbecue sauce all over while trying to impress a girl once. I remembered Noah being friendly—he even made friends with the teacher, which was weird. And nobody ever talked about him. There were no scandals, no gossip. I mean, it wasn't like there was a massive rumor mill functioning at Lincoln, but it seemed like everybody knew something about somebody. With Noah, though, you only knew what he told you. And he seemed like the kind of dude who was so open that he'd tell you anything if you asked. So, nobody did. He fit perfectly into that little category Mallory came up with: the boring people.

"Yeah."

"I didn't know he and Hadley knew each other," I said.

"Oh, he and Hadley were super close," she responded in monotone.

"Seriously?"

"Yeah." She looked at me like I was crazy. "He was at her funeral. Didn't you see him?"

"I guess not."

Monday, September 26

Dear Parker,

I can't live like this anymore. I'm tired of feeling so sad all the time. I was so happy when we were together, but that's in the past. I've stopped checking social media because you and her pop up constantly and you don't even use it and I don't follow her.

People talk about you guys. Nobody talked about us. They didn't care. But now that you're her boyfriend, you're, like, famous. It drives me crazy.

And when I see you in the halls, it's even worse. I can't stand it. You're everywhere I turn. You'd think I'd be jealous or something, but all it does is make me hate myself more. Whenever I see you, this obnoxious voice in my head says, "See that? Hadley, see that? That's proof no one loves you. That's proof you're not good enough. You're garbage. You deserve this. Everyone's laughing at you. Everyone knows you're feeling like garbage and they don't care. They think it's funny."

I try to shut it up. But it just gets louder. Louder, louder, louder. Until it's all I can hear.

So if you ever wonder why I turn around when I see you in the hallways, that's why. Sometimes I don't want to see your brown eyes and then overthink until my stomach hurts.

Kenzie says I need to forget you, but she doesn't understand. She's never been through this. She says I deserve better. It's just hard to believe. If I don't deserve you, how could I deserve better than you?

The line after that was scribbled out, the letter ending in:

I hope you burn in hell,
Hadley

"Wow," I said.

I looked at Kenzie, and she was crying.

"Kenzie," I said, putting the box on the coffee table and scooting next to her. "Are you okay?"

"She was struggling so much," she cried. "And I wasn't there for her."

I didn't know what to say. *I* was the reason she struggled.

"I was never there for her. I was a horrible friend. She thought I was too good for her because I never let her in. When she called to talk about her boy drama, I got so annoyed. I didn't understand why it was such a big deal. And then, when she stopped talking about it, I thought she was becoming more mature. But no. She was just dealing with it in silence." Her voice broke on the last word, opening the dam. "We used to drive places in my truck. We'd roll the windows down and turn the radio up, and she'd sing to it at the top of her lungs. She always made up her own harmony, and it bugged me so much. But now, I would do anything to hear her sing again."

My chest ached. Without thinking about it, I wrapped my arm around her shoulders and pulled her into me. She resisted at first, but it wasn't long before her warm tears soaked into the front of my T-shirt. "You were not a horrible friend," I told her.

"I was," she cried into my chest.

I held her for a few minutes, scanning my brain for something—anything—to say that might make her feel better.

"She wrote you a letter," I said.

She looked up at me. Brown streaks and smudges bordered her eyes. "She did?"

I wiped the puddle under her left eye, and she flinched slightly at my touch.

"Yeah," I replied.

She sat up and scooted away, wiping her own tears now.

I flipped through the letters in the box until I came across the one that said, *Dear Kenzie.*

"I can read it," I said.

Thursday, January 13

Dear Kenzie,

You're my best friend. I wish I could tell you how grateful I am to you, but it's so hard. It's hard to tell people you love that you love them and much easier to just let them forget, going through the motions of every day. What terrifies me the most, to the point of keeping me up some nights, is the thought of losing you.

I know that when some girls get boyfriends, they start to ignore their best friends to the point of making them believe they don't care anymore. Kenzie, I want you to know that's not the case. I know I do spend a lot of time with Parker, but it's important that you know that you will always be my best friend, no matter what.

Kenzie, you are amazing. When I first started talking to you all those years ago, I never thought you would actually enjoy spending time with me. Back then, to me, you were this gorgeous, popular girl who was smart and nice and amazing at soccer. I didn't ever believe someone like that would think someone like me was cool. And Kenzie, you still are all those things, but today you are more. You are my best friend. You pick me up when I am down. You are the only one I can tell all my secrets to. You actually try to make the world a better place, the way you are constantly trying to better yourself and with how kind and friendly you are to everyone around you. I don't know how I got to be so lucky to have a best friend like you. Thank you.

Love,
Hadley

Contrary to what I had hoped would happen, the letter made Kenzie cry even harder. I scooted closer and wrapped my arms around her, and she let me hold her with no hesitation this time. I felt the rise and fall of her chest against mine. Her arms wrapped loosely around me, with her face buried into my shoulder. As she cried, I ran my fingers along her back.

When she pulled back, she stopped to look at me. With our faces mere inches apart, butterflies swarmed in my stomach.

I panicked, although I wasn't sure if it was because of the butterflies or the fact that I made things worse. "I'm sorry, Kenzie. I thought it would help."

"No, you're good." She wiped her eyes and moved over, recreating the space between us. "I just miss her so much."

I found myself feeling disappointed that she wasn't right next to me anymore, but I pushed the feeling down. "I know."

"I just hate it. I hate that this is all we have left of her." She checked her phone. "It's getting late. I should probably go."

As she stood up, I grabbed her hand. "Wait."

She froze, just looking at me.

"It's probably not safe for you to drive like this," I explained, letting go of her hand. "Let's just keep talking until you feel better."

"Okay." She sniffled as she sat back down. "What do you want to talk about?"

I searched my mind for good topics—happy topics. "What's your favorite childhood memory?"

"My favorite childhood memory?" She thought about this

for a moment, her chin resting in her hand. "Well, when my two oldest siblings and I were super young, we used to go to my grandma's house in Washington for a few weeks every summer. She'd tell us stories and take us to the park to feed the ducks." She perked up—just a little. "She also had a bunch of apricot trees in her yard, and we'd walk around with little baskets to collect the ones she picked. I'd eat so many apricots during the summer that I wouldn't want any until the next year." A small smile tugged at the corners of her mouth, and I found myself smiling, too. "I always crave apricots when it gets hot."

"Do you still go out to see her?"

She looked down. "No. She passed away a few years ago."

"Oh."

"It's okay though. She was in a lot of pain towards the end. She's in a better place now."

"Hmm."

After what felt like an eternity of silence, she spoke up again. "Why aren't you religious?"

That caught me off guard. What kind of question was that? "I don't know. I just don't believe in God, or any of those other things that make people religious, I guess."

"Why not?"

It felt like such a silly thing—to ask someone why they *don't* believe in something. "Well, aside from the lack of evidence, I guess, I just don't want to."

"Again," she said, "why not?"

"Because ... because how could there be a god who lets such horrible things happen to people? How could he allow murder and rape and terrorism and violence to happen to these people he claims to love? Why would he make people die? Why would he kill Hadley when she was only seventeen?" I was raised without religion, although my dad's side of the family was Christian. They were some of the biggest hypocrites I'd ever met, telling my dad he'd go to hell for not taking us to church, and then going around stealing money from each other and having secret affairs. Even with these shining examples of god-fearing men and women in my life, I was never one of those "angry atheists" people talked about. I didn't care. But I did get angry when they said crap about people—especially young people—dying and going to a better place. That's what people said about Hadley when she died. But she was just a kid. The best place for her to be was *here*.

Kenzie stared at the floor, and, for a moment, I thought she was mad at me. "He didn't kill Hadley. He didn't do any of those things." She didn't seem mad. Just solemn.

"But he didn't stop any of it either."

"I know, but he can't just stop us from doing what we're going to do. If he controlled us, what would be the point?"

"What would be the point of what? Is there no point to life unless you're suffering?" I picked at a scab on my arm. "Why does he want that so badly?"

"Because there's something better after you die," she said. "It makes the suffering worth it."

"I just don't buy it. I'm sorry."

"That's okay," she said. "You don't have to."

Her response surprised me. I'd expected more of an argument, not acceptance. The Christians in my life always had to shove their beliefs down your throat—as if your acceptance of the garbage they preached made it valid. When I was a kid, my aunt screamed at me for saying I didn't believe in God. But Kenzie seemed so confident in this idea that there was somewhere better than here. My disbelief didn't sway her. "Thanks."

"So," she said, "you don't believe in God. Fine. What do you believe in?"

"I—"

"And please, don't say 'science.'"

I chuckled, feeling the tension dissipate. "I wasn't gonna say 'science.' I was gonna say I believe in ... people. I believe that people have a lot of power, and they can use that power for bad or good. I guess most people do both most of the time. I believe in family. I believe that everyone has the responsibility to be the best person they can be, although no one will ever be perfect. I don't know. Stuff like that."

"I believe in a lot of the same things," she said.

"Yeah?"

"Yeah." There was a comfortable silence for a while. Then, "This is super off topic, but can I ask you something?"

"Anything."

"Were you single when you met Hadley?"

"Why do you ask that?"

"I was just wondering." When I didn't respond right away, she sheepishly added, "You know, you kind of have a reputation for bouncing from one relationship to the next."

I wanted to be offended, but I was aware of my reputation. "Um, okay. Well, yes. I was single. I'd been single for, like, two months before Hadley and I met."

"Two months isn't a lot of time."

"So, what? What's your point?" How my attempt to comfort Kenzie turned into her judging me for my dating history, I didn't know.

"How could you be ready to be in another relationship with someone after only two months of being single?"

"Well, I don't know. My relationship with Jessica—my

girlfriend before Hadley—wasn't that serious." Jokingly, I added, "I was ready to be in another relationship before it was even over."

She didn't laugh.

I dropped my grin. "I'm kidding. Kind of. But, you know, sometimes relationships just don't work out. There's no need to be devastated every time. You just move on."

"But if a relationship means so little to you that it's easy to move on, why get into it in the first place? If you don't care that much, then why don't you just stay single?"

"Well, it's not that I don't care. Sometimes, I just don't feel the same way about the person I was dating. Am I not allowed to change my mind?"

"Well, yeah, you can change your mind. But if you're someone who changes their mind a lot, then why not take the time to make sure it's what you really want? So you're less likely to change your mind."

"I don't know …" I combed my fingers through my hair. "I don't like to let opportunities pass me by. And if I meet someone I feel like I have a connection with, then I don't see the point of waiting around."

She shook her head. "I just can't think of it that way."

"Oh yeah? Then, how do you think about it? Let's scrutinize your dating life now. How many boyfriends have *you* had?"

She ran her finger along the surface of one of the couch pillows and mumbled something.

"Sorry, I didn't catch that."

She looked me in the eyes and spoke louder. "I've never had a boyfriend."

"I don't believe that for a second."

"Well, it's true."

"How have you never had a boyfriend?" I knew a lot of guys were into Kenzie. How could they not be? She was gorgeous and confident and smart and … a lot of things. She was a lot of things.

"I never wanted one."

"Why?"

"It's a long story."

"I've got time."

She braided the strings on the pillow together for a moment before stopping and sighing. "Okay, well, first of all, my father isn't actually my father."

I stared at her. "What does that even mean?"

She laughed. "Yeah, that doesn't make any sense. Well, um …" She ran her finger along the pillow again, and I resisted the urge to grab it from her and throw it across the room so she'd say what she was going to say faster. "I mean my father isn't my biological father. My mom got pregnant with me when she was in high school. With somebody else."

"Okay, and …?"

"And my mom lost everything. She was one of the best soccer players at her school. She was going to play in college. But she didn't even get to go to college—she barely graduated high school. Because of me." She tightened her ponytail. "She had to take care of me because her boyfriend at the time—someone she thought she was so in love with—bailed. He didn't love her back, and the moment he realized she was pregnant with his child, he made it clear." She took a deep breath. "Obviously, I don't remember it, but I know the first couple years of my life were some of the hardest for her. And I don't think she started to believe in love again until she met my dad—stepdad, I guess, technically—years later at church. He was just a twenty-two-year-old guy who fell in love with a single mom." A smile formed on her lips at the end of the sentence. "He treated me like I was his own. That's real love. And that's what I want to wait for.

"All these counterfeits in high school aren't just pointless, to me, but they're dangerous. I mean, no offense, of course. Dating makes you happy, and that's great. But I know myself. When I fall for something, I fall hard. Like soccer, for example." She sighed, twirling a lock of hair around her finger. "So, it's better not to give myself the opportunity to fall at all. And also, I owe my mom because she gave up everything for me. I have to be good at soccer. I have to get into a good college, and I have to be able to pay for it. If I got a boyfriend, it would only distract me from those things."

This was the Kenzie I knew from dating Hadley. The Kenzie who was busy—so busy I talked to her probably twice during the months I was with her best friend. The Kenzie who had things to do—things to accomplish. The Kenzie who didn't ever want to get distracted. And this was why she felt guilty. Her need to make it up to her mom didn't just interfere with her ability to be some lucky idiot's girlfriend, but it made her a less present friend to Hadley. How could I blame her for that though? Unlike me, she had a good reason.

"Bold of you to assume that dating makes me happy," I said.

She looked at me, and her blue eyes were so striking that I almost regretted saying anything. "What do you mean?"

"I don't know," I said. "I don't know if I *am* that happy."

I didn't elaborate, and she didn't ask me to. Part of me was appreciative of that. But she knew. We both knew. Although, I didn't want to admit it to myself. I shouldn't have been offended by what Kenzie said about my reputation. I knew about it. And there was some truth to it. At the end of my relationship with Hadley, I thought that being with Mallory would make me happy.

Now, I was with Mallory, and I didn't feel happy. But I knew it wasn't her fault. And it would be stupid to ruin a perfectly good thing the way I always did just because my life felt so screwed up right now. I just had to push through, I guess.

"Hey, Parker," she said.

"Yeah?"

She motioned to Hadley's letter in the box. "Thanks for telling me about this."

"Of course."

"If we find letters for anybody else, I think we should give them to them. I think that would help a lot of people."

I looked at her and smiled. "I think so, too."

Slowly our conversation transformed into something completely different as we talked about our families and future plans and a million other things. In the world outside this cabin, I'm sure time passed. Inside, though, it felt as if time stood still, and it was just us and nothing else.

I realized how false this illusion had been as yellow sunlight seeped through the blinds.

When I woke up, I was in the same position I had been in when we were talking, but with my arm wrapped around Kenzie's shoulders. Her head rested against my cheek, and my first inclination was to kiss the top of it. Then, my brain woke up with the rest of me. "Kenzie," I said. "Kenzie, wake up."

Slowly she opened her eyes to mine. Then, she jumped, pushing herself off me. "What happened?"

"I guess we fell asleep." I sat up, wincing when I felt how stiff my neck was.

She reached for her phone on the coffee table. "It's 9 a.m.," she said. "And my mom has called me, like, fifty times." She put the phone back and rubbed her eyes. "She's going to kill me."

I picked up my own phone. I also had a bunch of missed calls from my mom and a text that read, *Where are you?? Ps.. Mallory asked where you were and I felt like Mom of the year telling her I have no idea where my own son is. Call me asap.*

"Same," I said. Someone was going to kill me. I wasn't sure it would be my mom though.

Chapter

Twenty-Two

After saying goodbye to Kenzie, I got in my car and drove as fast as I could, almost doubling the speed limit where I knew the cops didn't hang out. Maybe the high speed wasn't necessary, as the damage had already been done, but I needed to get back to town so I could fix my mistake—or beg for forgiveness, at the very least. I'd texted my mom to let her know I was on my way home, but she wasn't the one I worried about.

Deterred by a red light, I realized I'd been driving in silence, so I turned on the radio.

Upon hearing three chords play in the chorus of "Manic Monday," I hit the off button. "Not today," I grumbled. It was literally Saturday.

At home, my mom stood in front of the kitchen stove.

Her eyes met me at the door. "Parker."

I sucked in a breath. "Hey, Mom." She had her frilly pink apron on. She only wore that when she made cookies. This was confirmed when I saw the blue-and-white-striped ceramic bowl on top of the oven and oven mitts on her hands. The faint aroma of melting chocolate chips wafted toward me. "Baking?"

"Wanna tell me why you didn't come home last night?" she asked, a fake smile plastered on her face.

"I was at Gage's," I lied. "We fell asleep while we were playing video games."

She pulled her oven mitts off and crossed her arms, leaning back against the stove. "If that was the case, then why did you tell Mallory we had family night last night?"

I sighed. Couldn't lie myself out of this one. "So, she called?"

"She came over."

"What time?" I asked, feeling my stomach drop.

She pressed the home button on her phone, resting it on the counter beside her. "Oh, about an hour and a half ago."

"Wonderful."

"Parker, where have you been going every Friday? Mallory said you and Gage haven't been speaking, so I know you haven't been at his house."

I took a seat, putting the box of letters on the kitchen table right next to me. "I haven't told anyone because I don't know how to explain it."

Instead of saying anything, she waited for me to continue.

I gestured to the box. "Remember when I told you about these?"

She tilted her head to look at them. "The letters you got from Hadley's parents?"

"Yeah," I said. "Well, I told Hadley's best friend, Kenzie, about them, and we've been reading them together."

"So, then Kenzie's the one you were with last night?"

"Yeah …"

"Parker, I told you I don't like you staying over at—"

"It wasn't like that," I said, interrupting her. "I didn't mean to stay over last night."

"Then, why did you?"

"We fell asleep," I said. "It wasn't supposed to happen. But she was upset because … she misses Hadley, and I didn't feel like it was safe for her to drive while she was crying like that, so we decided to stay a little longer and talk. And we ended up falling asleep."

"Okay," she said. "But why did you feel like you had to keep this whole letter-reading thing from Mallory?" She walked over to the table and sat in the chair next to me. "Why'd you keep it from me, Parker?"

"Because Mallory gets jealous, and I don't want her to get the wrong idea about what we're doing. And no offense, but I know that you'd let it slip in front of her, and I didn't want to risk that."

"Okay, so I said *one* thing in front of Jessica *one* time. How long are you going to hold that over my head?"

"She never treated me the same after that."

"Honey, lots of boys say they want to marry their mom when they're little. She's the weird one for thinking it was anything other than an innocent little kid thing."

I stared at her.

"Anyway," she said, "you're not doing anything wrong. If you tell Mallory, she'll understand."

"No, she won't."

"She will. If this is something you feel like you can't tell her about, then either you need a more understanding girlfriend or"—she waited for me to meet her eyes—"you're doing something you know you're not supposed to."

"I told you, it's not like that."

"Okay."

I put my head in my hands. "I don't know how to tell Mallory."

"Parker." She put her hand under my chin and lifted it until I met her eyes. "Are you sure nothing's going on with this girl?"

No. "Yes."

"Not even emotionally?"

Definitely not. "Yes."

"Then I think you know what you need to do." As if on cue, the timer went off. "One sec." When she opened the oven door, the aroma of chocolate chip cookies swept through the kitchen stronger than it was before. "I made these to surprise your brother. They're still hot, but you can have one."

I scraped one off the pan with a spatula and picked up the scalding pile of goo with my hand. "Thanks. I'm gonna go take a shower."

After showering, I drove to Mallory's house. In my mind, I rehearsed what I would say to her, but every train of thought drifted off, leading to Kenzie. Kenzie crying. Kenzie smiling. The way it felt to wake up with my arm around her and her head laid up against mine. The way I felt so understood by her.

Focus.

But it was to no avail. By the time I reached Mallory's doorstep, I had no idea what I was going to say. And I felt terrible. I shouldn't have been thinking about Kenzie so much. Did I have feelings for her though? No. No, I had a girlfriend whom I loved and that's why I was here.

I took a deep breath, then knocked on the door. Mallory opened it, standing there in one of her tighter-fitting StudCo shirts and a pair of jeans.

When we locked eyes, she slammed the door shut.

"Mallory." I knocked again. "Mallory, please open up."

She swung the door open. "What do you want, Parker?"

"I just want to talk."

She looked back into the house, then stepped onto the porch, shutting the door behind her. "Okay, let's talk. Do you want to start with the part where I spoke to your mom this morning, and she had no idea what I was talking about when I asked how 'family night' went?"

"Yeah—"

"Or," she said, dragging out the R, "maybe we can talk about how you weren't home yesterday like you said you'd be, or this morning, for that matter."

"I—"

"Or—"

"Mallory," I pleaded. "Stop. I get it."

She put her hands on her hips. "You can start anywhere. These were just ideas."

I sighed, running a hand through my hair. "Okay, I admit it. I wasn't as honest with you as I should have been."

"Parker, you flat-out lied to me."

"I know, but—"

"Are you cheating on me?" The hurt shining in her eyes made me nearly double over. For the first time, I realized just how bad this was.

"No," I said softly. "I promise I'm not."

"Then, where were you last night? Your mom said you didn't come home."

"I know, and I can't tell you right now," I said, carefully, "but I promise I will tell you later." *When it's over. When it doesn't matter anymore. When I can think of a way to do it without it sounding bad.*

"Why can't you tell me now?"

"I just can't. But I will. I promise."

"How can I trust that?"

"Because I love you. Because I'd never purposely do anything to hurt you." That much was true. And that's why I couldn't tell her now. She wouldn't get it, and it would just hurt her. But with time, I'd find a way to explain. And then it'd be okay.

She looked down at the ground, then back at me. Tears pricked the corners of her eyes. "I don't need this, Parker. I can't put up with much more of this."

I pulled her into me. "I know. I'm sorry."

The next Monday in class, I couldn't focus. Instead, I thought of the time Hadley and I had gone to the coast.

It had been misty and overcast, with a sharp chill lingering in the air. She sat on the towel across from me in a hoodie and jeans. I remembered her shivering, rubbing her arms over her sleeves in an effort to warm up.

"You cold?" I asked.

"Yeah." She smirked. "You should come warm me up."

I returned the smirk. "You should come here."

She giggled, before crawling over and making a spot for herself under my flannel-clad arm. "Okay." She leaned her head on my chest, and her body felt warm against mine.

I shifted so she'd feel more comfortable and moved her hair over her shoulder.

"I love the sky like this," she said.

"Why?" I asked. "It's constantly gloomy."

"Yeah, but I like that."

"It being constant or gloomy?"

"Gloomy."

"You just like being sad," I'd accused her.

She'd leaned her head back and looked at me. "I do not like being sad."

"Yeah, you do!" I said, laughing. "You love rainy days and writing poems and watching movies with sad endings. You like being sad."

She moved her head, no longer facing me. "You can like those things and not like being sad." Then she looked at me and smiled. "Actually, this is something I've been thinking about since we talked about osmosis in chemistry. Because it's kind of like osmosis. If you have sad things on the outside, then it's like the sad things on the inside are in equilibrium, and they don't come out as much. And then you don't feel as sad. Does that make sense?"

I thought about it for a second, enjoying her warmth. I wasn't sure if it made sense. "I think so."

Then I had kissed her.

"Parker," Stephen, the football player who sat next to me in English, whispered, pulling me off the beach and back into class. "What chapter did she say?"

"Um. I don't know."

Stephen grimaced. "Well, if I'm going down, at least you're going down with me."

I faked an apologetic smile and shifted my gaze to the board, pretending to pay attention to it, as my mind drifted back to that moment on the coast. It was the moments like that that I preferred to have define the relationship I had with Hadley. Things used to be easy like that. She'd share these theories with me—about emotions or music or nature—and I'd just look at her and think about how lucky I was to be with someone so beautiful and intelligent. The way she viewed the world, in the beginning, never failed to amaze me. She saw beauty in the sky, in the pain, in the joy, in everything.

But it got hard. I couldn't deny that. It got so hard with her sometimes. She'd always been deep, but then she fell deeper and deeper and deeper until she was in a place where I couldn't reach her. It was a dark place; I knew that. But I never knew quite how dark it was. She never told me.

Then, when she came up from that dark place, she brought pieces of it with her. Pretty soon, you could feel the darkness just by being around her, as if it floated in the air. It penetrated her skin. She turned from a girl who was so excited about life to a girl who wanted to hide from it, first by asking to leave parties early, eventually getting to the point where she didn't want to attend them at all. It penetrated our relationship. It told her there was a threat to us and she became extremely jealous. If I simply looked in the direction of another girl, she got upset. When I took more than a couple hours to text her back—even if I was at school or at lacrosse or with friends—she freaked out. Sometimes she would say something. But most of the time, she would just shut me out. She wouldn't tell me what was wrong—she just made it clear that something was.

But the funny thing was, there never was a threat.

Until there was.

By then, the threat looked like an escape, and I clung to it.

Now, though, I questioned everything. As I'd watched the connection between Hadley and me dissipate, I felt confident that she was the wrong girl for me and that Mallory was the right one. Now, the same destruction that doomed Hadley and me loomed over my relationship with Mallory. For so long, things were *so* easy. She was *so* perfect. Now, the more time I spent with her, the more I saw Hadley's Mallory instead of my own. It was getting to the point where I didn't even recognize the girl in front of me anymore.

Before, it was so obvious that Hadley was to be blamed for our end—not the way it ended but the fact that it needed to end. Now, I wasn't so sure. Maybe it was me. Maybe I was not only to blame for breaking up with her but for bringing us to the point where we needed to break up in the first place. Because I changed my mind. Because I stopped trying. Maybe I was doing the same to Mallory and me.

Or maybe Hadley was responsible for the damnation of both relationships. Now, she got her revenge from the grave.

"Fourteen."

"Huh?"

"Fourteen," Stephen repeated in his gruff, meathead voice. "That's what chapter we're supposed to read to tonight. I figured I'd clue you in since you're lost in la-la land or whatever."

"Right," I said. "Thanks."

During the period between class and lunch, I saw Kenzie passing through the cafeteria. "Hey," I called, walking up to her.

She turned around and smiled at me. "Oh, hey, Parker."

"Listen, I need to talk to you about Friday."

"Friday?"

I turned around. The voice asking the question didn't belong to Kenzie but to my girlfriend.

"Oh. Mallory." I stood there, completely dumbfounded. *Say something. Anything.* But I couldn't. I just watched in anticipation of everything around me suddenly bursting into flames.

"So, she's the one you've been spending all your Fridays with? She's the one you slept with the other night?"

"Oh no," Kenzie said, putting her hands up in defense. "It's not like—"

"I'm not talking to you," Mallory barked.

"Mallory," I said, "listen."

Before I could explain myself, the warning bell rang.

Kenzie shifted her feet. "I'm so sorry. I really need to—"

"Go," Mallory commanded.

Kenzie did as she was told, leaving us alone.

"You lied to me." Tears pricked the corners of Mallory's eyes. "You're cheating on me."

"Mallory." I reached for her hand, but she pulled it away from me. "Mallory, I promise I'm not."

"But you *have* been spending your Fridays with her?"

I swallowed, staring down at the scuffed-up floor beneath me. "Yes."

"What have you been doing?"

I couldn't tell her about the letters. She wouldn't understand. "I told you already. I can't tell you right now, but I will later."

She shook her head. "No. Okay? No. That excuse stood on thin ice before, but it's not acceptable now. Especially now that I know there's another girl involved. Especially *her*." She wiped her eyes. "If a relationship doesn't have trust, what does it have?"

Now, the hallway was clear, with everyone either in class or sitting down at the tables in the cafeteria. Normally, I'd worry about making a scene, but, luckily, there weren't a lot of people around to hear us. "I'm sorry I lost your trust. I messed up." I watched her glossy blue eyes stare up at me. It would be so easy. *Just tell her the truth.* "I'll do anything to make it up to you. I promise."

"Anything?"

My shoulders relaxed. "Yes. Anything."

"Swear you'll never talk to her again."

"I—huh?"

She wiped under her eye and straightened her posture. "Promise you'll never talk to her or see her again, and we can put this behind us."

"But, Mallory, there's gotta be—"

"If our relationship means anything to you, then not seeing her anymore shouldn't be that big of a deal."

"Mallory, you don't understand. If you just let me explain. I can explain sooner than later. I don't need to wait." The time I thought I'd bought was slipping away. I'd have to tell her everything now, as bad as it may come out. It was better than losing Mallory. It was better than losing my time with Kenzie.

"I don't care about your explanation anymore. Nothing you say is going to make this better. Just promise she won't be in your life anymore, and we can move on."

"Mallory—"

"Promise, or we're over."

I sucked in a breath. I couldn't have both, so what meant more to me? What was more important? Friday nights with Kenzie, or Mallory and the last semblance of the life I'd been watching myself destroy for the last four months? I released my breath. "Okay," I said. "I promise I won't talk to her anymore."

Chapter

Twenty-Three

I didn't want to stop talking to Kenzie. She was the only one who seemed to understand me. She was the only one I really felt like myself around. After the crap show my life had been lately, she felt like my one and only best friend.

But Mallory was my girlfriend. I couldn't keep sneaking around. I couldn't keep lying to her. That's something I didn't want to do anymore.

I had to make things right.

As I texted Kenzie that night, the phone felt like a cinder block in my hand: *I need to tell you something.*

Before I finished drafting the follow-up text, she called me.

I took one shaky breath before answering. "Hello?"

"Hey," she said. "You wanted to talk?"

"Yeah," I said. "I, um … I was just going to text you."

"Were things pretty bad with Mallory?" she asked. "I was going to call or something, but I didn't want to create any problems."

"Um, yeah. No worries. Things were pretty bad with Mallory, but they're good now."

"Oh, that's good."

"We need to stop hanging out," I blurted.

A pause. "What?"

I cleared my throat. "I'm sorry. But we can't do the Friday thing anymore. We can't meet up or talk or anything anymore. Mallory thinks I'm cheating on her."

"But you told her you're not, right?"

I couldn't tell if she was distressed or irritated. Maybe a little bit of both.

"Yeah, but I don't think she believed me."

"Well, did you tell her we've just been reading Hadley's letters?"

"I tried to, but she wouldn't let me explain. She didn't want to hear it."

"Of course." She scoffed. "Parker, if she won't even listen to you, then why don't you just break up with her? You said so yourself that you're not hap—"

"Stop," I warned. "I don't want to talk about this anymore."

"I just don't understand why you stay with her."

I felt a lump in my throat. "You don't need to understand," I said. "You've never been in a relationship. You can't understand."

"Well, I wouldn't ever *want* to be in a relationship if it looked anything like yours."

The lump got bigger. I couldn't argue with her. What could I say? Why couldn't I think of anything? What she was saying was wrong. My relationship was just fine. Wasn't it?

I remained silent.

After a long pause, she added, "So, I don't get to read the rest of my best friend's letters?"

"I'm sorry, Kenzie."

Another pause and then—"Fine. Have a nice life."

Click.

The next week, on my way to our lunch table, I passed Gage. For a brief moment, we made eye contact.

He was the first one to look away.

Two months had passed since I told him to leave me alone, and he did. Gage had been my best friend for six years. I told him everything. We did everything together. Now, we were nothing more than strangers passing one another awkwardly in the halls. I was the one who did this to us.

I did the same thing to Kenzie. When no one understood, she did. When no one was there, she was. She never let me down. But I screwed it up. I let her down, and I was the only one who could be blamed for the downfall of our friendship.

At least I had Mallory.

"Parker!" Mallory greeted as I took my seat next to her and her friends.

"Hey," I said, not wanting to interrupt the conversation I walked into.

"Anyway," Ben said to the group, "I've just been getting everything ready for the University of Northern Oregon next fall."

"I'm still so excited that you got accepted," Brittany said.

"Thanks." Ben chuckled. "My mom's pretty excited, too. She's told everybody about it. Aunts, uncles, grandparents, family friends. I took the trash out the other day and one of my neighbors, who I've never even talked to before, was like, 'Congrats on the University of Northern Oregon, Ben!' It's unreal."

Mallory sighed. "It was so smart of you to do early action. I was gonna do that for Aldrich, but I didn't get my letter of recommendation on time. I'm dying to find out if I got in."

"Man, I bet," Ben replied. To me, he said, "Parker, aren't you applying to Aldrich, too?"

"Yeah," I responded.

That was the plan, at least. For years, the University of Northern Oregon had been my dream school. I was going to go there and become a doctor. Now, it was too late to apply. Not just for early action, but in general. The Parker who still planned to go there would have been devastated. The Parker who already made up his mind to attend Aldrich University with Mallory might have been a little disappointed. Now, I couldn't make myself care. My dream of attending UNO in the fall would never happen, and it wasn't too late to apply to Aldrich, but I couldn't see myself there either.

I couldn't see myself graduating high school. I couldn't see myself attending college. I couldn't see myself becoming a doctor. Nothing felt real or attainable or worth it anymore.

This truth had been here for months. With Kenzie, it was manageable. It was easier to ignore. But now that I hadn't spoken to her in almost a week, it stared me directly in the face. Now, surrounded by my high-achieving friends, I was alone in it. Completely alone.

"Ah, I'm just so excited," Brittany said. "You guys are going to college; I'm getting my cosmetology license. This calls for a celebration! We should go to JP's on Friday before the basketball game."

"Down," Ben said. "So down."

"Same." Mallory elbowed me. "You can actually come this time, too!"

She hadn't asked if I was free on Friday, but I guess, since everything with Kenzie was over now, I was.

Brittany squealed. "Yay! It'll be so fun. Ooh, speaking of sports," she said, looking at me, "isn't lacrosse season coming up?"

"Yeah," I said.

"Final season!" Ben cheered. "Are you excited, man?"

Mallory cut in. "Parker's not doing lacrosse this season."

Both Ben and Brittany's expressions dropped.

"Oh no," Brittany said. "What happened?"

"Nothing." I shrugged. "I just decided not to do it."

"But you'd be on varsity, man," Ben said. "You're one of the best players."

"That's what I've been trying to tell him," Mallory said.

Brittany offered a reassuring smile. "Well, I'm sure you have a good reason for opting out this year."

In my peripheral vision, I noticed Mallory roll her eyes. I didn't think anyone in the group was meant to see it. Either way, though, her feelings about the topic were clear.

When Friday came, I awoke from a nap ten minutes before I was supposed to be at Mallory's house, picking her up to go to JP's. I couldn't sleep at all the night before and felt exhausted by the time school ended. I still felt exhausted, but it was something I'd have to push through.

When I turned on the bathroom light, I saw my blue razor. The blades had been taken out and sat in a puddle of water on the counter, next to the handle. Aborting my previous mission to take a quick leak, I picked up the razor's handle, bounded to Chase's room, and threw open the door.

Chase lay in his bed, eyes closed with headphones in both ears. I stood over him and stared until his eyes opened.

He was startled when he saw me but quickly replaced his surprise with a scowl and sat up. "What are you doing in my room?" With me being busy and Chase being a hermit, we hadn't really talked in a while. I forgot how pissy he got when people entered his room.

I held up the razor. "Why are you tearing apart my razors?"

He examined the dark blue handle. "Where did you get that?"

"On the bathroom counter."

"Weren't you supposed to go somewhere today?"

"Don't change the subject," I barked. "Why'd you tear apart my razor?"

"I thought it was mine," he defended. "I'm sorry."

"Okay? I still don't get why you tore it—"

"Get out of my room." He hopped out of bed and shoved me. "Chase."

Undeterred, he pushed me to the door. I didn't fight back but didn't move on my own, either, so he shoved me through the doorway. "Stop coming into my room."

After he slammed the door in my face, I stood in the hall and looked at my now useless razor. Toward the door, I yelled, "Don't be surprised if you find more hair than usual in your razor! I need to shave … things." I sighed and pulled out my phone. When I saw what time it was, I realized I would have to pee fast.

After Mallory got into my car, I threaded my fingers through hers, our hands resting on the console.

"This is nice," she said, after a moment of driving—the only sound being the hum of the tires gliding against the road. "I don't remember the last time we held hands like this."

I glanced at her. "I'm pretty sure we held hands a few days ago—at your house."

"No," she said, rubbing her thumb across mine. "We made out. No hand-holding."

"Well, that's basically the same thing," I joked. "If not better."

"No. It's not."

I pointed up with my index finger. "I know we've held hands at school."

"That's different," she protested. "At school, in front of people, hand-holding is, like, possessive. When we're alone, like this, it's close. I feel connected to you." She sighed. "It's been a long time since I've really felt connected to you."

After a moment of consideration, I said, "Mallory, I want to tell you what I've been doing with Kenzie."

I looked at her, and her dark blue eyes focused on me. I had her full attention. She wasn't going to cut me off this time.

I continued, "You remember Hadley? My ex?"

"Yes."

"Well." I took a deep breath. "She left behind these letters, and Kenzie and I have been reading them together."

"That's what you've been doing?" she asked.

I breathed a sigh of relief. "Yeah. That's pretty much all we did."

"I have a hard time believing that," she said flatly, taking her hand away. "If you're going to keep lying to me, you might as well come up with something that doesn't sound so fake."

My stomach dropped. "I'm not lying to you, Mallory. We've seriously just been reading letters from Hadley."

"I thought she died in a car accident. But you're telling me she wrote a bunch of letters before she died?"

When I realized what she meant, I said, "No, they're not suicide notes. They're letters she'd written years ago."

"Well, then you should go to therapy," she snapped. "Sneaking around and lying to me about something like that isn't healthy. I can't believe you're so hung up on someone you *supposedly* broke up with years ago that you're getting together with another girl every week to reread love letters she wrote you."

I despised the way she said *supposedly*. She didn't get it. And we weren't *rereading*. But it didn't feel worth it anymore to clarify. "Maybe there's a reason I haven't told anyone about this."

"Yeah," she said. "Maybe it's because you know you're doing something wrong." She sounded like my mom, but her words didn't feel well-meaning. They felt vindictive.

"It's too hard to explain right now."

"So, that's it?" she asked. "That's the story you're gonna go with?"

"It's not a story."

"Are you serious?" I felt her stare at me. "You are not serious."

My hands hurt, so I loosened my grip on the steering wheel.

"So, this is why you've been so distant? Is this why you stopped talking to Gage? Is this why you're not playing lacrosse this year?" When she paused, I looked over and her eyes widened in horror. "I can't believe this. It's *consuming* you. Parker, I'm not kidding. You need therapy. Like, what happened was sad, and I get being sad, but it's been *six months*, and you're letting it control your life. You need to get help."

"I'm *fine*." I realized I was driving too close to the curb and jerked the steering wheel.

"You are absolutely not fine," she said. "This is not normal."

"So, what? How does it affect you?"

"Seriously? How does it *not* affect me? I'm your girlfriend, Parker. And aside from the fact that I care about you and want you to do well, this makes me look really bad."

"Well, I'm sorry I make you look so bad," I said.

She threw her hand in the air. "Did you even listen to the first part? Parker, I care about you."

She cared about me? If she cared about me so much, then where was she this whole time? How did I know we'd have this exact conversation if I told her the truth? Because I knew she *cared* about me? "Whatever."

"Fine. Don't believe me. But I seriously hope you get help for this. If not for you, then for me." We rounded the corner, and the yellow JP's sign came into view. She added, "Please don't talk about this in front of our friends. This whole thing is humiliating."

I pulled the car into a stall right next to the building. "Fine," I said. "Let's never talk about this again."

Chapter

Twenty-Four

After school a couple of Mondays later, I walked the long way around the building to get to my car. On the field, my lacrosse team practiced. Well, not *my* team, I guess, but *the* team. Honestly, it sucked to see them on the field without me. This was supposed to be my year—mine and Gage's.

"Hey," Mallory said, walking up to me. "What are you doing over here?"

"Oh," I said, turning my attention to her. I'd forgotten that her last class got out around here. "Just walking to my car."

She looked around. "Did you park by the tennis courts today?"

"No."

"What are you doing, then?"

I shrugged. "Just wanted to go for a little walk."

"Okay." She narrowed her eyes. "Well, anyway, I'm glad I caught you. I have a proposition."

Since agreeing not to talk about Hadley, our relationship had been pretty stable—other than that undeniably tense dinner with our friends at JP's. Since then, Mallory and I held hands to feel close, talked to each other, and hung out more than we had in months. I had a hard time trusting this *okay-ness,* but Mallory seemed happy and that's what mattered. I didn't want to be that guy who lied to his girlfriend or made her feel ignored. I didn't want to throw away a perfectly good thing just because I got distracted. What worried me, though, was how often I thought about Kenzie. I knew it was wrong, but I missed her.

"What's the proposition?"

"Well," she said, twirling a strand of wavy hair with her finger, "I still need to attend a school event to meet quota this week, so Sarah and I were planning to go to the girls' soccer game on Thursday. You want to be my date?"

Girls' soccer.

Kenzie.

Mallory had to know Kenzie played soccer. Was this a test? Was I supposed to say no? Maybe it didn't matter that much.

"Sure," I said carefully. When she was still smiling, I said, "I'd love to go."

"Awesome." She kissed me on the cheek. "I've got to get going, but I'll see you tomorrow."

All day Thursday, the fluttering in my stomach wouldn't go away. I had no reason to be nervous, and yet ...

Mallory and Sarah had to stay after school for a student council meeting, so I met them there. I arrived late to the soccer field, and the game had already begun when I found them sitting on a yellow blanket.

From behind, I wrapped my arms around Mallory, hoping it was her and not just another girl who kind of looked like her from the back—like that one time—and whispered, "Guess who?"

She turned her head, smiled, and kissed me on the cheek. "My super cute boyfriend?"

I smiled back. "Bingo."

When I took my seat, Mallory gushed, "Sarah brought this blanket to sit on so our legs wouldn't get all itchy. Isn't that nice of her?"

"I brought it for selfish reasons. It just happens to be big enough for all of us," Sarah said, flicking her hand.

"Well, I am grateful," Mallory said.

"How are we doing?" I asked, stretching my legs out across my section of the blanket.

"The game just started," Mallory said. "They've just been running around so far."

"Gotcha." I let my eyes find and focus on the ball. When it got passed to a tall girl in a long blonde ponytail, my heart stopped momentarily. Kenzie's face was flushed, and she led the ball to the other side with determination, dribbling it to match the length of her strides on the muddy field. Even after she passed the ball to another girl on the team, my eyes followed her.

When I realized what I'd been doing, I shifted my attention to Mallory. I reached for her hand and she grabbed mine.

"So, what did you think of that book?" she asked Sarah.

"The Regency one?" Sarah asked. "It was all right. I feel like it fell a little flat though."

"Oh, really?" Mallory shifted to lean closer to Sarah, slightly pulling my hand with her. "I liked it. But I stalked the author online, and turns out, she's super boring. It almost ruined the book for me."

I tuned them out as they continued talking about Regency novels and boring authors.

From the field, Kenzie's presence captivated me once again. Her forehead gleamed with sweat. Her passes were swift and her shots fierce. I'd never seen her play before, but now I regretted that. She was a natural, as if she was born to play soccer, brought into existence with the sole purpose of winning this game.

While barely paying attention, Mallory and Sarah still managed to cheer when everyone else did. It was one of those skills they'd mastered by being members of student council all these years—the ability to appear interested, especially when they were anything but.

I returned my attention to Kenzie, feeling impressed by the way she seemed to lose herself in the game.

That's how I felt when I played lacrosse.

Sarah sighed. "We should have gone to the Dance Company concert last night instead."

"Ugh, I'm feeling that, too," Mallory agreed. "Girls' soccer is so boring."

"I like it," I chimed in.

Mallory glared at me. "Nobody asked, Parker."

"You do have to admire the way they dedicate themselves to the game," Sarah said. "I don't think I could ever do it."

"Seriously." Mallory snorted. "Some of them look kind of stupid though. Especially that blonde one in the back. Kenzie Bennett."

I felt a pang in my chest at the mention of Kenzie's name.

"Really?" Sarah asked, shifting her body to see.

"Just look at her," Mallory said. "Her face is so red; she looks like she's about to pass out. And she runs around with her mouth open like a dog."

She did this on purpose; I knew it. And she knew I couldn't say anything at the risk of looking like I hadn't moved on from what we agreed to put behind us. Even after telling her about Hadley's letters, it felt like she was still convinced I cheated on her with Kenzie. She just had to get me to admit it.

Sarah smacked the ground. "Oh my gosh, I see it now. At least she doesn't look as bad as that chubby girl with the black hair. Poor girl legitimately looks like she's about to fall over."

"I need to go," I said.

Mallory shot me a look. "Why?"

"I feel sick."

"Parker—"

"No, really," I said. "I gotta go."

I stood up. Without meaning to, I looked back at the field and made eye contact with Kenzie. For a moment, it felt like time froze—just like that time at the lake house. Like then, it couldn't last. She returned her attention to the ball, and I turned mine to getting away from Mallory and Sarah as fast as I could.

Chapter

Twenty-Five

Friday night, my family gathered at the dining table. My mom made tacos, and I stuffed my face while Dad complained about the new guy at work. Beside me, Chase sat with two tacos on his plate. He didn't eat them; he just messed up the insides with his fork.

When there was a lull in the conversation, I asked, "So, why are we eating together? Do you guys have an announcement to make or something?"

Mom glanced at Chase and his tacos, then gave her attention to me. "Why do we have to have some kind of announcement to make? We did family dinner all the time when you boys were little. Plus, a certain somebody had this great idea to do family night on Fridays, and I'm just trying to honor his wishes."

I sighed.

After taking a bite, Dad waved a taco-filled hand in my direction. "Hey, son. Let this be a valuable lesson not to lie about things you don't want to come true."

I rolled my eyes. "Lesson learned."

Mom gave me a sympathetic smile, then looked at Chase again. "Chase, baby, you haven't eaten any of your dinner. Is everything all right?"

"I'm not hungry," he mumbled.

Mom rubbed her temples. "How many times do I have to tell you not to eat junk food after four? This is how you ruin your dinner."

"Sorry. Can I go to my room now?"

"You're not going to eat even a little bit?" she asked.

"I'm not hungry." Chase stood and pushed his chair in. "Goodnight."

We all watched him walk away. Once he had disappeared into the hall, Dad said, "Is it just me, or does he seem moodier than usual?"

Mom sighed. "I don't know what to do. The parenting book I've been reading said this is pretty normal behavior for boys his age."

"You've been reading a parenting book?" I asked.

"Well, can you blame me?" With her fork, she gestured to me. "You're living a double life." She gestured to the hall. "And he never comes out of his room. Sometimes I don't think I was cut out for raising teenage boys."

Dad patted her hand. "You're doing just fine."

She smiled at him, and I took advantage of their sweet moment. "Can I be excused, too?"

Mom dropped the fork. "Whatever."

"What?" I asked. "I ate all my food."

"Get out of here," she said, shooing me away with her hand.

It felt weird to stay home on a Friday night. Even before Kenzie, when things were normal, I always went out with Gage or some of our friends from lacrosse. It was funny how you take away lacrosse and your best friends just go with it. Of course, Mallory was always a strong contender for passing the time, but she was still irritated about me leaving the soccer game yesterday.

When I got to my room, Hadley's box of letters stared me down, as always. It had been a month since I last read a letter with Kenzie and three months since I'd read one on my own. It felt wrong in a way, but this was how it had to be. I couldn't see Kenzie anymore, but I felt like I owed it to Hadley to finish reading her story—even though all it seemed to be about anymore was her hatred for me.

I was alone. There were no friends to distract me. Just me and this box.

I pulled it off the dresser and read the first letter.

Thursday, October 6

Dear Parker,

My world is black. Waking up every day is torture. I was getting ready for school the other day after lying in bed an hour longer than I should have. I looked in the mirror and realized I don't want to live anymore.

It's not your fault, not really. My life has always been meaningless. You kind of just made me realize it.

So, thanks for that.

Well, my eyes are burning, so I'm going to end this now.

With love,
Hadley

P.s. This is my last letter to you.

Panicked, I pulled out the next letter.

Saturday, October 8

Dear Parker,

Okay, this is actually my last letter to you.

I've been thinking about how I can do this. I don't want to leave a mess for my family. They're busy as it is. Cleaning up their dead daughter would be the last thing they need, but it's not like I can just disappear. I mean, I guess I could, but that would lead to people looking for me and I don't think that would make it any more convenient. It needs to be fast, clean, and obvious.

My chest feels tight again. My head is spinning. This happens every day. It starts with one thought. Then, that thought turns into two. Then, three. Now, I'm stuck in a spiral of thoughts that don't end and they make me so dizzy, but my body won't let me pass out. It forces me to stay awake, listening to the thoughts pound against each other in the walls of my brain. I'm never gonna make my parents proud. No one's ever gonna love me. You lied to me, Parker. The only person who could claim to love me was faking it. My friends don't really like me. I don't have any friends. The only way to escape this and stop being a disappointment to everyone is to leave. I need to die.

I just want this to stop.

I hate you, Parker. It was more manageable before you. You've turned me into a monster. No, you showed me who I really am. For a second, you made me think I wasn't worthless.

Now, I'm more worthless than ever. It's obvious. I don't know if I should thank you or curse you, although I did become accustomed to the illusion. I hate you, Parker Everett. Goodbye, until I see you in hell.

Hadley

A horrible feeling punctured my stomach, like I could throw up.

Without thinking, I pulled my phone from my pocket and brought up Kenzie's contact. Before I hit the call button, I stopped myself.

I can't do this. I can't talk to her anymore.

But I *had* to.

I found a link to "Party In The U.S.A." and sent it to her.

Within a few minutes, she replied, *???*

Can you meet up tonight? I really need to see you, I texted back.

One minute passed.

Then another.

Then, *Okay*.

Chapter

Twenty-Six

"Yeah," Kenzie said. "Hadley was suicidal." We were back at the lake house, and she sat a good distance away from me on the couch. From the window, minimal light seeped in from the recently set sun.

"And you knew about it the whole time?" I asked. Why hadn't she mentioned it before?

"No. She didn't tell me about it until way after the fact. It ..." She paused. "It was really hard to find out about something like that."

"I can imagine."

"I should have known though." She rubbed the corners of her eyes with her fingers. "I didn't see her a lot during that time, but when I did, she acted weird. She started giving me her bracelets—the ones she really liked. And she just seemed so off. I should have known something was wrong."

"I don't think I would have known."

She looked at me. "Yeah." After a moment of silence, she

cleared her throat. "Well, do you want to read a few more?" I'd certainly get in trouble for this if Mallory found out. Fortunately, she was sleeping over at Brittany's house tonight. She didn't usually text me when she was with her friends. In fact, she wasn't a big texter in general. It was something that bugged me when we first started dating, but I'd come to appreciate it recently. And, as much as I wanted to be the good boyfriend, tonight, I needed this.

I nodded and pulled out the next one.

Monday, October 17

I paused briefly. *October 17.* That felt like something, but I didn't know what.

Dear Parker,

I'm shaking. That's why my writing looks so bad. It's hard to control the pencil. It's hard to control the tears. It's hard to see through them. I am here and I am alive and I don't think I want to die.

I swear, Parker. I swear to God that I was ready. I scheduled texts on my phone. One to my mom, my dad, Reagan, Daniel, Kenzie. One to you. They aren't very long or complicated. They were just to say goodbye. Scheduled to go off tonight at midnight. I figured that would give me enough time to do what I needed.

I can't breathe.

My parents are having dinner with my dad's coworker, Gary. I figured they'd be out late enough. It would give me enough time. I wasn't sure what drug would be best. I think that it probably doesn't really matter, just as long as I took enough of it. I grabbed a few bottles just in case. Four of them. I didn't write a suicide note. I figured the texts would be good enough.

I took the pill bottles to my room. Four pills from each bottle. One for each year I've been alive. I put them in a bowl and shook the bowl a little to mix them together. I guess it didn't really matter if they were mixed. I was gonna swallow them at the same time, anyway. I had a bottle of orange juice to wash them down. It was going to hurt a little, I think. Trying to swallow them all at once. But I wanted to feel something for the last time. I can't remember the last time I really felt something.

After I mixed the pills on my bed, I went over to my vanity. I sat down and looked in the mirror. The girl in the mirror wasn't me. I couldn't look her in the eyes, knowing what I was about to do to her. I took a deep breath, poured the pills into my right hand—they barely fit—and closed my eyes.

Then, from the bed, my phone buzzed.

It made me angry.

"Don't get up," I told myself. "Don't stop. You're almost there."

But my hand froze. I couldn't move it any higher. I squeezed it until the pills stabbed my skin. Then, I put them back in the bowl and stood up. I doubted the text would be important. Probably just from my service provider or something. I was gonna check the phone and then start over. I would turn the phone on silent so it wouldn't stop me again. I was gonna do it this time.

But when I pushed the home button, the text that showed up wasn't from the service provider. It was from Kenzie.

It said, "Hey Hadley. You just popped in my head and I

realized we haven't talked all day and that made me sad haha. How are you doing, girl?"

For the first time in so long, I felt the pang of emotion I was craving. I started crying. Uncontrollable sobs. And I realized that I do not think I want to die. I'm a mess. My life is a mess. I don't know what to do. But I don't think I want to die.

I don't want to die. I don't want to die. I don't want to die.

Hadley.

When I finished reading, I looked at Kenzie and caught her staring at the floor. "Are you okay?"

She looked at me, then straightened her posture. "Yeah. I just didn't know it was my text that … I didn't think it was my text that made her change her mind."

I didn't know how to respond, so I pulled out the next few letters and read.

Tuesday, October 18

Parker,

The morning after you decide to end your life—and then don't—is a weird one. After I wrote that letter last night, I went through and deleted all the texts I had scheduled. Now, I'm just alone with this secret. The secret is that I'm not supposed to be here, but I am. My mom came into the kitchen while I was eating breakfast and seeing her made me want to burst into tears. The idea that I almost didn't see it, that I almost made it so I would never see her again … it's too much. My father came into the kitchen, just a few minutes later, to grab his lunch from the fridge before running out the door to leave for work. It made my mission to keep myself composed even more difficult.

My parents are so consumed in their busy lives. So blissfully unaware of what almost happened last night, of the darkness that's been living inside me for so long now. I can't really blame them, though. They're not the only ones who don't know. In fact, nobody knows what I'm going through. And I used to think nobody cared, either. But Kenzie texted me all night and my mom hugged me this morning before she left and I think … maybe people do care. At least a little bit.

And then there's Noah … this totally random and formerly anonymous boy who keeps popping up everywhere—in my mind and at school.

I saw him today in the lunch line. It had been a while since I'd actually eaten lunch at school. I usually just go straight to the table where my friends are, but I want to be healthy. Haha, I guess that's laughable to use "healthy" and "school lunch" in the same paragraph or whatever, but you get it. I want to try.

Anyways, I was in front of him so I didn't see him at first. After a few minutes of waiting, I heard his voice ask, "Hadley? Is that you?"

I flipped around, feeling my face get hot upon recognizing him.

"It is you!" he said, his face erupting in a smile. "I swear, I was staring at the back of your head for, like, five minutes straight trying to figure out if it was you or not. I didn't want to say anything and look stupid, but I couldn't take it anymore. I'm glad I was right." He laughed, paused, then stuck his hands up. "I promise I'm not stalking you."

I laughed, too. "I didn't think you were stalking me. ... until now." The "until now" came out kind of forced, so it sounded more like a serious accusation than me trying to be playful.

He didn't seem to notice, though. "Okay, so I've got to know. Clearly, I'm new to the school and, from what I've noticed, the food here isn't the same as what they served back in Idaho. I chose the spaghetti line because I feel like spaghetti's your safest bet. What do you think?"

"Oh, it's fine," I said, taking a few steps forward, moving with the line, "if you're okay with mystery meat."

He stepped forward, too. "Mystery meat? You're kidding, right?"

"They say it's hamburger, but I don't really think hamburger's supposed to look like that," I said.

He laughed. "You're hilarious."

After he said that, my face flushed and I froze, not knowing what to say.

Why am I like this?

I forced myself to thank him. It was so awkward, Parker. I don't know if he noticed, but we didn't really talk a lot after that.

"Well, I'll talk to you later!" He waved to me, after grabbing his lunch, and walked away.

I felt stupid after our encounter, but at least I felt

something, I guess. I'm still in shock, honestly. From last night. It feels weird to still be here. I'm scared I'm gonna try again and not be able to stop myself and I just don't know what to do. I think I'm gonna text Kenzie and ask if she wants to hang out this weekend. That might be good.

I don't know,
Hadley

Thursday, October 27

Dear Parker,

Part of me wonders if there's still that part of you that hates high school gossip. The part of you that was humble and carefree. I wouldn't be surprised if it's gone, to be honest. You seem like a completely new person with the way you stand in the bleachers at basketball games and walk with your arm around Mallory. You're so preppy now. I never thought that day would come.

Anyway, I thought you'd be interested to know that Brittany and Ariel were talking about you again in physics (they always talk about you, and the other 85 people in your new clan). It was something about how they were worried for the fate of your relationship with Mallory because you had an argument during lunch yesterday, but then everything was okay because you were making out after school. Oh! And then Ariel found out that you left this girl in band (I was never in band?) to be with Mallory. Oh! How scandalous!

For such popular people, you'd think they'd have better things to do with their lives than talk about other people all day.

I was so ready to go home after school. I had a headache, I hated everyone, and my last bit of will power was dwindling.

Noah always seems to catch me at these moments.

On the way to my bus, I heard, "Hey, Hadley!"

I turned my head to see his smiling, freckled face. "Hey," I muttered before turning back around.

"How are you?"

Why was he still talking to me? "I'm okay."

"Just okay?"

I shrugged. "Yeah. Just okay."

He was persistent. "Well, is there anything I can do? To help you be more than just okay?"

I smiled, in spite of myself. I've run into Noah a few times and we always have pleasant conversations, but it's weird to think he would really care about how I was feeling. "I don't think so. But thank you."

He frowned, like he wasn't satisfied with that answer. "Okay."

He didn't say anything else, so I just turned around and kept walking.

"Wait. Hadley."

I turned back around. "Yeah?"

"Do you want to hang out sometime?"

I was a little shocked to hear that. "Hang out? With you?"

He laughed. "Yeah, with me."

I'm such an idiot. Who else would he be talking about? "Okay. Um, yeah. Sure."

He nodded, smiling still. "Okay cool."

Then, he gave me his phone number.
What the heck??

Until next time?
Hadley

The mention of Mallory's name, yet again, struck me. When I glanced at Kenzie, she was still focusing her attention on the floor, and I could tell the mention of Mallory's name made her uncomfortable, too. We didn't talk about my girlfriend when we first met up tonight, and I didn't want to. I hurried to read the next one.

Saturday, October 29
Dear Parker,
So, Noah actually texted me. He's just as funny over text as he is in person. I'll spare you the details, but I think I might kind of like him? Not like I liked you. Not really. I don't know.
Anyway.
We met at the park by my house and walked to the ice cream shop. I don't remember the last time I'd been there, but when we were younger, Reagan and I would walk to get ice cream all the time. That's back when we were a lot closer, but I cherish the memories. I'm glad I never went with you because I feel like it would have been ruined for me after we broke up.
But it's different with Noah. Walking into the pink, vintage-themed parlor brought me back to my childhood, but it also felt new going with him. It was like two happy

memories were merging into one, leaving out the bitterness of Reagan slowly becoming too busy and mature to go anymore and the fear that things could turn bitter with Noah.

At the counter, he pulled out his wallet.

I pulled out mine, too, but he said, "It's okay, Hadley. I'll pay for you."

"Are you sure?" I asked him. "I can pay for myself."

He waved me away. "Nah, I'm the one who asked you to hang out. Let me take care of this."

I wasn't really sure what to say, so I just let him. Recalling the memory, I kind of get butterflies. It was really sweet of him.

I'm not really sure how the conversation started, but we talked about last year.

He had a lot of friends in Idaho, but he wasn't popular. He did choir and track and went to competitions a lot. He said he was bummed out that he wasn't able to audition for choir at Lincoln, but planned to join the track team when the season started.

Honestly, I could have listened to him all day. It threw me off when he asked about me. In fact, I stammered for, like, five minutes straight before I was able to answer him. But I told him about my writing—not this, but, like, the poetry and short stories. I also told him that I like to read, and turns out, so does he! He prefers fantasy, though, while I tend to stick with realistic fiction.

Ugh, Parker. He's so smart. And kind. And funny. And fun. And I think ...

Maybe I do like him?

I don't know.

Love,
Hadley

I put the letters at the bottom of the stack, avoiding eye contact with Kenzie.

But I couldn't avoid it forever because she asked me, "So, what's going on, Parker?"

I looked at her. "What do you mean?" The window behind us showcased darkness once the sun had fully set, leaving us with only the harsh yellow light from the ceiling. The sense of Hadley's presence that the letters had simulated began to fade, and the air felt stiff. I felt trapped.

"Well," she said, gesturing to me, "you're here. You said you didn't want to talk to me anymore."

"I know," I said.

"So?"

"I don't know."

"Is this a onetime thing, then?"

"I don't know."

"And Mallory?"

My shoulders slumped. "I don't know."

"Do you know anything?" Sharpness colored her tone.

"All I know," I said, "is that I miss you. And I didn't want to be alone tonight. I want to finish Hadley's story, but I can't do it alone."

"That's pretty selfish."

"What do you mean?"

"Well, you're allowed to abandon me at any moment because you're afraid to tell your girlfriend the truth, but whenever you need me, you expect me to be there for you."

"I don't expect you to be there for me."

Holding my gaze, she stated, "But I am."

Through my mind ran dozens of comebacks. *Well, that's your choice.* Or *I know I'm being selfish, but I can't help it. I'm just trying to figure things out. I'm trying to survive.* Or *You're only there so you can read the letters.* Or *You just don't understand.* Or … *Whatever.* But in the end, all of these sentiments fell flat because … "You're right. I'm sorry." She was always there for me, and I took her for granted. She agreed to read these letters in the middle of nowhere because I didn't want to be seen by anyone we knew. She was the only one who didn't act like something was wrong with me. Hell, she met up with me in under an hour after I texted her tonight with no context.

"Well, thanks, I guess." She remained sitting there, stiff like a board.

"Also," I said, "I did tell Mallory the truth."

This caught her attention. She shifted her body more to face me. "You did?"

I nodded.

"How did it go?"

"Just like I thought it would," I said, rubbing my face. "She didn't understand."

Her blue eyes softened. "I'm sorry."

"It's whatever." I leaned back into the couch and snorted. "This whole thing is such a mess."

She leaned back, too, and sighed. "Yeah."

It wasn't funny, and I knew she knew that. Nothing was funny about mourning the loss of your best friend or ex-girlfriend. Nothing was funny about lying to everybody close to you about what you're doing every Friday night. Nothing was funny about Hadley being suicidal or dying or being the center of drama in our lives when she wasn't even around to create or perpetuate it. But in this knowledge, we were alone, together.

"This is horrible to say," I began, "but I can't help but feel like her death could have been avoided if her parents hadn't made her drive that day. Hadley hated driving."

Kenzie furrowed her eyebrows. "No, she didn't. She loved it."

"No? She was terrified of it."

"Maybe when she was sixteen and first learning how," she said. "I mean, that's kind of how most people are. But I've been in the car with her. She loves ... loved driving," she corrected. "It made her feel free."

"Oh."

As I drove home that night, my conversation with Kenzie played on repeat in my head. *She loved driving. It made her feel free.*

Mist filled the open highway, and the moon was barely visible behind the fog and clouds. I turned on my fog lights to see in front of me better.

When I read the date at the top of that first letter tonight, it felt familiar. I couldn't figure out why. *October 17.* It wasn't a birthday. I didn't think it was an old anniversary.

Suddenly, a large brown object filled my line of sight. I slammed on the brakes. A deer turned its head and stared at me with wide neon-yellow eyes. After it stared thoroughly into my soul, I reminded myself to breathe. It hopped away, and I slowly put my foot back on the gas pedal.

I could have hit that deer. I could have died.

Then I realized.

October 17 was the day Hadley died.

She got into that car accident exactly one year after she tried to kill herself.

Chapter

Twenty-Seven

I woke up and walked downstairs to the kitchen. Outside the window, it was still dark. Maybe midnight. When I rounded the corner to where the dining table was, I saw a girl with long dark hair sitting in one of the chairs, her back to me.

"Hadley?" I asked.

Slowly she turned to face me. Her dark eyes were big and sad. On the table in front of her was a piece of white paper, and she held a pen in one of her hands.

My heartbeat accelerated. What was she doing in my kitchen? "What are you writing?" I asked.

"Come see," she said in a melancholy, half-hearted tone.

I did as she instructed, feeling scared but not knowing why.

I came to her, but before I had a chance to look at the paper, she said, "Your fault."

"Huh?"

"Your fault." When my eyes focused on the paper, I saw that she was right. *Your fault* was scrawled all over the piece of paper in her wavy handwriting. I couldn't read it, exactly. But I knew what it said. *Your fault.*

I took a step back and saw that it was written all over the tabletop, too.

I looked down and it was written all over my hands. All over the floor. I looked at her in desperation, and she had it written all over her body and clothes in black ink.

With that same melancholy voice, she said, "You did this to me, Parker. It's your fault."

"She's right," another voice said, coming in from the hall. It was Noah Porter, wearing that blue, green, and white plaid shirt I remembered. How did he get in my house? "She told me everything. It's your fault."

Then I woke up, for real this time, in a cold sweat. Immediately, I sat up and brought my hands to my eyes. They were clean. There was no handwriting anywhere.

I let out a sigh of relief and reached for my phone, charging on the nightstand. It was 9 a.m.

I unlocked the phone and called Kenzie. *Answer. Please answer.*

When she did, relief washed over me. "You said Hadley became really close to Noah Porter? Like, they were close right before she died?"

"Um, yeah. Why?"

"We need to talk to him."

"Why?"

"We just need to talk to him. I have some questions I want to ask. Do you have a way of getting a hold of him?"

"He's not on social media very much," she said. "And I don't have his number."

"Oh."

"Hadley texted me his address once. I could probably find it, but—"

"That's perfect. Can you take me to him?"

"I mean, I could give you his address, and you could go see him," she said. "I feel a little weird showing up to his house out of nowhere."

"Kenzie, it'd be weirder for me to show up to his house out of nowhere. Will you please just come with me?"

"What do you need to ask him anyway?"

"It doesn't matter right now," I said. "I just really need to see him. Will you come with me?"

After a long pause, I was sure she'd say no.

But she surprised me. "Yeah. I can."

Kenzie and I met up Saturday evening, exactly one week later, at the lake house. A steady rain fell over her as she covered her head with a jacket and ran from her truck to my car. Once she'd settled into the passenger seat, she pulled the visor down and tightened her damp ponytail in the mirror. "I haven't talked to Noah since the funeral." She popped the visor shut and looked at me. "I still feel really weird about this."

When I put my hand on the back of her seat, she flinched. While backing up, I said, "Well, thank you for coming with me anyway." I stopped the car, put it into drive, and looked at her. "I really appreciate it."

"Of course." Her voice came out quiet and unsure, which was weird.

Once we pulled onto the highway, she returned to her talkative and confident self, making me feel like the sudden timidness was a figment of my imagination. Between small talk, she fed me the directions to Noah's house from her phone.

After a lull in the conversation, she asked, "So, how are things going with Mallory?"

The mention of Mallory's name shot guilt into my stomach.

I almost reminded myself that I wasn't doing anything wrong by going to see Noah with Kenzie, but I was this time because I'd promised Mallory I wouldn't talk to Kenzie anymore. "Good," I said. "I haven't seen her much this week. She's been busy with student council and stressed about college and stuff. Her acceptance letter to Aldrich's supposed to come any day now, and she's freaking out."

Kenzie snorted. "I know how that goes."

"Oh yeah. Have you heard back from Seattle yet?"

"I'm not super worried I won't get in, but also"—she paused, drawing in a breath—"you never know. It's just nerve-racking knowing there's a group of people in another state with the fate of my entire future in their hands. Are you still undecided about where you're going?"

Kenzie was the only one who knew I hadn't applied to any colleges. It was one of the many things we talked about the night we fell asleep together. Her dream was to go to the University of Seattle, and mine was … undecided. I told her because I felt like she was the only person who wouldn't judge me for that.

So far, I'd been right.

"Yup."

Instead of acknowledging my response—probably out of pity—she looked down at her phone. "I don't remember it taking this long to get to Noah's house."

"It's not too bad."

When we finally arrived at Noah's house, the rain had stopped, and the sun was setting. Solar lights lined a cobblestone path to a wooden door. Shrubs and trees decorated the yard. The home reminded me of some kind of cottage in the woods—but with a modern twist.

We stopped at the door. A gray tabby cat mewed at us, then

rubbed against my legs. After doing the same to Kenzie, it scampered away, and a heavy nervousness replaced the space between us.

Kenzie looked at me. "Ready?"

"Of course," I lied. I took a step forward and knocked.

A few seconds passed and nobody came, so I rang the doorbell.

Then the door opened to reveal a guy our age with short, side-parted red hair, wearing a faded college T-shirt. It was Noah Porter. He squinted at us, then raised his eyebrows in recognition. "Oh, hey. Kenzie! How are you doing? And Parker, right?"

Kenzie said, "Good," the same time I said, "Yeah."

He stood there, waiting for us to say something else.

Neither of us did.

He gestured to the inside of his house. "Did you want to come in?"

"Yeah," Kenzie said. "Thanks." When Noah turned his back, she made a face at me like, *Well?*

I cleared my throat. "Nice place you got here." And it was. Following Kenzie through the door, the first thing I noticed was the sweet smell of baking bread. There were pictures all over the wall adjacent to the door. Below the pictures stood an ebony table with a framed wedding photo and blocks that spelled out *FAMILIES CAN BE TOGETHER FOREVER.*

"Oh, thanks, Parker!" Noah led us straight to the living room that housed an olive-colored couch, matching chairs, and a glass coffee table. Adjacent to the living room was the dining room with a round, stained table and a modest chandelier. The wall behind the table had two doors.

"Noah," a thin woman with frizzy red hair called, poking

her head through one of the doors. Her eyes widened when she saw us. "Oh, I didn't know you had friends over."

Noah gestured to us. "This is Kenzie and Parker, Mom. They just stopped by."

"Oh. Well, can I get you two anything?" she asked us. "I just made some bread for a church activity. There's an extra loaf if you'd like to try a slice."

Kenzie smiled, flicking her hand. "Oh no, thank you. We're good." She was so awkward in her effort to be polite. It was cute.

Noah's mom grinned. "Well, if either of you changes your mind, don't hesitate to say anything. We have plenty. Noah, will you go get Nathan?"

"Yeah." To us, he promised, "I'll be back in a sec."

Once Noah had disappeared into another room, his mom untied the apron she'd been wearing and draped it over one of the dining room chairs. "So, are you two friends from school?"

"We go to his old school," Kenzie said. "Lincoln."

"Oh, okay." Noah's mom scrunched her nose. "You know, I feel so bad about pulling him out of that school. You probably know already, but we were staying with Noah's aunt for a bit while this house was being built. I didn't know it was out of Lincoln's boundaries until just before we moved in. I think it worked out for the best though. It would have been hard for him to stay after Hadley ... did you guys know Hadley?"

Before either of us could respond, Noah returned with a small brown-haired boy—probably about ten years old. He got his mom's attention when he coughed.

Kenzie and I glanced at each other.

Noah's mom looked uncomfortable, clearly caught off guard by his sudden reappearance. She picked up her apron and said, "Nathan, why don't you come back to the kitchen with me? I'm going to show you how to use the mixer."

The kid looked horrified but followed his mom back into the kitchen.

Kenzie looked puzzled, and I guess I did, too, because Noah laughed. "He had an accident with the mixer last time. She's going to teach him how not to make smoothies with it."

Kenzie laughed uncomfortably. "A good skill to have."

He grinned, then led us farther into the living room where he sat on the couch. "So, what brought you guys all the way out here?"

After shooting each other another look, Kenzie and I took a seat.

I cleared my throat. "We actually came to talk about Hadley."

His cheery expression fell. "Oh. What did you want to talk about?"

I felt Kenzie's eyes land on me. She didn't know what I wanted to talk about. Truth be told, I wasn't sure if *I* even knew what I wanted to talk about anymore. The dream I had last week just felt so real.

She told me everything.

Did she tell him everything? Did he know, then, if her accident was really an accident? Because if it wasn't, then I wouldn't want to read the rest of the letters. I wouldn't want Kenzie to read them either. That'd be the one exception to my belief that her story needed to be told. Nobody needed to read about how horrible I was that I led her to kill herself. It was bad enough knowing I almost caused it the first time. If she did kill herself, I would get rid of the letters. I didn't want to know her reason for doing it. I didn't think I'd be able to live anymore knowing that I was the reason the world lost a beautiful person.

Looking at Noah now, I wondered if I made the wrong decision by driving all the way out here and dragging Kenzie with me. Was this insane? I wasn't sure, but I needed to know the truth about Hadley's death. This felt easier than reading about it.

I asked, "You and Hadley were pretty close before she died, right?"

Noah looked at Kenzie, as if for confirmation, then looked back to me. "Yeah, we were really good friends."

"Were you more than friends?" I blurted. Maybe it was an inappropriate thing to ask, but it felt important to know.

He looked down and blushed. "I don't know. Maybe. I wanted to be, for sure. Someday."

That last word *someday* floated in the air among us, as if it was its own entity. In it contained so much broken hope, like a shattered promise of the life Hadley could have had.

"Do you think she liked you, too?"

Kenzie nudged my shin with her foot. "Parker."

"It's okay. I know you guys dated for a while. Is this about that?"

"No, uh—"

"Hadley left behind some letters," Kenzie interrupted.

Noah's eyes widened. "Really? To me?"

"No." She gestured to me. "To him."

"Oh."

"But they're more like diary entries," she quickly added. "We don't think that he was actually supposed to read them. She started writing them years ago, but—"

"It's not important," I snapped. Part of me was annoyed that she told him about them. It wasn't any of his business. But then

I saw the look of hurt in her eyes after I cut her off and felt bad. I softened my tone as I spoke to Noah. "I just wanted to know what Hadley was like the last few weeks of her life. It seemed like you knew her in a way we didn't."

He rubbed his chin. "I don't really know how to answer that. She was the same as she's always been, I guess."

"No, like"—I took a deep breath, feeling anxiety bubble in my chest—"I'd see her all the time in the halls. She seemed so happy, but she wasn't really, right?"

Noah stared at me for a long time as if he was trying to figure out if I was being serious. "You know Hadley suffered from depression, right?"

Kenzie and I both nodded.

"Well," he said, "a lot of the time, it's not something that just goes away. Like, Hadley was happy. She got excited about things and had dreams for the future and everything. But she still struggled with her depression sometimes. I don't really think the two have to cancel each other out." He looked at Kenzie. "I mean, you know, right? You were her best friend."

Shooting a look at me, Kenzie said, "Yeah, I know."

"Yeah, so—"

Noah's mom called from the kitchen. "Noah! Five minutes!"

"Okay!" he called back. To us, he said, "I'm really sorry. I should have mentioned I don't have a lot of time to talk. My mom has a Relief Society—a church—thing tonight, and I offered to go and help set up. But was there anything else you wanted to talk about before we go?"

There were a billion things I wanted to talk about and so many questions I could have asked. Maybe I didn't know a lot about depression, but I thought it meant you weren't happy. So, how did it make sense that she had it and was happy? What did he mean when he said, *She still struggled with her depression sometimes?* If her depression didn't go away, did that mean her suicidal thoughts stayed, too? Was that really what the rest of the letters were going to be about? What if things did get better and then got worse right before the end? What if she realized it was the anniversary of the day she almost died and decided to pull the wheel into oncoming traffic? What if pulling the wheel had been the plan all along?

Before I could formulate just one question, Kenzie asked, "How have you been doing?"

Noah smiled softly. "I'll be honest; I've been having a really hard time with it. Hadley was my best friend. It's been months, but I still think, 'Oh, that must be her,' when my phone rings. As much as I hate to admit it, my mom was right. I wouldn't have been able to keep going to Lincoln after that. It would have been too hard without her. I mean, everything else is already so hard without her." He sighed. "But I don't know. Sometimes God has another plan. I don't understand it, but I know he does."

I refrained from arguing with him. If God was real, then what a stupid plan.

"Noah." Noah's mom stepped through the door. "Did you hear me?"

"Yeah, Mom," he said. "They'll be leaving in a minute."

To us, she said, "I'm sorry to rush you out like this, but just know that you are welcome here anytime."

She disappeared back through the door, and Noah asked us, "Was there—"

"No." I stood up. "Thanks for talking to us. We'll be going now." Nothing Noah could say would change anything at this point. I should have realized that before coming out here.

Kenzie and I had nearly escaped before Noah's mom chased

after us with a gallon-sized Ziplock bag of bread slices. We thanked her and tossed the bag in the back of my car before starting our drive back home.

The first few minutes of the drive were silent. Fragments of our conversation with Noah swirled around in my mind. *Hadley. Depression. Dreams. Struggled. Someday. God.*

Eventually, Kenzie broke the silence. "Is that really why you wanted to see him so badly? To ask how Hadley was before she died?" She sounded angry. Maybe even hurt. "I know it seems like I was never there for her, but I was still her best friend. I spent time with her. I could have told you what she was like."

I sighed, rubbing my temple. I didn't want to tell her about the dream. I didn't want to talk about my suspicions. "I know, but it's different. You said it yourself. Noah and Hadley got really close, and it's clear that they liked each other. People tend to be more open with the people they like than with their friends. That's why I said he knew her differently, not better."

Whether or not Kenzie had a response to this, I didn't know because she turned, shifting her attention to the window. The area bordering this part of the highway was flat, and it was getting increasingly darker as the light faded from the sky. I doubted anything she saw was all that interesting.

"If it makes you feel better," I said, "talking to him didn't really help."

She turned back to face me. "It doesn't make me feel better. I wanted it to help. I know seeing him was important to you. Although, I still don't really understand why."

"I didn't realize that's all he was going to say," I mumbled. "That it was God's plan for Hadley to die. I mean, does he really believe that? Do people really believe that? I'm so tired of hearing that." I felt a lump in my throat, and it pissed me off. I couldn't stop as my breaths became shorter and my voice became louder. "That everything happens for a reason. That she's in a better place. That this God everybody loves wanted her to die."

Kenzie didn't say anything.

"And then," I said, "they not only believe that crap, but they *say it*, too. They say it like they're doing something."

"Can you pull over?" she asked. "You're getting heated, and it makes me nervous with you driving."

I quickly pulled to the side of the road and put the car in park, pulling my hands away from the steering wheel in an *Are you happy now?* gesture.

"Thanks," she said.

I took a deep breath and looked at her. She just sat there, staring at the glove compartment with her arms crossed, and it made me feel stupid for freaking out. "Kenzie—"

"No," she said, "listen. I've been thinking a lot about the conversation we had that one time—when you asked if our purpose in life is to suffer, and … I've decided that it's not. The fact of the matter is that, in life, there is suffering. People do things to hurt other people. And to hurt themselves. And it's not because God doesn't exist, or that he doesn't love us. It's just how it is. And I know it sounds absolutely ludicrous to say that God has a plan, but he does. Even when we don't understand it." She looked at me. "I know he has a plan because I've seen it. I've seen him take suffering and make beautiful and necessary things happen with it. In October, I lost my best friend in the whole world. But then I gained you."

In the steady silence of the car, the sound of my own breathing suddenly became obvious, along with my beating heart. I studied Kenzie, sitting there in my passenger seat. A shadow cast over her face, but her blue eyes pierced through it.

"It doesn't seem like a fair trade-off," I said. I meant it to come out as a half joke to lift the tension now thick in the car, but it came out shaky and insecure.

She snorted. "Maybe not." She cleared her throat, her expression transitioning back to serious. "But you really do mean a lot to me, Parker. I felt so alone and misunderstood, and you changed that." She looked down, picking at her nails. "I'm really grateful to have you in my life."

My head felt fuzzy as I looked at her, feeling so much *love* in that moment. As if by instinct, my hand reached out and cupped her chin, slightly, directing it up until her eyes met mine. Under my fingertips, her skin was soft. I felt her swallow. Maybe something should have told me not to touch her this way. Maybe I would have ignored it.

"I can't put into words what you mean to me," I said, stroking her cheek with my thumb. "You make me feel a peace I haven't felt in years."

Slowly her lips opened into a natural, innocent smile that shot butterflies into my stomach. Without thinking, I leaned in slightly and she did, too. We gravitated toward one another slowly until our faces were mere inches apart, hovering over the console. Her eyes were so beautiful. This time, they reminded me of a pool in the summer, with sea green stretching into sky blue. A slight copper color lined her pupils.

Then her lips touched mine, just for a moment.

She pulled back. "Oh my gosh, I'm so sorry."

Her sudden jerk threatened the dream I found myself in. I didn't want it to end. Not yet. Without saying anything, I leaned back in, placing my hand between her shoulder blades.

A nervous smile took over her face, and she leaned in closer. At first, our lips found each other cautiously. Hers were soft. They moved slowly and then with more urgency. With one hand, my fingers found and twirled the loose baby hairs at the nape of her neck while my other hand rested along the curvature of her spine. Her fingers crept through my curls.

As I kissed her with my eyes closed, images of her filled my brain. Kenzie at Hadley's funeral, with her long hair falling into loose curls against her back. Kenzie at the basketball game when her eyes were wet and red. Countless images of Kenzie sitting next to me on the couch, letters in her hands. Images of Kenzie sitting across from me by the fireplace—orange light dancing on her face. The time I woke up with Kenzie next to me, feeling the ghost of her touch for the rest of the day—wanting so badly to kiss her on the head, just to know what it would feel like to be close to her. Now, we were closer than we'd ever been. I drew her closer.

I inhaled the scent of coconut and gardenias. She smelled so fresh and new. The perfume Mallory always wore was never very flowery. She often smelled like vanilla.

Mallory.

Immediately, I broke away.

Kenzie backed away, too, up against the door. "Parker, are you okay?"

"Mallory," I spoke almost breathlessly.

She gulped. "Oh. Parker—"

"Do you have any idea how she would feel if she found out?" I raged. "She was right. I'm a horrible boyfriend. I'm cheating on her." The whole time, I thought Mallory was so off-base, feeling jealous of Kenzie. But she must have seen it coming. She knew I was in love with Kenzie long before I did. My despair grew as I thought of Hadley. *Hadley.* I did the same thing to Hadley. Hadley killed herself because of what I did and now I was doing the same thing to Mallory.

"Parker—"

The anger I felt at myself jumped out at her. "You shouldn't have kissed me."

"I—"

"No, you don't get it," I said. "This is going to ruin our relationship. You shouldn't have done that."

The apologetic look in her eyes transformed into anger. "Okay, I get that you're upset," she snapped, "but you kissed me, too. Maybe I crossed a boundary the first time, but you were not innocent in that."

"Please. Just. Stop talking." I gripped my head. "I can't think."

She touched my arm. "Parker—"

"I said stop!"

Immediately, she withdrew her hand. "You know what?" She gripped the door handle. "I don't need this."

I watched, helpless, as she opened the door and walked out. "What are you doing?"

"I'm walking home." She slammed the door.

I rolled my window down and called after her. "Are you serious? It's, like, fifteen miles to your car. It would take you hours to walk. And it's getting dark."

Without looking back, she yelled, "Oh well!"

"Kenzie, get in the car!" I shifted my car into drive and drove alongside her.

"No, actually, I like walking," she said, sarcasm embedded in her tone. "It feels so much better than being in a car with you."

"Kenzie, I'm not kidding. Get in the car."

"Screw you."

"It's late. You're going to get killed. Please don't do this."

"Don't worry about me. I'd hate to ruin anything else for you."

In the rearview mirror, I saw headlights quickly approaching.

Clearly, she saw them, too. She looked back with a flash of determination in her eyes.

"Kenzie," I pleaded.

This wasn't like her. She wouldn't do it. And yet she ran ahead, waving her arms to get the driver's attention.

In horror, I watched as it pulled over.

"Kenzie!" I screamed. I hopped out of the car and ran to her.

Too late. She climbed into the backseat of the car, and they were gone.

Chapter

Twenty-Eight

After watching Kenzie leave in a stranger's car, I got back into mine as fast as I could and drove after them. When I lost them in a more congested part of the highway, I felt hopeless. The whole time I drove, I called her, hanging up and redialing, over and over again. I drove around aimlessly for a while, my eyes twitching between the road in front of me and the shoulder. When I realized I wasn't going to find her, I drove back to my house. It was the only thing I could think to do.

At home, I paced my bedroom floor. *Should I call the police? Should I try to get ahold of her parents? Should I trust that she made it home okay?* I called her two more times, shoulders relaxing when I heard her voice the second time. "Parker," she said through the phone, "what do you want?"

"I just wanted to make sure you didn't get murdered," I said.

"Thanks for your concern, but I'm fine."

"Are you home?"

"I'm on my way home." There was static on the other line. "The car turned out to be Noah's mom's. After they made it to

their church, Noah dropped his mom off and drove me back to
the lake house."

The lake house! Obviously. I should have checked there.
"How did you know it was Noah's mom's car?"

"I didn't until I saw them in it."

So, she essentially chased after a car she thought was a
stranger's? "That's lucky it was Noah. It could have been a serial
killer."

"Well, I guess I'm lucky like that," she said. "Is that all you
need?"

"Well, I, um." I paused. I wanted to make the situation
better, but I didn't know how. I didn't know if I wanted to go
back to the kiss, where I had her in a way I hadn't realized I
wanted so badly, or go back to before all of that when I had her
in a way that didn't feel so fragile. In this moment, though, I knew
I didn't have her at all. "I guess."

"Great. Then I'm gonna hang up now."

The line went silent.

I let the phone drop to the floor and collapsed onto my bed.

I did it. I really did it this time. I lost her. I still had Mallory
and the options to either tell her what happened or put it behind
me, but it didn't really matter anymore.

Before school even started on Monday, my stomach was twisting
with anxiety. I hadn't told Mallory about the kiss yet, but that was
the least of my worries. I walked through the school hallways,
scanning the crowds for Kenzie. I eventually found her in front
of her locker.

Walking up behind her, I called her name.

She jumped, then slammed the locker. "I don't want to talk to you."

"Still?"

She whipped her head to face me. "Seriously?"

"I know you're mad," I said, "but—"

"Mad?" Her eyes glossed with anger. "Try infuriated. Betrayed. Hurt." She threw her hands up. "Call it whatever you want, I don't care. I just don't want to be anywhere near you right now." Books in her arms, she began walking away.

"Wait, Kenzie, please. Can we just talk about it?"

When she turned back around, her face was red and tears gathered in the corners of her eyes. "I don't care about the kiss. I never expected anything more from you than a friendship. But those things that I told you? I meant them. And it was hard for me to say it because you keep letting me down. Over and over again." Her voice shook. "We get close and then you get scared and try to sweep me under the rug and leave. But I always let you come back. Because I care about you." She tried to wipe away the tears as soon as they formed. "I made myself so vulnerable to you, and then you—you—" Emotion overcame her, and she didn't finish the sentence. She threw her hands up, turned around, and walked away.

I stood there, paralyzed as she faded into the crowd of students making their way to class. Then, I looked around and realized that people were watching. They were listening. They heard everything. And for the first time, I didn't care. Because I hurt the one person I cared about.

When I made it to my own locker, I was surprised to find Mallory standing there. "Oh, hey, Mallory."

"Why didn't you answer any of my calls or texts yesterday? Was something wrong with your phone?" she asked, more concerned than angry.

It was the anxiety of knowing I had to tell her the truth that prevented me from returning any of her calls or messages— another decision I thought I could postpone. "Um, yeah," I lied. "I'm sorry."

"Whatever. I'm not worried about that. Let's just focus on the fact that you have something to tell me."

I froze. There was no way word could have traveled that fast. It had only been five minutes, at most. "Yeah?"

"Yeah," she said, craning her neck in anticipation of what I had to tell her. It confused me because the energy she had was nervous—but in an excited way. After about a second of me not saying anything, she said, "Okay, you're playing dumb. That's fine. I'll go first." As she spoke, I could tell she was trying to hide a smile. Now, she released it, jumping a little as she said, "I got in!"

Still confused, I tried to mimic her excitement. "You got in?"

"Yes! I got into Aldrich! I didn't think they'd release decisions early, but, wow, it made for an epic Sunday." She waved her hand as she spoke. "I mean, it could have made for an epic *Friday* if the idiot postman didn't put the letter in my neighbor's mailbox, but it was still epic nonetheless."

My face fell. Aldrich. Of course.

"What's wrong?" she asked. Then her expression dropped, as well. "Oh no. Did you not get in?"

"Mallory, I didn't apply."

She took a step back. "You didn't apply?"

I shook my head. "I'm sorry."

"That's …" She looked down and raised her eyebrows. "Wow. I mean, we've been planning to go there together forever, but I guess I understand if you found a college that was a better fit for you." She looked me in the eyes. "Where did you apply to, then? Where are you planning to go?"

"I didn't apply anywhere," I admitted.

"You didn't apply anywhere? Like, you haven't applied to any schools at all?"

"No."

"Then—then, what are you planning to do after graduation?"

"I don't know."

She looked away and snorted. "I don't know why this surprises me. You've been so weird the last few months. You've been hanging out with another girl behind my back. You ditched your best friend of six years. You refuse to play a sport you've always loved. Now you have no plans for the future." She locked eyes with me. "I don't even know who you are anymore."

I chuckled. "Me neither."

She shook her head. Her voice was higher than normal as she said, "Parker, I can't do this anymore. I've felt so much pressure this last year. And you—you haven't been supportive at all. In fact, all our relationship has been recently is a waste of time and energy, and I just can't. I don't have any more of that to waste. It's over."

"You're breaking up with me?"

"Yes. I am." She stepped back, then looked at me and grinned. "I am, and it feels good." She shook her head. "I thought losing you would hurt, but turns out, it's exactly what I need." Looking into my eyes, she said, "Have a good life, Parker. I hope things work out for you."

Then she turned on her heel and walked away, leaving me alone to watch another girl I'd loved fade into the distance. I'd never had a girl break up with me before. As Mallory had said, I'd thought it would hurt. But it actually felt good.

Chapter

Twenty-Nine

A few days had passed since everything went down at school, leaving me almost entirely in solitude except for the classes I attended each day. I thought about Mallory and her easy acceptance of our breakup. Of course, I'd stopped eating with her and the student council kids, taking lunch, instead, to my car. When I saw her in the halls, we didn't acknowledge each other, but she didn't seem torn up. I thought about how nearly two years with her washed down the drain as if it had been nothing the entire time. If she'd heard about what happened between Kenzie and me, she didn't show it.

I thought about Kenzie. I thought about how I'd found someone who'd lost themselves after the death of Hadley like I did. I thought about how upset she was on Monday and how I couldn't be there for her—how I was the reason for it all. I didn't even see her in the halls; I'm sure she found different routes to avoid me. I thought about Saturday night, feeling her arms around me in the car as we kissed. I missed it, but even more, I missed our long conversations in the lake house—the ones we didn't plan. The ones that came when we didn't talk about Hadley and the letters. I thought about the night she took me to that weird, Portland-esque pizza place when the weight of Hadley's letters started becoming too heavy to bear. I thought about our conversations about religion—how she respected my views while standing firm in her own. I thought about seeing Noah and then Kenzie asking him how he was doing. I knew she meant it. She genuinely cared about people.

There was another person I'd been close to who genuinely cared about people, and I thought a lot about him, too. Gage and I had been best friends for six years. I told him almost everything, and I wished, more than ever, that I could tell him what was happening now. I wished I could tell him how I lost myself in the face of another's death. I wished I could tell him about Kenzie and Mallory. I wished that I didn't tell him to leave me alone when being alone scared me more than anything. I wished I knew how he was doing. I wished my pride didn't prevent me from reaching out to him now.

I thought about my future, too, surprisingly. I thought about how I had no idea what I was going to do with my life. Time passed and it passed, and it moved on without me.

Most of all, though, I thought about the girl to whom time didn't grant a future—planned or unknown. I thought about the pain she went through. I thought about how I was, yet again, the one who caused it. In an effort to escape our relationship, I suffocated her. I bound her with hopelessness and thoughts of suicide. Everybody said her death was an accident. A car accident—unplanned, unknown. But I couldn't shake the fear that I'd caused it—that I was the reason she killed herself that day. As afraid as I was of the possible revelation, I didn't want to stop reading—just in case.

That Friday, I grabbed the box of letters from my dresser and began to read.

Sunday, October 30

Dear Parker,

Today was a bad day. I couldn't find the motivation to get out of bed until one in the afternoon. When I finally emerged from my room and trudged into the kitchen, my dad saw me and said that I was lazy. It stung. I know I'm lazy, but I don't feel like I can do anything about it. I can't help it. It doesn't feel like a choice. I mean, logically, I should want to get up and do something—anything—productive, like studying for the SAT, doing the piles of homework I have due tomorrow, clean. I don't know. I just couldn't find a reason to live today.

And it's funny the way it happens. Yesterday, I felt complete bliss hanging out with Noah. Then, today, I felt utterly hopeless. I don't understand.

Thanks for listening,
Hadley

Tuesday, December 6

Dear Parker,

Noah and I have hung out after school at least once every week. I've never felt as comfortable around anyone as I do with him. It's not that he's perfect or even extraordinarily charming. But something about him is irresistible to me. He's real. And genuine. He doesn't hide his feelings or thoughts to seem cool. In fact, he says the dorkiest things all the time, but they don't come out dorky. They come out confident because he isn't ashamed of who he is. I always thought that, in order to be able to have that, you had to be cool or popular.

Something else that I really like about him is that he's not just confident in himself, but he's confident in other people. He sees something in me no one ever has before—not even you. And, normally, it's not a big deal when people think highly of you. Like, we all have a facade. We have a face we put on for the world so that they'll think more of us than we actually are. But, that's the thing, Parker. At this point, Noah has seen me without my facade. Last time we hung out, I had been overthinking all day and was in the middle of a spiral by the time we were together. I didn't hide it. I couldn't. I felt insecure. I couldn't shut up about the stress and worries I was feeling. And it didn't scare him away.

And I think that's really cool,
Hadley

Saturday, December 10
Dear Parker,

What did I do what did I do what did I do what did I do. I told Noah.

That's what I did.

I don't know. It just ... it just came out. When we were getting ice cream, he was telling me about his friend from Idaho who was super upset because his cousin committed suicide. He was worried about him. But he didn't blame the cousin. He said, "He was so consumed in darkness that he felt like his only option was to die." He seemed really sad about it.

And it just struck a nerve with me. I haven't thought about it as much in a while. It was like a memory I was trying to suppress. I didn't tell anyone about it. I was so ashamed. But the way Noah talked about it, I just ... I couldn't stop myself. I blurted, "I tried to kill myself in October."

He looked at me and his eyes were blank. "You ... you what?"

I clamped my hand over my mouth. "I did not mean to say that out loud."

"You tried to kill yourself? In October?"

"Yeah, but it's not a big deal. That was forever ago."

"Hadley, that kind of is a big deal. Why ... why did you try to kill yourself?" The way he said "kill" made it seem like it was painful to say, like it stuck in his throat and he had to force it out. It made me immediately regret saying anything. The way he looked at me with so much pain in his eyes hurt.

He knows I get stressed and worried. And he knows that I feel sad sometimes. But, looking at him then, it felt shameful to admit that those were the reasons. Who tries to kill herself because she can't stop overthinking a past relationship? Who tries to kill herself because she feels ignored by her parents? Because she feels sad but doesn't have a reason to? Or because she felt so numb no matter what she did? Thinking about the reasons why felt the same as thinking about all the reasons why Noah should've gotten up and left right then and there and never talked to me again. "I felt like the world would be a better place without me in it." It wasn't a complete lie and it felt less selfish than the more prominent reasons.

A philanthropist, he'd think of me.

He stared at me. Then, "Do you still feel that way?"

I shook my head. "No. Of course not."

"I don't believe you."

The ice cream parlor we sat in was eerily quiet. We were the only customers there, but I was scared the employees would hear us. I remember pulling on my sleeves. "Well, I don't know what to say," I said.

"Why do you feel like the world would be better without you?"

I told him I didn't want to talk about it.

After a long pause, he said, "It wouldn't be, you know?"

I cocked my head. "What do you mean?"

"The world wouldn't be a better place without you in it. It would be a terrible place. It would be a world I wouldn't want to live in." He looked sad, as he stood up with his paper ice cream bowl in hand, and I hated myself for making him feel that way.

"Please don't be mad at me," I said.

His expression softened. "I'm not mad at you, Hadley. But I'm worried about you." He walked to the garbage to throw away his bowl and mine. After returning, he asked, "Have you talked to a counselor?"

I shook my head.

"I think you should," he said.

"I'd rather not."

He took his seat again. "Why?"

"Counselors are for people with real problems. I don't want to take away resources from someone who needs them more."

"Hadley, that's not—"

I shot him a look.

"You don't have to do anything you don't want to do, but I want you to know I'm here for you." He touched my hand, sending electric currents through my skin. "If you're feeling suicidal or stressed or sad or alone. It doesn't matter. I'm your friend and I care about you and I promise nothing you say will ever change that."

Thanks for listening again,
Hadley

I slammed the letter onto the bed.

I needed to get out of here.

My keys lay on my cluttered desk. I needed to drive somewhere. I couldn't leave the letters here though. If anybody saw them, then they'd know. They'd know. Not even Noah could save her. She killed herself because she couldn't stop overthinking our relationship.

I scooped the stray letters into the box and carried it under my arm as I reached for the keys. Outside, I started the car, shifted it into reverse, then pulled out of the driveway. I drove out of the neighborhood and followed the highway until it turned into the canyon I used to drive through with Hadley. The sun lingered above the horizon, washing the trees and road in warm light. For the first time in days, it wasn't raining. When I glanced at the passenger seat, I swore I saw her—singing, laughing, smiling at me. We had been so young when we drove through this canyon together, learning about life as new drivers and stupid sixteen-year-olds. For that brief moment in our lives, we had been in love.

The image of a smiling Hadley disappeared, and my mind circled back to that last letter I read.

Two months after her initial attempt, she still felt like she should die. Because of me.

She also said that she was suicidal because she felt numb. But I was the reason she felt numb. And I was the first reason she listed for feeling that way. And she said it before: she was better off before me. She was lonely, but then I made her depressed. I made her want to kill herself. And she did. If it was two months later and she still felt that way and Noah said she was still depressed, then what would stop her from killing herself last October? Nothing. Nothing would. Nothing did. She did it. She killed herself.

A car with a Texas license plate passed me over the solid yellow line and honked. I was seven miles under the speed limit. Breaking from my thoughts momentarily, I sped up.

Hadley had so much to offer the world. She was going to be one of the greatest writers this world had ever known. She would have written things more profound than letters to an ex-boyfriend. More than two people would have read them. Now, it would never happen. It would never happen. And it was my fault. I denied the world the opportunity to truly know Hadley García.

The sun began its descent into golden hour. I checked my phone. There was no service.

I drove to the spot where I'd kissed her for the first time on one of our canyon drives. It was a ledge that overlooked the valley. At the time, the sun was setting. Her dark silhouette in front of the golden sky made me think of the Golden Suns music video for "Here with You." I told her so. She told me to turn the car on and play the song. I did. We kissed again, and then she asked me to dance with her. I wasn't much of a spontaneous dancer, but nobody was around. Nobody could see us, so I said yes. I danced with her. It got cold. We got inside the car. She looked at me and smiled. I told her I loved her. She said she loved me, too.

I wondered if Noah ever drove her through the canyon. I wondered if he ever told her he loved her. Maybe he wanted to. Now he would never get to. Because Hadley killed herself. Because of me. I killed Hadley.

I flipped around at the spot and drove back down the path I took to get there. By the time I exited the canyon and reached the main highway, I had been driving for two hours. The sun continued to descend for the night. Once I'd reached a spot where my phone had service, it vibrated multiple times. While trying to pay attention to the road in front of me, I quickly checked my phone and saw multiple missed calls from both my parents and a text from Mom that said, *Call me asap.*

I pulled over to the shoulder.

"Parker," my mom said when she picked up. It sounded like she was crying.

"Mom, what's going on?"

She mumbled something, her jumbled words being punctuated by sobs. The only word I could make out was "Chase."

"I can't understand you," I told her. "Slow down."

"Your brother." She was hysterical. "Chase. He's in the hospital."

Blood rushed to my ears. "Chase is in the hospital? What happened? Is he okay?"

"He tried. To kill. Himself." She let out big, heaving breaths between words. "There was blood everywhere."

My head burned and the road spun in front of me. "What?"

"Chase tried to kill himself."

I didn't say anything. The air in my lungs began to feel heavy. It had to be a nightmare. It couldn't be real. It wasn't real.

She continued after taking a long, deep breath. "I'm sorry, Parker. I don't want to worry you. I'm still processing this. He's okay now. He's in the hospital recovering. But I wanted to let you know what's going on. Other than your dad and me, they're not allowing visitors right now. We're actually waiting in the hall while someone talks to him. They'll give us more information later, but that's what I know now."

Was this some kind of sick joke? "Okay."

"I love you. Please be safe. I'll probably stay the night with Chase, but your dad will be home later tonight."

"Okay," I said, phone trembling in my hand. "Love you, too."

What was going on? How could this happen? Why would my brother try to do that to himself? Chase tried to kill himself. The same thing that Hadley—but it was Chase.

Chase.

How? Why?

I turned around and stared at the box of letters in my backseat.

It was because of them. Because of me. Because of who I was when they were written. Everything was wrong. My little brother was in the hospital, and Hadley was dead. The evidence was in the letters. I knew it. I couldn't finish reading them, and I couldn't let anyone else read them either.

I had to destroy them.

And I knew exactly how.

I nearly forgot to check my blind spot when I spun my car back onto the road. Cars sped up behind me, but I slammed my foot on the gas to stay ahead of them. It wasn't too far from here.

By the time I got to Kenzie's lake house, the sun had almost completely set, but there was still enough light to find my way around through the fog. I parked my car on the vacant parking pad and stumbled down the wooden stairs, box of letters in hand. This was it. I just had to get them to the water, and I'd be done with all of this. It would all be over. The nightmare would be over.

To the side of the house was a dock that floated over the lake. It was all that separated me from the vast body of water, which would have seemed to have gone on forever if it wasn't for the surrounding forest. I felt like a moth flying toward the light as I made my way to it.

I laid the box on the dock and sat down beside it. "I'm sorry," I muttered. "I'm sorry."

For several minutes, I sat there, thinking about how sorry I was for all of it, truly. I thought about Hadley's letter. Noah said something about the darkness becoming so much that the friend felt like his only option was to die. That was what happened to Hadley. The darkness was too much for her. She never recovered from how she felt. The same thing happened to my brother—the pain became too heavy.

Chase … How did I miss what was going on? Why couldn't I see that he was drowning in the darkness, too? How could he attempt to end his life right under my nose? With me in the room right across the hall from his? What did I do wrong?

"I'm sorry," I screamed. "I'm sorry!" My desperation echoed against the trees around me.

For what felt like an eternity, I stared at the box of letters in front of me. I took the lid off and ran my fingers along the dry paper, feeling the sharp edges. They could cut me if I let them.

I almost did.

With trembling arms, I replaced the lid and picked up the box. As I stood, I slowly raised the box above my head. I took two careful steps toward the edge of the dock. "Goodbye, Hadley."

"No!" I heard someone scream behind me. Two arms wrapped around my waist and pulled me down. As I fell, the lid came off the box, making some letters fall onto the dock. One fell into the lake. In a frenzy, Kenzie moved from underneath me, grabbing the letters and putting them back where they belonged. She shoved the box away from my reach. "Parker, what are you doing?" Her voice came out high and forced. Her face was red and eyes watery.

I sat up. "I need to get rid of these." I brought my knees up and buried my face into my legs. "I can't do this anymore. I can't do it."

"You can't. This is all we have left of her," she cried. When I looked up, I saw that she had tears streaming down her face. "Why would you do this?"

"Because," I said, trying with everything I had to keep my emotions contained.

"Because why?"

I looked her in the eyes. I couldn't hold back anymore. I broke down into tears. "I killed her, Kenzie. I killed Hadley."

Her eyes widened, the look of despair she wore turning to confusion. "You what?"

"It wasn't an accident," I told her, my words falling between sobs. "She turned the wheel. She crashed her car on purpose."

"Parker, what are you talking about?"

Louder, I said, "Hadley killed herself that day. She killed herself because of me."

"Is that what the letters say?"

I shook my head, my tears falling more urgently. "No, but I know. The signs are everywhere. In the letters. With Noah. He said her depression never went away. It got worse. She killed herself."

She stared at me, her pupils twitching back and forth over me like I was crazy. Slowly she said, "Parker, Hadley didn't kill herself."

"She did," I cried. "She did. And then my brother did. He tried to. It's my fault."

She put her hand on my shoulder. "What? Your brother? What happened?"

"He's in the hospital," I said, not able to meet her eyes. "He tried to kill himself like Hadley did."

"Is he okay?"

I wiped my eyes. "I think so. I don't know. I just found out." The hospital wasn't allowing visitors. Should I have gone, anyway?

Kenzie scooted next to me and grabbed my hand with both of hers. "Parker, listen to me. Hadley did not kill herself."

"She did."

She dropped my hands, grabbing my face and forcing me to look at her. "No. She didn't. Hadley died in a car accident."

"But she had depression."

"Yes, she struggled with depression," she said, letting go of my face. "Not suicide. She was getting help. She was doing good. She had bad days, but they weren't that bad after a while. Not to the point of ending her life. Not after she got into therapy."

"How do you know?"

"Because I know," she said. "She's my best friend. Yeah, the beginning of junior year was a super low point for her, but it got so much better." She gestured to the box. "Did you read the rest without me?"

"Only a few."

"Read the rest of them," she said, "I think they'll get better. They have to." She looked at the water. "She did."

A moment of silence passed among us, and I felt the daze I'd been in slowly melt away, bringing me back to reality. With Kenzie here beside me, there was so much I wanted to say, so much I wanted to tell her. "I messed up so bad," I said.

"Parker, it wasn't your fault. Her mental health was bad. You can't take responsibility for that just because you broke up with her."

They were the words I needed to hear, even if they weren't the ones I expected. "Thanks," I said. "But I mean I messed up with you."

"Oh," she said. "Yeah, you definitely did."

"Will you forgive me?"

"I want to," she said. "But if I forgive you, then I'll want to trust you, and I don't think I can do that again. Not when I keep getting hurt like this."

"I hate that I hurt you," I said, trying not to cry again. "You were right. You are always there for me. And for the past three months, you've been the only person who has been there for me. I've been an idiot. And I messed up. And I understand if you can never forgive me or trust me ever again. But I swear I will never hurt you like that again. If I do, then I'll be the first one to walk away and never come back." I paused, then blurted, "But I'm in love with you."

I didn't mean to say it, but I couldn't take it back either. And although I'd said those words over and over throughout my life, this time, they felt heavier. I meant them. I had never felt as close to anyone as I did Kenzie. I loved her.

She looked taken aback but quickly regained her composure. "I heard Mallory broke up with you."

"She did."

"So ..."

"So, it needed to happen. I fell out of love with her months ago. I just didn't realize it."

"Right."

"I mean it," I said softly. "I know it sounds fake, but she knew what was going on long before I did." I sighed. "I didn't want to admit it because I didn't want to break up with her. I hurt Hadley so much, and I didn't want to do that to Mallory. I didn't want to do it to anyone again. Mallory also felt like the one thing that didn't change after Hadley died, and I didn't want to let go of that. But I screwed up. I made things worse."

She sat there like she was trying to take it all in. "Do you really mean that? Do you really feel that way about me?"

"I do."

She looked away—at the water again. Trying to see what she saw, I looked, too. The lake reflected the dark orange glow of the sky, almost like it was on fire. The trees and hills around it were black. When she turned her head back to face me, we locked eyes. She said, "I love you, too."

Chapter

Thirty

Kenzie and I stayed on the dock, talking for a while. About Chase. About Hadley. As we sat next to each other, I experienced a weird mixture of guilt and relief to have her back. And as much as I couldn't stop worrying about Chase, I felt comforted to know I wasn't alone in it. At least for now.

With the sunset, the cold breeze threatened to penetrate our bones. I told Kenzie goodbye and walked back to my car, holding on to the calm I felt before the inevitable storm that awaited me.

Driving back home, my head hurt from all the tears and spinning thoughts. Hearing Kenzie say that Hadley got better made me want to believe it. Maybe, with time, I eventually would. I could only hope the same for my brother. I had no idea what state he was in. Or what his reasoning was.

After I parked the car in front of my house, I gripped my steering wheel and took a deep breath. Tonight, I'd spent so much time thinking about the past. I was afraid to face the present and all that it had in store.

When I walked inside, my dad sat at the kitchen table.

"Hey," I said, hanging the keys on the hook by the door. "How is he?"

With his elbow propped on the table, he rubbed his face. "Better. Why don't you sit down?"

I did as I was told, sitting down in the chair next to him. Part of me considered sitting in the chair at the other end of the table. Maybe if I could create distance from my dad, I could create distance from the situation, and it would somehow cease to exist. "So, he's doing better, but they still want to keep him overnight?"

Dad sighed. "They don't take these suicide attempts lightly."

"He really tried to do it?" I was scared to ask how he did it. I didn't need another vision like that stuck in my head. But part of me wondered how far he got. If he was able to change his mind like Hadley did, or if he was only still here because someone found him in time. "Who found him?"

"Your mother." He shook his head. "I hate that she had to be the one to see him like that, but if she hadn't …"

He didn't finish his sentence, giving me the answer I'd been hoping against. If my mom hadn't found Chase when she did, he wouldn't still be here.

"Do you know how long he's going to be in the hospital?" I asked.

"It depends on how much progress he makes while he's there," Dad said. "But it will probably be a few days, at least."

I waited a long time before I posed the next question. "Do you know why he did it?"

"The psychologist who talked to him didn't go into a lot of detail with us, but it seems like this was triggered by a bully at school."

My teeth clenched at the thought of some kid at school making my brother do this to himself. "Is he going to be okay, Dad?"

"I think he is. Things are going to be pretty different for a while, but he's getting the help he needs, and that's what matters."

"How's Mom doing?" Was she still as upset as when she had called me?

Dad ran a hand through his salt-and-pepper hair. "She's blaming herself. She's blaming that stupid parenting book. She's trying really hard to keep it together for Chase, but being the one to see him like that will probably stick with her for a while." He paused. "She'll be okay though."

I nodded, swallowing the lump I felt forming in my throat.

"You didn't ... you didn't know about any of this right?" he asked.

I shook my head.

"I didn't think so."

The image of my torn-apart razor in the bathroom flashed in my mind. Was this why he took it apart? So he could hurt himself with it? "Did he cut himself?"

"Yeah."

"I should have known." I was an idiot. The signs were right there. Right under my nose. If I hadn't been so consumed in my own life, then maybe I would have noticed. Maybe I could have stopped this.

Dad put his hand on my shoulder. "Parker, we don't need another member of this family blaming themselves because they didn't know. It's nobody's fault. And the important thing now is not to dwell on what we should have known or should have done but to give Chase a loving environment for his recovery." He looked at me as he said, "All we can do is move forward. Together."

For the next couple of days, I kept coming back to what my dad had said about not dwelling. Dwelling was all I'd done since Hadley died. I lived with her through letters and flashbacks, afraid to face the uncertainty of my future with the knowledge that hers would never exist. It wasn't a fun way to live, but it was the only way I could think of. Because how are you supposed to let go of something like that? How could moving on from Hadley's death or past suicidal ideations benefit *her*? She was gone, so how could I give *her* an environment for recovery?

Maybe she wasn't the one who had to benefit. Maybe the benefits were only available to the people still living. That was the difference between Chase's situation and Hadley's.

Chase got home from the hospital Wednesday morning. After school that day, I knocked on his door.

"Come in."

I opened the door slowly. "Hey, Chase. How are you feeling?"

From his bed, he looked at me with dark circles under his eyes. "Physically," he said, "I feel like crap. But mentally, I feel a little better."

I took a seat at the chair by his desk. "What happened?"

He looked at the door. "It's stupid. You wouldn't get it."

"Try me."

"It's a really long story."

"I've got time."

He sighed. "Okay, well, I guess I'll start off by saying that things have sucked for a while now. But I thought, for a minute, that they were getting better." He paused and looked away, as if whatever he was thinking about pained him. For a moment, I didn't think he was going to tell me anything. Maybe he thought the same thing.

But then he said, "There's this girl in my English class. Her name is Summer. And she's gorgeous, with long red hair and big hazel eyes. She's also smart and funny and kind and popular and extremely out of my league." He looked down. "So when we were put next to each other on the seating chart, I was really surprised that she was talking to me. Like, she didn't just talk to me when we had to for assignments, but she asked me questions about different things and seemed interested in what I had to say. Because English is last period, I started walking her out to where the buses meet. It was really cool, but after a while, this guy in ninth grade started showing up, waiting for her.

"After the first two or three times, I figured he was her boyfriend or something, so I stopped walking her out and tried to keep my distance in class, while still being her friend. But then she asked for my phone number."

"Really?" I asked. "Sounds like she was into you."

"Yeah, that's kind of what I thought. I'm not like you though. Girls don't like me. There's not a single girl who wants to be my girlfriend, let alone twelve or however many you've had. So, I was excited when she started texting me. We texted every day, sometimes for hours at a time. She asked me all these questions about my life and stuff." His face turned pale, and he looked like he was about to throw up. "After a few weeks, I found out that she wasn't texting me. Her boyfriend was texting me, pretending to be her."

"Are you serious?" Now *I* wanted to throw up.

He nodded, looking as if he was going to cry. "It really sucked, but whatever. It was too good to be true anyway. Summer was nice, but I guess her boyfriend convinced her it would be funny to give him my number to mess with me. She just went along with it like making him happy was more important than not humiliating me." He rubbed his eyes. "I didn't know what to do, so I just stopped talking to her, and then the teacher changed the seating chart, so I didn't have to worry about it being awkward. But then he posted screenshots of our texts online, and everyone at school found out. They started calling me all these slurs. They told me I was stupid and a pervert. Some people wouldn't stop insisting I was gay since I was texting a boy. Some of Summer's guy friends told me I should kill myself. They said I should have known someone like Summer would never like me like that."

His words echoed in my mind. It felt like someone had punched me in the gut. After I recovered from the shock, anger filled my chest. "What's the boyfriend's name?"

Chase shook his head. "It doesn't matter."

"Seriously?" I asked. "Why are you protecting this kid? He obviously doesn't care about you."

He sighed. "His name is Cole."

"Cole what?"

"McGrady," he muttered.

"I don't know a Cole McGrady. I know a Jackson McGrady though. Are they brothers?"

"I don't know. All I know is Cole's in ninth grade and plays football." He locked eyes with me. "Promise you won't do anything stupid."

"I'm sorry, Chase, but I don't make promises to protect idiots who hurt people I care about."

"Whatever."

"Chase?"

"What?"

"Why did you try to end your life?"

His neck turned red. "I thought it would be better," he said. When I didn't say anything, he continued, "I felt depressed. At school, I was a nobody. No one cared whether I was there or not.

Then I became a loser, and everybody told me every day that they
didn't want me there. I thought I'd do them a favor. If I wasn't
here anymore, then some people would be happy, and other
people just wouldn't notice. Summer proved that nobody will
ever like me for who I am anyway. I got tired of holding on to
false hope. I'm still tired."

"You're wrong," I said. He tried to respond, but I cut him
off as I got up from the chair and sat beside him on his bed. What
he said reminded me of one of Hadley's letters. I didn't want him
to feel the way Hadley had felt. Chase and Hadley were both too
good to feel that way. "You're wrong that people wouldn't notice.
People would notice. People you don't know that well would
come to your funeral and cry. Friends you had years ago and don't
talk to anymore would lose their minds over your death. Lives
would be changed in a really awful way. And Mom, Dad, and I
wouldn't know how to live anymore."

I put my hand on his shoulder, and he looked up at me with
tears forming in the corners of his eyes. "But guess what, Chase?
After you die, that's it. There's no coming back from it. You don't
get to rub it in anyone's face. You don't get to have revenge. You
don't get to feel the satisfaction of knowing that—it turns out—
people do care about you and miss you. You don't gain anything
from that because you're dead." I removed my hand, gesturing as
I spoke. "And who freaking cares if nobody likes you? For one,
that's not true. People like you. But let's pretend, for a minute,
that people don't. Let's pretend nobody does. Who are they to
say that you don't deserve to live? That you don't deserve to be
happy or to be yourself? They don't have that right." I touched
his shoulder again, hoping so desperately that I had his attention.
"Okay, Chase? You have just as much of a right to be here as
anyone else. Nobody is better than you." By the time I stopped

talking, I realized that I had hot tears streaming down my face, just like Chase did.

"I want to believe that," he sobbed, "but it's so hard."

For the first time in years, I had the strongest urge to hug my brother. I wrapped my arms around him and said, "I know, but you have to promise me that you'll make yourself believe it. You have to believe it because my life would be so dark if you weren't in it. I love you, Chase."

He cried harder, whimpering as he said, "I love you, too, Parker."

When he calmed down, I pulled him away and said, looking him in the eyes, "It's going to be okay. We're going to get through this."

Chapter

Thirty-One

Thursday, January 12

Dear Parker,

Hey! It's been a while. Today, I had the fun opportunity of sitting in the counseling office. Yep, that's right. Noah broke me down.

Honestly, it was kind of terrifying. I could hear my heart pounding. Noah sat with me while we waited and I was so scared he was going to hear it, too.

Maybe he could hear it or maybe he saw the look on my face, but he said, "You've got this. Don't worry."

His warm voice and encouraging smile calmed my nerves a bit, but telling me not to worry is like telling someone with chickenpox not to scratch. I just can't help it.

I didn't tell him that, though.

He checked the time on his phone.

I told him, "You can go if you want. I'll be fine."

Then, he slid it back into his pocket. "No, it's okay. The bell doesn't ring for a few more minutes."

As if summoned by this, a girl with a long brown braid appeared. "Hadley García?"

My rapid heart palpitations returned. "Yeah, that's me."

She smiled super wide and it made me feel better. "Awesome! Mrs. Kelly is ready for you now!"

I glanced back at Noah and he grinned. "You got this," he mouthed.

I nodded back at him, forcing myself to smile, then followed the girl to the office around the corner in the back. "Erin Kelly" read the plaque on the glass. Inside was a thin woman with red glasses and honey-colored hair. She looked like a mom, but like a cool one.

When she saw me standing outside the doorway, she smiled. Her teeth were super straight and white. Except for the wrinkles, she looked like she could be a celebrity. "Hadley?" she asked.

I nodded, just standing there like an idiot.

"Please, come in."

I obeyed her command.

"Will you also close the door? It will give us a little more privacy."

Again, I did as I was told and then sat in the chair across from her at the desk.

She straightened a stack of papers on her desk and then looked at me. "So, I hope we don't have you too disappointed. I know your assigned counselor is Mrs. Houston, but she's on maternity leave, so I'm filling in for her for a while."

I didn't care. I saw Mrs. Houston twice a year to talk

about my grades. Our meetings lasted about five minutes and she messed up and called me Hallie at least once each time.

When I didn't say anything, Mrs. Kelly continued. "So, I see you've requested this meeting today. Before we talk about your reason for that, I'd like to get to know you a little bit, Hadley. What kind of things do you like to do for fun?"

I answered her question, then answered the one about my family, and then answered the one about what my favorite classes are.

When she asked me what prompted me to make the appointment, I broke down. I don't remember the last time I cried so hard in front of another person before, but ... it felt good. I felt clean. I've been pretty embarrassed about it all day, but the feeling of peace that's been with me since makes me not really care. I'm going back next week, so that'll be fun.

Well, I'm physically, emotionally, and mentally exhausted, so I'm gonna go to bed.

Goodnight,
Hadley

                                   Thursday, January 26
Dear Parker,

Okay, so I went to my third counseling session today. And I told Mrs. Kelly about you! That was actually pretty embarrassing, honestly, but I'll spare you the details. I told her about the letters and she thinks it's really good that I have an outlet for expressing my feelings. It was kind of funny to hear her put it that way, but I guess that is how this whole thing started out. An outlet for loneliness. And, you know what? Looking back, I'm not as lonely as I once was. When I started back in middle school, I didn't feel like I had anybody. Now, I have Noah and Kenzie and Mrs. Kelly, even though she's a counselor haha.

But I guess it does come in waves.

Like, last night, I had a dream that I was sitting on the beach. There was a hole in the sand underneath me and it kept expanding, making me slowly sink. I didn't realize until you appeared. When you saw me, you came and put your arms around me. I could smell that cologne you always wore too much of and I felt safe in your embrace. Of course, I woke up and you weren't there. I was alone in my bed, left with nothing but an emptiness in my chest.

I was sad for the rest of the morning—not because I missed you but because I felt the emptiness in the first place. I don't remember the last time I felt this way. I've been doing so good. Then, just one stupid dream and it knocked down all the progress I made. Then, I saw you at lunch sitting with all your cool and popular friends. And Mallory sat so close to you, she might as well have been on your lap.

But I was fine because I meet with Mrs. Kelly around lunchtime, so I was able to talk about how I felt. I didn't want to. I felt so stupid. But she coaxed it out of me and, instead of making me feel stupid about it, she actually told me my feelings were normal. I guess a lot of people go through it.

Also fun fact: Mrs. Kelly says I show signs of depression and anxiety. She said that I should start meeting with a therapist because a therapist would be able to give me more help than what she's able to provide as a counselor. That means I need to tell my parents about how I've been feeling.

Things were going pretty well until she said that.

I don't know, Parker. Counseling has been really cool because Mrs. Kelly makes it seem like I'm not crazy. Like, the way I've been feeling isn't just in my head. And the thought that I can get to a point where I don't feel this way all the time or as often or as strong, I guess ... I don't know. It feels unreal.

But I don't want to talk to my parents about it. I can't.

Anyway,
Hadley

Over the past week, Chase spent a lot of time doing his outpatient therapy with the hospital. My parents made dinner every single night, and we ate together, just like we did when Chase and I were younger. My mom had found a list of conversation starters to use at the table to encourage Chase to talk without making him feel like he had to. And slowly he began to open up about what he was feeling and what had been going on in his life. I could tell that something he wasn't sharing still bothered him though.

I thought about this as I sat through my second-period class one day. The teacher had left us to fill in worksheets.

Breaking me from my thoughts, I heard a girl's voice say, "Hadley."

I looked around and tracked the voice to Joelle, a girl who sat two tables over.

The guy she was talking to was Aaron, someone else I

vaguely knew. He said, "Yeah, I remember that day. But I didn't really know her."

"I didn't know her super well either," Joelle said, "but I remember her being so nice. She always complimented me on my outfits, and it turned a lot of really bad days around. When I found out that she died, I stayed home from school for a week. She was such a good person, and it kills me to think she's gone."

"Yeah," Aaron responded. "It's sad. She was a good person."

"Yeah." Joelle had a dejected tone. "I still think about her all the time."

I turned my attention back to my worksheet. There were so many people who cared about Hadley. I knew this, but it still came as a surprise. She wasn't just a ghost who floated around in my life or Kenzie's. Her loss was felt by every person who ever knew her. Like at the funeral, I wished she could have seen this. I wished Chase could have seen this.

On Friday, Kenzie and I met at the lake house, although we didn't really need to read the letters in private anymore. She told me how soccer was going while raindrops pounding against the roof competed with her voice. A harsh gray light filled the room, and it made me wonder how my team was doing. I'd heard there was a lacrosse game that night. Some of the members hated playing in the rain.

After describing her most recent game, she asked, "What's wrong?"

I didn't realize I had been zoning out. "Oh. Nothing."

She nudged my shoulder with her hand. "Come on. Tell me."

I sighed. "I'm happy that things are going well for you this season. It just makes me realize how much I miss lacrosse."

"You really loved it, didn't you?"

I nodded, smiling at the thought. "Yeah."

"You should see if they'll let you back on the team. Didn't the season just start a few weeks ago?"

I leaned back. "I can't do that. Coach would never let me back on, after missing preseason and tryouts. Plus, I'm not registered anymore."

"Oh, that's true," she said. "I forgot about that."

But the more I thought about our conversation, the more my desire to get back on the lacrosse team grew. I knew it was too late. I knew I'd missed my chance. But when I walked past Coach Deming's math classroom the following Wednesday, I couldn't reason myself out of trying.

I took a deep breath, then stuck my head in. "Coach!"

Since third period had just gotten out, nobody was there except for Coach Deming. From his desk in the corner of the room, he peered up at me through his wire-framed glasses. "Everett!" He stood up, taking his glasses off and putting them on the desk. "Long time no see! We've really missed you on the team."

I walked over to him. "I actually wanted to talk to you about that. I want back on the team."

He raised his eyebrows. "You want back on the team? Everett, the season's already started."

"I know," I said, "but I've done lacrosse with you for years. And I know I messed up by not trying out, but I miss it. I miss my team."

"Well, I understand that, but we have new players on the team," he said. "And those players have worked hard. They've paid attention to deadlines. They didn't just come in partway through the season expecting a spot on the team."

I pulled my fingers through my hair. "I know. And I'm sorry. It's just been a really rough year for me."

He smiled sympathetically. "Thompson had mentioned things have been rough."

"Gage?"

"Yeah. He's been really worried about you. I probably shouldn't be saying anything, but he told me about your falling out. He's come to me about what to do, but I advised him that the best thing to do was give you space when you asked for space."

"I didn't know he was asking for advice about me."

"Yeah," Coach said. "He cares about you a lot."

"Hmm." I knew Gage would go to Coach Deming about things sometimes. I never thought he talked about me though. I figured Gage ignored me because he was still mad I wasn't doing lacrosse. Was it because Coach told him to give me space? I guess that's what I'd asked for.

"Everett, I don't know the details of what's been going on in your life, but I'm sorry you've had to go through whatever it is. I know senior year is hard enough already. If there weren't rules about this kind of thing, I'd let you back on the team in a heartbeat. But the reality is that I can't."

"I understand," I said. "I just figured it was worth a try."

"You fight for what you want," he said. "That's something I've always admired about you. And I want you to know that just because you didn't play senior year doesn't discount all those years of hard work. Remember that, okay? You're still a great player, and Lincoln has been forever changed by the passion and hard work you've put into this team."

"Thanks, Coach. I guess I'll see you around."

As I turned and headed for the door, he said, "I'll see you around, kid. Come support us at the games, okay? You're still a part of the team whether you play or not, and I'm sure the guys would love to see you."

I forced a laugh. "Of course, Coach. I'll see you then."

"And Everett?"

"Yeah?"

"A friendship like you and Thompson have is a once-in-a-lifetime kind of thing. I'd try not to let whatever's been keeping you down get in the way of it. And I wouldn't freeze Thompson out for too much longer."

"Okay, Coach."

When I left the room, the hall was empty except for one kid making his way to the drinking fountain. I didn't think anything of it until I saw his face. I'd seen it before. It was in a picture I found after stalking Jackson McGrady online a few nights ago. My body filled with rage, but I tried to push it down. At least until I could confirm it was him.

I walked up to him. "Cole McGrady?"

He turned around to face me, wiping his mouth with his sleeve. "Yeah?"

Within an instant, I drew my fist back and punched him in the stomach as hard as I could.

He yelped, hands flying to cover his stomach as he fell back against the wall. "What the hell? Why'd you do that?"

I turned around, not intending to drag on the encounter.

He called after me. "Hey, aren't you a senior? I could have you arrested for aggravated assault of a minor!"

I turned back around. He stood only two feet away from me. I took a step forward. "You could, but you're not going to because I could have you arrested for incessant bullying and harassment leading to the attempted suicide of a minor, impersonation, and libel." I also knew this from my online search the other night. I took another step forward, grabbing him by the collar of his shirt, adrenaline boiling within me. "Of course, we don't have to have any problems. You will apologize to Chase and take down those posts." I pulled his face closer to mine. His hazel eyes widened with fear, and sweat bubbled at his hairline. "And if you don't and I hear that things get worse, and not better, then we're going to have some major problems. Do I make myself clear?"

He swallowed, nodding profusely. "Yeah."

Still holding on, I said, "And don't you think for a second that just because I'm a senior I won't be able to do anything next year. Chase may not tell me everything, but I know a lot of people, and I hear a lot of things. I'm not going anywhere."

He nodded again. "I understand."

I released my grip, pushing him backward. "Good." With that, I turned around and began walking.

"Wait," he said.

I turned back around. "What?"

"You said attempted suicide. Did … did Chase try to kill himself?"

I silently cursed myself at the realization that I'd just shared Chase's most vulnerable secret with the kid responsible for ruining his reputation. But it was too late to deny it. "Yeah."

His face went pale. "I didn't mean for that to happen." He shook his head. "I didn't mean for it to go that far. I just wanted him to stay away from my girlfriend."

"That's not what it looked like. It looked like you saw a kid talking to your girlfriend and took it as a chance to fulfill some sadistic fantasy of yours." I swallowed the lump beginning to form in my throat. "If you didn't mean for it to go that far, you shouldn't have taken it that far. Actions have consequences, Cole."

"I'm sorry," he said, a tear welling in his eye.

I shook my head. "I'm not the one you need to apologize to."

Chapter

Thirty-Two

Tuesday, January 31

Dear Parker,

Okay, so I told Noah about how Mrs. Kelly said I should talk to my parents about my mental health issues, and he got really excited about it. Like, too excited. I don't know. It kind of freaked me out.

I was like, "I'm not gonna do it, though."

His expression dropped. "Why not?"

"Because I can't."

Again, "Why not?"

"They don't believe in stuff like that."

"Oh," he said. "So you've talked about it with them before?"

"Well ... no."

He squinted. "Well, then how do you know?"

Like it wasn't obvious. "Because they're my parents. I know them."

He smiled that comforting smile of his. I wanted to hate it, but it never fails to make me feel at least a little bit better. "I think you'd be surprised, Hadley. Parents have a way of being there for their kids when they really need it."

I wanted to say, "You don't get it." But I didn't.

I think he read my mind, though, because he sighed and then said, "I have to tell you something."

This really caught my attention.

"I also have depression and anxiety."

My jaw had to have dropped. "Really?"

He nodded. "Yeah. I take pills for it."

"How long have you had it?"

"I started not feeling like myself at the beginning of high school. I struggled for a long time and couldn't figure out why I felt the way I did. I felt like something was wrong with me. I had some really low lows, too. When my grades started to tank and I wasn't leaving my room very often, my parents told me they were worried about me. I thought they'd be mad at me, but they were super understanding. And I was able to get the help I needed after a while. I also learned that you really can't just positive think yourself out of mental illness."

I couldn't believe what I was hearing. "I can't see you not being happy. You just seem like you have your life so together. You don't seem broken at all."

He laughed. "First of all, I promise you I don't have my life together at all. I'm a complete mess. But you're right: I'm not broken. And neither are you."

He asked me again if I'd consider telling my parents

about it. I told him I'd consider it. It's the least I could do. But I'm not making any promises.

I don't like getting out of my comfort zone, but I have a feeling that I'm gonna have to get super used to it being friends with Noah.

Best,
Hadley

                           Monday, February 6
Dear Parker,

"Hadleeeeeeeeeyyyyy," is how Noah greeted me today in the halls.

I immediately felt my face go red. To have someone recognize me and greet me in front of people. To be known publicly. I wasn't used to it. I smiled at the attention but felt shy when I quietly said, "Hey, Noah."

It was his turn to have his face go red. "Oh my gosh, Hadley. Did I embarrass you?"

Even redder. "No, I promise you didn't."

His blush faded, though. Then he grinned at me, his red freckles being pulled up to his light blue eyes by his smile lines. "Did you have a good weekend?"

I smiled back at him. It was uneventful, but I couldn't stand the thought of disappointing him. "Yeah, it was pretty good." Pause. "How was yours?"

"It was pretty good. Did you ...?"

Talk to my parents. "No."

He frowned. Softly. "Did you think about it, at least?"

"Yeah, but thinking about it and actually doing it are two very different things."

He chuckled. "True."

I just nodded or something.

His eyes lit up. "Hey. Do you think it would be easier if you had someone to go to them with?"

"I mean ... maybe. Why?"

"I could go with you if you want."

"Really?"

He grinned, nodding his head. "Yeah!"

"I don't know." Bringing home a boy who my parents didn't know about to talk about an issue they didn't know I had. I could picture my dad's face immediately and it wasn't pretty.

"Hey, no pressure. I just want you to know I'm here for you and I want you to do what's best for you. No matter what it is."

UGHHH. Why did he have to say that?? "Okay. If you'll come with me, I'll do it."

He grinned. That stupid, gorgeous grin that I love. "Awesome."

I'll keep you updated,
Hadley

On Saturday, I knocked on Chase's door before opening it and sticking my head in. "Hey, Chase?"

"Yeah?" He sat at his desk doing homework.

"Can I come in?"

He looked up at me. "You basically already did."

"Sweet." I walked to his desk. "How's it going?"

He pushed his homework to the side. "Good. Can I help you?"

"Yes!" I said, sticking my index finger in the air. "Do you want to go to a lacrosse game with a friend and me?"

He squinted at me. "I thought you hated lacrosse now."

"I don't hate lacrosse," I corrected him. "I'm just not playing this season. But it's still my team. I gotta go and support them." I wouldn't admit it to him, but the thought of going to a lacrosse game terrified me. Would I be able to watch my team out there on the field without me? Would it be like being on the sidelines but worse? I wasn't sure. But I couldn't get what Coach Deming said about Gage out of my head. He cared about me. He missed me. And I missed him. I thought about texting him or something. But Kenzie and I decided it would probably mean more if I went out to support him.

"What time are you going?"

"I'm leaving in fifteen minutes."

"That's not a lot of notice if you really want me to go." He looked at his homework and scowled. "But I'm tired of this, so I'll go."

I clapped my hands together. "Great. Meet me in the car in fifteen minutes."

When almost twenty minutes had passed of me waiting in my car alone, I wondered if Chase had stood me up. I unbuckled my seatbelt to go look for him, but then he walked out of the house and approached my car. He tried for the door handle, then banged on the window when it wouldn't budge.

I unlocked his side of the car. "Easy," I warned as he slid into the passenger seat.

"Well, then, unlock it next time."

Typical moody Chase. I couldn't help but smile.

I pulled out of the driveway and Chase said, "So, something weird happened yesterday."

"Oh yeah?"

"Yeah. Summer and Cole apologized to me."

I froze. "Really?"

"Yeah," he said, raising an eyebrow. "It was super random. But Summer was crying. She was actually crying in class, too, after I caught her staring at me. When class was over, she asked me to walk out with her to the buses, and Cole was there. He said he was sorry about pretending to be Summer and that he deleted all the screenshots he posted. The weirdest thing was that he looked like he actually meant it."

"Oh," I said, trying my best not to sound suspicious, although I was still surprised. I didn't think the kid would actually apologize. "That's great."

"Did you have anything to do with that?"

"Oh, you know what?" I pointed to my stereo. "I'm gonna let you have free rein over the radio today. You can play anything you want. My treat."

"Parker, I told you not to—"

"Oh," I said, reaching for the volume dial. "Emo music! Your favorite!" I turned the volume up loud enough to drown out his voice, and he gave up talking.

When I pulled into Kenzie's driveway, he turned the music down and asked, "Who lives here?"

"Kenzie."

His eyes widened. "A girl?"

I unbuckled my seatbelt. "Yep."

"Does Mallory know?"

I looked at him and smiled. "Yeah, uh, Mallory and I broke up."

"Seriously?"

I nodded.

"I knew you two wouldn't last," he said, shaking his head.

"Why do you say that?"

He shrugged. "It just didn't seem right."

I didn't know how to respond to that, so I didn't.

Walking up to Kenzie's door, I wiped my damp hands on my jeans. It didn't seem right for me to be this nervous to see her, but I was. This was our first time hanging out in broad daylight. It would be the first time people saw us together at a school thing. It was a big deal.

After I knocked on the door, the dogs went crazy for a minute before a stocky man with a blond cul-de-sac hairstyle answered. He scolded them, then narrowed his eyes at me. "Yes?"

"Is Kenzie here?"

"No," he said, matter-of-factly. "You must have the wrong house. There is not, nor has there ever been, nor will there ever be a Kenzie Bennett who lives here. Good day." With that, he shut the door.

Left alone, I looked over at the house number. I'd been here before. How could this be the wrong house? This was the right address. "Wait," I said to myself. "I didn't say her last name."

As if on cue, a voice from inside progressively got closer, saying, "Dad, that's not funny!" Then the door opened to reveal a slightly winded Kenzie, ponytail sticking out the back of a denim baseball cap. "Hey, Parker."

From the hallway, her stepdad said, "I was just kidding around!"

She turned back to face him. "Yeah, whatever! I'll be home in a few hours!" To me, she said, "I'm sorry. My dad's a huge dork."

I waited for her to close the door, then interlocked my

fingers with hers. "That's okay. I like him." I could get along great with a dad who liked to mess with people for fun.

She blushed, squeezing my hand. "He is awesome. I'm excited for you to meet him under different circumstances."

I smiled at her. "I am, too."

At my car, I let go of her hand, and she slid into the back middle seat. Once we were all situated, she stuck her hand out up front to my brother, who had probably sunken back into his seat as far as he could possibly go. "You must be Chase. I'm Kenzie."

"Hey," he replied, not looking at her but shaking her hand awkwardly.

I was amused. Chase thought Kenzie was cute.

"Parker's told me a lot about you," she said, completely undeterred by his shyness. "It's an honor to finally meet you." Then she asked him about his hobbies.

Shifting my eyes between the road and my brother, I watched in amazement as he slowly came out of his shell, to the point of grinning and even laughing at what she said. Before Mallory, my girlfriends never hung around my family enough to ever really get to know Chase. Mallory did, but she did little more than acknowledge him. She also talked to him like he was a little kid. It wasn't something I ever thought too much about until now.

I parked close to the football field. As we got out of the car, Kenzie asked Chase, "Do you like to play sports?"

"I used to play soccer," he said. "But not anymore."

Her eyes lit up. "Why not?"

He stared at the grass while we walked. "I stopped playing when I got into middle school because it's a lot more competitive now."

"Did you like it though?"

"I mean, I did."

She waved her hand in the air. "Then, who cares if it's competitive? I'm sure you're a great player, but even if you're not, there are plenty of ways to play on a team. You should do it if you like it."

"You should listen to her, Chase." Stealing Rick the Pizza Guy's line, I said, "Kenzie is a very wise woman."

He turned his attention to me. "Then, why don't you play lacrosse anymore?"

I rubbed my neck. "We're not talking about me right now."

Kenzie shot me a sympathetic smile. Then to Chase, she asked, "What grade are you in, again?"

"Eighth," he replied.

She gasped. "My brother's in your grade! Do you know Ross Bennett?"

"I do. Kind of. He's one of the popular kids, and he seems really nice. But I don't think he knows who I am."

"Oh, I can introduce you guys. He's on the soccer team, too. I'll ask him to practice with you."

Chase shook his head. "Oh no. No, that's okay."

"I'm gonna do it anyway. He loves meeting new people. Also, he's really into anime, too, so I think you guys would get along super well."

Chase's eyes widened. "Ross Bennett watches anime?"

Kenzie looked down. "Crap. That's one of those things I'm not supposed to tell people."

I wanted to kiss Kenzie right then and there, but I refrained. She seemed to really care about Chase, and I could tell that he liked her, too.

We found a spot near the top of the bleachers. Looking around, it was pitiful. These bleachers were always filled for football games, but only families, girlfriends, and the occasional student council members actually watched lacrosse. Before, I was too busy playing to care.

The high-pitched whistle of the referee sounded, pulling everyone's attention to the field. My heartbeat sped up and memories came flooding in. My first time on the field. Making my first pass. My first time playing varsity. The adrenaline rush. The way the world slowed down and my heartbeat sounded in my ears whenever I played. Six years later and it never went away.

"Oh, it's starting." Kenzie sat up to get a good view of the players.

My eyes followed the ball as it made its way back and forth across the field. From one teammate to the next. In the air. Into the net. Our team scored. Everyone on the bleachers cheered.

Kenzie's hand found mine, and we interlocked fingers. She rested her head on my shoulder, and I kissed the top of it.

I was not a nail-biter but found my free hand in my mouth by the time we entered the fourth quarter. We were tied twelve to twelve with Mountain View, and the game could go either way at this point.

Kenzie took a deep breath and let it out. "It's so close."

"Yeah," Chase added, "this is way more intense than any of the games you've played in."

I punched him in the shoulder. "That's because the other team never stood a chance whenever I played."

Kenzie rolled her eyes. "You're so full of it, Parker."

I whipped my head to face her. "What? It's true."

She laughed. "I came to a few of your games with Hadley. I think you have a more rose-colored memory of what went down."

Before I could think of a comeback, the ref's whistle sounded.

"What happened?" I asked.

Chase answered, "Somebody got injured."

I sat up taller to see. "Who?"

On the field, players surrounded the injured kid who was lying in the fetal position. It was someone on my team.

Ending the mystery, the announcer boomed. "Player Forty-One, Trevor Smith, is injured. The seriousness of the injury is being assessed."

The bleachers grew quiet as spectators exchanged cheering for hushed whispers and silent anticipation. On the field, my team took a knee.

Trevor was a midfielder. My position.

He was assisted off the field.

My adrenaline spiked and I stood up. Kenzie said something. It wasn't until I was six feet away, running down the bleachers, that I registered what she'd said. "Parker, where are you going?"

This was my chance. This was my chance to make things right with Gage. To get to play with him one last time. I'd fill in for Trevor somehow.

At the bottom of the bleachers, I waved erratically until Gage noticed. From the field, he mouthed my name, cocking his head.

I waved him over, and he broke away from the team to meet me.

"Parker," he said. "What are you doing here?"

"I came to see you play," I said. "Is Trevor okay?"

Gage glanced back at the commotion. The athletic trainer assessed Trevor while the rest of the team watched in anticipation. "I don't know. He won't be able to play the rest of the game for sure."

A beat later, clapping sounded from the team, with the spectators promptly joining. Using the athletic trainer as a crutch, Trevor got to his feet. Shifting his weight to his right foot, he flashed the crowd a thumbs up. Then the trainer assisted him off the field.

"Well," Gage said, "looks like he is okay. But he still won't be playing for the rest of the game."

"I can help," I said.

"What?"

"You guys are short one of the best players. I can fill in for him."

He raised an eyebrow. "How are you going to do that?"

"I don't know," I said. "Maybe I can wear someone's jersey. I'm not registered, so I can't use mine, but—"

Gage placed his hand on my shoulder. "Hey. Parker. It's okay."

His words stopped the forward motion of racing ideas in my mind. "It's okay?"

Gage smiled. "Yeah. We're going to be okay."

"Okay," I said, nodding slowly. "You got this. I guess I'll just go back to the bleachers, then."

The referee's whistle blew—Gage's cue to get back on the field.

He turned his head to look at the referee, then returned his attention to me. "We're going to be okay, Everett."

As he ran back to the field, I nodded at him. "Okay, Thompson."

On my way back to Kenzie and Chase, I replayed my interaction with Gage. *We're going to be okay.* The team would be okay. And I knew this. I mean, we'd had plenty of injuries before. And I knew what I had suggested was an illegal move. I just thought, maybe, that's how I could make it up to him. Show him that I wanted to be friends again. To be there for him. But they were going to be okay.

I could respect that.

But why did he need to say it twice?

When I rejoined Kenzie and Chase at our spot on the bleachers, Kenzie grabbed my hand. "What was that all about?"

"Just felt like saying hi," I said, squeezing her hand.

For the last quarter, I watched my team play without me. And they were amazing. I loved watching Chase get so invested as he watched from the edge of his seat. I loved whenever Kenzie got stressed and squeezed my hand tighter. And in spite of myself, I loved watching the guys I learned to truly love and respect play. I never thought I would love *watching* them so much. But I did. And peace washed over me at the thought. Lacrosse was my thing, but it was behind me now. And I was okay with that.

When we inevitably won, I was probably the first person to jump up from the bleachers and cheer.

As the team erupted in cheers from the field, Gage stood just on the outskirts of the crowd, with his helmet in hand, staring at the bleachers—staring at *me*, I was pretty sure—and grinning.

And then I got it.

He wasn't talking about the team.

He was talking about him and me.

We're going to be okay.

"I'll be right back," I told Kenzie and Chase.

Snaking through the groups of people trying to make their way off the bleachers, I met Gage's line of sight on the field.

As he started walking toward me, I shouted, "That was incredible, man!"

"Thanks, man," he said, halting just in front of me. He wiped his forehead with his arm. "Thanks for coming tonight. It really means the world."

"I'm glad I did." For a moment, we just stood there and

stared at each other. It was like we were playing a game of apology chicken, waiting for the other to make the first move. But we both knew who had to be the one. "Listen, Gage, I'm sorry. I'm so sorry. I was an idiot and a jerk. I should never have said those things to you on Christmas Eve."

"No, Parker, I'm sorry. I wanted you to play this season because I knew how much lacrosse meant to you, but you were struggling, and I should have seen that a lot sooner than I did. I was a sucky friend."

"It wasn't your fault," I said. "I pushed you away. And I didn't need to freeze you out like that."

He opened his arms. "Same. I've really missed you, man."

"I missed you, too," I said, joining him in a bear hug. "There's so much I need to tell you."

He pulled away. "Uh, yeah. I saw you with Kenzie Bennett up there. That's not what I think it is, right?"

I laughed, rubbing my neck. "I think you already know."

He shook his head, a wide grin on his face. "Oh, Parker."

Chapter

Thirty-Three

Kenzie sat across from me on the wooden floor of the lake house. Her long blonde hair fell in loose curls, not in a ponytail for once, and her blue eyes shined. "Are you ready?" We didn't think today would ever come, but here it was. Today, we would finish reading Hadley's letters.

I took a deep breath. "Let's do it."

Friday, February 10

Dear Parker,

Today was utterly exhausting. But I'm happy. I'm euphoric. I'm proud of myself.

"Are you ready?" Noah asked, meeting me at my locker after school.

"Ready?" I took a deep breath. "That's debatable."

He beamed at me, melting my worries away. "I'm so proud of you, Hadley. This is gonna be so good."

I smiled back. I couldn't help it. "Thanks for coming with me."

He grabbed my hand and squeezed it. "Of course."

Butterflies. Butterflies. Butterflies.

We went to his house for a few hours since my parents didn't get home until later. When the time came, I rode in the passenger side of his car, to my house, not saying a word while the butterflies started to feel less exciting.

"I'm excited to meet your parents," Noah said.

I wanted to throw up.

When we walked through the door, my dad was watching TV with his feet on the coffee table. He looked startled when we came into the front room. "Oh, Hadley." Then, he noticed Noah. "Who is this?"

Undeterred, Noah zipped around the couch to where my dad could face him comfortably. "Hi Mr. García. I'm Noah."

Dad glanced at me.

"He's a friend from school," I said.

He shifted his gaze back to Noah, returning his handshake. "Well, Noah, it's very nice to meet you. Hadley told me she was going to see a friend, but she didn't tell me a friend was coming over to see us." He looked at me when he said the last part.

He was probably annoyed because I didn't give him enough notice to practice playing bad cop before I brought a new boy home.

"Uh." Noah looked at me.

"I'm sorry, Dad. I just had something I wanted to tell you and Mom. And Noah came to support me."

His eyes widened with horror. "What do you need to tell us?"

I picked at my nails. "Oh, nothing. It's kind of stupid, actually. Not really a big deal."

I glanced at Noah and he smiled at me, motioning for me to continue.

"No," I corrected. "It is a big deal. It's something I really need to talk to you about."

Dad glanced at Noah, then me. "Carrie!" he called, still looking at me.

My mom's voice rang from her office. "Yeah?"

"Will you come in here? Hadley has some news for us."

Mom came out, giving Noah that same questioning look that Dad did. For a moment, I thought that maybe having him come along wasn't the best idea.

"Hadley," she said in a worried tone. "Is everything all right?"

I felt a lump in my throat. This was so uncomfortable. It wasn't supposed to go like this. "Yeah."

Noah introduced himself, then came back to me. "Would you prefer for me to go outside so you can have some privacy or do you want me to stay?"

"Are you going to leave?"

"No. Not unless you want me to. I am one-hundred percent here for you and whatever you want to do."

I bit my bottom lip, thinking. "Um ... will you wait outside, but don't leave?"

"Of course." He excused himself and there I was left with my parents.

On my own.

I couldn't get out of this now.

"Hadley, who is that boy?" my mom asked, still careful.

"Are you pregnant?" my dad asked.

"No!" It was so abrupt and I didn't even think of the possibility of them thinking that. "Not at all. That's not what I wanted to talk about."

My dad heaved a sigh of relief. "Good."

My mom sat by my dad on the couch. I couldn't make myself move, so I stayed standing up, picking at my cuticles. "So I've been meeting with my guidance counselor at school."

Their eyes were glued to me and I started to feel super hot. My mom asked, "Why?"

"Well, uh. Noah talked me into it. Because I've been feeling ... not super good. And, um." I literally just stammered. "It's been really good, actually. And Mrs. Kelly, my guidance counselor, wanted me to talk to you. She says that she thinks I have depression and anxiety. But she wants me to meet with a professional because they can help more than she can."

"Depression?" my dad asked, a hardness in his tone. "What do you have to be depressed about?"

"Shh," my mom scolded. "Your counselor said that?"

"She did," I told them.

"I don't understand. Why would she say that?" She looked panicked.

"Well, um. We've been talking for a few weeks now and I've just been telling her about how I've been feeling."

"And you've been feeling depressed?"

"I guess," I said. "I didn't think that's what it was. But I've been feeling really low. Sometimes sad, but mostly low and numb. Sometimes I worry about the future. A lot. And the past. Even more than the future. I get this awful spiral of thoughts sometimes and I feel like I can't stop them and then my head starts to hurt a lot and my stomach aches and then I just feel low. And the lowness got so bad ..." Tears started to form and my throat got tight. In an effort to loosen up my throat, I let out a cry and then the tears flowed. I wiped the corners of my eyes, to no avail. "I tried to take my life. A few months ago."

A heavy silence fell over the room.

In the silence, I tried to wipe my tears, but they just kept coming.

My mom's head fell into her hand, with her elbow propped against her thigh. "I don't understand. Why? Why would you do that? What did we do wrong?"

"Nothing," I said. "I don't know why I did it. I just wanted to stop the thoughts. I wanted to stop feeling so broken. I wanted to feel something other than numbness and anxiety." I could barely get the words out. I didn't know if they could even understand a word I was saying. "I don't know. I don't know. I haven't felt that bad in a while now, but I still don't feel very okay. That's why I've been going to the counselor. It's been helping. The pain isn't as strong now, but it's still there. That's why she wanted me to tell you. She wants me to see a doctor."

My mom was crying now, too. She stood up and wrapped her arms around me, pushing my head into her neck. "Hadley, baby, stop crying. Please."

Through choked tears, I said, "I can't."

She started sobbing heavier, gasping deeply. She didn't say anything, but stroked my hair.

After a few minutes, my dad, who was still sitting on the

couch, said, "If you want to see the doctor, then we will get you into the doctor."

"But we can't afford it," I cried.

"Mija, you are more important than all the money in the world," he said. Then, he got up and wrapped his arms around my mom and me. "We don't want to lose you. We'll do whatever it takes to help you."

I was grateful they didn't make me talk after that. We just cried together.

After what felt like forever, I remembered Noah, who was waiting outside for me.

I went to the bathroom before going out. My mascara had completely abandoned my eyelashes, resting in charcoal streaks underneath my eyes and somehow in random places on my forehead and cheeks. I wanted to make myself look better, but there was no time. So I just wiped the streaks off my face with a cold, damp washcloth.

When I walked out, he was sitting on the wooden bench on our back porch, his backpack right next to him and homework on his lap.

When he saw me, he put his calculator down. "How'd it go?"

"A lot better than I thought it would," I said. "They actually didn't get mad at me. They just hugged me and cried." I paused for a long moment. "They said I could go to the doctor."

"That's great." He beamed. "Your parents are really cool."

I laughed. "Thanks. I'm glad you think that." I rubbed my temple, as I went over to sit next to him. My head felt so heavy. "I'm sorry. I look so awful."

He looked straight into my eyes. "I don't think so," he argued. "I think you look beautiful."

"You're just saying that."

"I don't just say things, Hadley." He said my name very matter-of-factly. "And I think you're so beautiful. And strong."

We looked at each other for a few seconds. I didn't realize it, but I was slowly leaning into him. He was leaning in, too. His fingers grazed my left cheekbone and, before I knew it, our lips were touching. His lips felt chapped against mine, but his breath was warm. The good butterflies came back as we kissed.

For the first time in—I don't even know how long—I felt okay and happy. So happy.

Sincerely,
Hadley

Monday, March 6

Dear Parker,

I met with my therapist for the first time today. Her name is Ashley and she's really cool. She's even younger than Mrs. Kelly, so that was weird. Like, she's not old enough to be a mom of teenagers. Maybe little kids, though. I don't know. She didn't talk about herself very much. I was pretty intimidated at first because she was so young and pretty, but she was so warm with me that I didn't care after a while. Our family doctor got us in touch with her and I definitely think he knew what he was doing because she's awesome. Also, turns out our insurance covers our sessions so it's definitely going to be a regular thing for a while.

After our session, I had dinner at Noah's house. And that was really nice because I love Noah's family. His little brothers are super cute and his parents are really nice to me. They always make me feel welcome.

After dinner, Noah walked me out to my car and I told him about my therapy appointment earlier.

He told me he was proud of me.

"It's hard, though," I responded. "With all the help I've been getting, I still feel weak. I still have days where it feels like the negative thoughts are winning."

He shocked me when he said, "You know, Hadley? That's going to happen and that's okay. If your negative thoughts win today, then just try again tomorrow. You don't have to win every battle to win the war."

"That sounds like something my new therapist would say," I said, laughing a little. "But I didn't think about it like that. Thank you."

He laughed. "Of course. And, also, you're not weak. You're strong. And ..." He hesitated, but then said, "God loves you so much."

He always acts hesitant when he brings up God around me because he knows I'm agnostic, but that doesn't fully stop him from continuing to do so. I know he likes me for who I am and doesn't want to change my beliefs, but I guess it's just who he is. He loves God and his religion and it's hard for him to not talk about things that he loves. I always listen without arguing, but the other week, I told him that if there was a

God, then he couldn't have cared about me. Then, he said something like, "Of course, God cares about you. How else do you explain Kenzie texting you at the exact moment you were about to end your life? God is the one who gave her the feeling to do it." Ever since then, I've been thinking about God a little differently.

Anyway, I looked into his beautiful blue eyes and said, "He better. He's the one who made me so messed up."

Noah is good. Can't complain (well, not too much. You know me).

Hope you are doing well,
Hadley

Wednesday, May 3

Dear Parker,

I know it's been a while since I've written to you, but I hope you are doing well. I saw you in the halls the other day and you looked really happy and honestly it made me happy that you were happy and I can say that now. It took me months. It had to take months of saying, "Oh, I hope he's happy. He looks happy and I'm happy for him." Months of not meaning it. But, Parker, right now I'm at the point where I feel like I'm allowed to be happy. I genuinely feel happy for you. Anyway, I can genuinely feel happy for you now. (Wow, sorry I wrote "happy" like 500 times).

As I passed you the other day, you looked at me and you smiled. It was one of those awkward half-smiles like you weren't sure if it would be reciprocated and I don't blame you.

That's how it's been for the last who-knows-how-long, but when you smiled at me, I smiled back. And I meant to say I was happy to see you. I was happy that I wasn't with you and that you were happy. (Haha, there I go again.) And when you saw that, you smiled even bigger and I knew that I finally got to this point and it's amazing, Parker. It's a wonderful feeling. I'm just so grateful for it and so, because of that, I want to inform you that this will be my last letter to you.

And I mean it this time. This is my last letter to you ever. Like Mrs. Kelly, Ashley said that she thinks it's wonderful that I write these letters and she said to use your name as often as I need to but, the thing is, Parker, I just don't feel the need to anymore. Honestly, I haven't felt the need to ever since she told me that. I feel like I can finally let go of this part of you that I've been holding on to.

When I saw you, I thought you were poetry and I just wanted to read you over and over again and I wanted to memorize every verse. But now I know people aren't poetry. They're people and they mess up. They make mistakes. They say they love you and sometimes they even mean it. That doesn't stop you from getting hurt and if you ever were a poem, you're one that I just have to stop reading now. And it doesn't feel hard to do anymore. It feels right. It feels like what I've been waiting for all this time.

Parker, I loved you. You were my first love, but I feel like I can let our story end and, no offense, but I'm so happy about that. I still want to be your friend and I'm grateful to have you as a friend now. I feel like we're at that point.

You're probably wondering about Noah: I'm in love with

him, but I know he's not poetry, either. He is also just a person. But he's a person that brings out the best in me when I'm with him. I can see him being in my life for a long time. I can also see myself—my flawed and imperfect, sometimes annoying, sad, but wonderful self—and I love myself. I mean that, too. I love myself and so I won't stop writing, even if it looks different from how it's been, because it helps me to get to know myself and my emotions even more. So, Parker, thank you for always being willing to listen, even though you don't know it.

I know that you will never read this. I just want to say it's been hard getting over you, dealing with what I thought was never-ending rejection and emptiness, but it's been nice being able to tell you this. In a way, it's funny. The most important things I've told you are the ones you'll never hear.

Anyway, I just wanted to say that it's really weird, to be honest—this sense of closure, but I'm ready for it. So, I don't know how to end this. I never really saw myself getting to this point. I never saw myself living to the point where you weren't the center of my world—something that was building me up or the thing that was destroying me. I couldn't imagine a life where you weren't there and now I can. I'm living it.

Not only am I healing from the heartbreak that our beautiful and naive love caused me, but I'm healing from the dead self-esteem and sadness that has lived within me for so long. I'm learning to manage my anxiety instead of letting it control me. I have my moments still, of course, but now it doesn't paralyze me. I have the tools I need to stop it from becoming a spiral. I'm also managing my depression. I'm feeling and living in a way that feels right.

So, thanks Parker. Thanks for everything and I hope you have a wonderful life. I'll continue to smile at you in the hallway when I see you again.

Much love,
Hadley

Chapter

Thirty-Four

My room was dark except for the neon glow of my alarm clock. It read *12:46 AM.*

I groaned.

Tomorrow was my high school graduation, and if I didn't fall asleep soon, I'd be a zombie for it. But something kept pounding in my brain, keeping me up. It was the same thought that had been pressuring me for over a month and a half now, ever since I read Hadley's last letter.

I covered my head with my pillow and rolled over.

I sighed.

It was no use.

I got out of bed, sat at my desk, flipped the switch of the lamp on, turned on my laptop, and began typing.

June 6

Dear Hadley,

I don't know if you will ever read this. Probably not, but, then again, you never thought I would read your letters. So I guess anything is possible.

I don't believe in an afterlife. I don't believe your spirit is hanging out somewhere, drinking something from a cloud-grown coconut or whatever. I know your boyfriend believes something like that and your best friend does, too, but I just can't bring myself to believe the same. But that's beside the point. Just because your spirit isn't hanging out somewhere, doesn't mean you're not as real as I am. It doesn't mean you're not here. Because one thing that all this has taught me is that death really isn't the end of a human being, even though I once thought it was. Even though you've been gone for eight months now, you still live.

Your memory continues to play in my mind. It plays in Kenzie's mind and Noah's. Your parents', your siblings', even in the minds of people who you never got too close to. You left behind a piece of you in the lives of everybody who has had the honor to know you, even if it was only for a moment. In that way, Hadley, you will never die.

I wanted to write this letter to you since you've written so many to me. And those letters, Hadley, have changed my entire life. So, your dream of becoming an influential writer came true. Congratulations.

I also feel like I owe you an update.

Mallory and I broke up. I'm not sure if you would consider that a good thing or a bad thing, but, for me, it was definitely a positive. I always thought it would hurt losing her, but it felt like taking a weight off my shoulders. Now, don't get me wrong. I don't think Mallory is a bad person. I know that you definitely had your issues with her, and to be honest, I completely understand. But another thing I've learned in the past few months is that people are not all good or all bad. As someone who tends to demonize my ex-girlfriends (I'm sorry about that, by the way), it was an important lesson for me to learn. Also, she is dating Ben now. Bet you didn't see that one coming! Just kidding. Everybody saw that one coming.

Gage and I had a bit of a falling out, but we're good now. Closer than ever, actually. Our falling out started because I didn't want to do lacrosse this year. (I was in a weird mindset.) But we moved on from that, and now I support the team as a fan instead of a player. It's perfect, actually, because I can go to all the games I want, but now I have a lot more time to dedicate to other ... interests (which I'll get to in a minute). Also, I know you loved Gage, so you'd be excited to know that he got into Princeton, and he'll be attending this fall.

As for my own college plans, my aspirations kind of died with you, and almost my brother. The plan was to go to Aldrich with Mallory, but I realized I didn't want to do that. I didn't know what I wanted to do. But I realized that's okay. It's okay not to know—at least, not to know everything. Right now, my plan is to go to Copperton Community College to get some of my generals out of the way. I'll live at home for at least the first year, and I feel good about it. That way I can be there for Chase. I haven't really been there for him in a long time. Then I think I'll transfer to the University of Northern Oregon. Still don't know what I'm gonna major in. Maybe I'll try to become a doctor. Maybe I won't. I don't know and, like I said, that's okay.

Since I've mentioned Chase, I should let you know that

he's doing a lot better! He started meeting with a therapist once a week. The guy's name is Roger! I don't know why, but I love that. According to Chase, he's a super old guy who likes to wear rainbow bowties. Dude can wear whatever he wants as long as he keeps treating Chase the way he does. With therapy, Chase has made so much progress. He's a lot more open, and he smiles a lot more. He also takes antidepressants now. My dad was pretty against them at first, but they're definitely doing good things for Chase. Things on the outside have improved a lot for him, too. After the kid who kind of ruined his life (long story) apologized, a lot of other kids started apologizing, too. Chase was annoyed that I said anything, but he got over it. Also, Chase is really good friends with Kenzie's brother, Ross, now.

Which brings me to Kenzie. We started hanging out a lot to read your letters, and I can't begin to describe what she's come to mean to me. Ever since turning twelve, I've never gone more than a few months without a girlfriend, but I promise you, I have never felt the way I feel for Kenzie for anybody else. She brings out the best in me and loves me through the worst. She's so intelligent and kind and hardworking. She knows what she wants and lets nothing deter her. At one point, she hated me, and I wasn't too fond of her either. But now I can't imagine a life without her, and I have you to thank for that. (It's not morbid if you don't think too hard about it ... I'm sorry.)

Another thing I've learned is that you can love something without having to possess it. You can appreciate it and let it change you and also let it go to be what it needs to be. That's what Kenzie and I have decided to do. She'll be going to the University of Seattle in the fall while I stay here, and we've agreed to just be friends during this time. I really don't know what it's like to be single for a long period of time. So, I'm going to be single and find out who I am when I'm not with somebody else. Don't worry though. I'm not going to let a girl like Kenzie pass me by. We're going to talk as often as possible, and when she's back for the summer, we're going to reassess how we feel about being in a relationship. I'm taking my single time seriously, but I feel like our odds are good. I know it's kind of weird since she's your best friend, but Hadley, I'm in love with her.

Also, before I end this, I should let you know what we decided to do with your letters. First of all, I feel like Kenzie and I deserve a ton of credit for not reading the ones that weren't addressed to us ... You know, the ones you mostly kept on the bottom of the stack. We did have to look at the first line, but that's just so we could know who to give them to. Noah was really grateful when we told him there actually was a letter for him after all. Mrs. Melton cried when I handed one to her. Kenzie talked about having hers framed. And the ones written to your family? Well, those weren't handed out individually. And there's a reason for that, I promise. Kenzie and I talked long and hard about what to do with the letters you wrote for me. I thought about keeping them, but I decided the memories I have of you are all I really need moving forward. No offense, but I actually wanted to burn them. Or throw them into the lake. But Kenzie didn't think that was right. After listening to her reasoning, I decided she had a point. So, along with their own letters, we gave my letters to your parents. They might think I'm the biggest jerk to ever associate with their daughter, but I know they'll appreciate having that piece of you with them.

Anyway, Hadley, I should probably let you get back to doing whatever dead people do (or don't do), but I just wanted to thank you really quick. Thank you for being you. Thank you for allowing yourself recovery. You have changed the lives of many by choosing to stay here as long as you did. You have changed my life in more ways than you will ever know. You were the person I needed. I'm sorry I couldn't be who you needed at the time, but I'm glad that you became who you needed.

Love,
Parker

Acknowledgments

You know how they say it takes a village to raise a child? Well, apparently that's true about writing books, too. I'm always afraid to write acknowledgments because I feel I'll inevitably forget to mention someone, as I've been supported by so many. So, I'm just going to go ahead and make sure I include everyone now by saying THANK YOU to you, dear reader.

Thank you to my editors Meghan Zalar and Heather Moore. Heather, I really appreciate you for the direction you provided and your willingness to answer all of my many questions in order to get this story where it needed to be.

I am grateful for my sensitivity readers, Amanda Garcia and Neff Rodriguez. Your honest feedback and kind words were so helpful when it came to representing my characters in the light they deserved.

Makayla, thank you for being my Oregon expert. I also loved getting all the reference photos you took of the trees and mist. Seriously, what a beautiful place!

Thank you to my other amazing beta readers and draft cheerleaders: Miggs, Devin, Allison, Michaela, Paige, and Tori. Whether you were in charge of giving me your honest feedback to make Letters from Hadley better or just encouraged me to keep writing chapters when I was in the trenches of drafting, you did a phenomenal job. And I am so grateful for you. Especially since you all let me pull you out of your beta reader graves to help me brainstorm cover designs and blurbs.

To my writing group: I firmly believe we were destined to come together. You started out as a critique group I was so scared to share my work with and became my most cherished friends and allies in the writing world. Brenna, Mandy, Stefani, and Karly—you guys are so amazing. You are the best cheerleaders and have written some of my favorite books. I can't wait to have all of them on my shelves.

Thank you to Layla Brown for designing such a beautiful cover and working with my vague descriptions of how I wanted it to look haha. You really made it come to life!

And to my husband. Just like Noah in the book inspired and encouraged Hadley, you inspire and encourage me every day. I love you so much, and I'm grateful for your help in my journey of writing and publishing this book.

To my Mom who has sacrificed so much for me and always encouraged me to pursue my dreams. And to all my friends and family who have supported me in my writing. Writing and publishing can be really hard, but having people treat you like you've already become a bestselling author before you've sold a single book is so encouraging. I truly believe I could write a whole other book titled "Acknowledgments" if I were to try and mention you all by name. Thank you for being so good to me.

Lastly, I want to thank God who has guided and inspired me throughout this journey and in my life. I truly believe this story is better because of Him.

Playlist

"Someone New" by Hozier
"The Funeral" by Band of Horses
"Good Grief" by Bastille
"Halls" by Andrew McMahon in the Wilderness
"Absolutely (Story of a Girl)" by Nine Days
"The Night We Met" by Lord Huron
"Weak" by AJR
"the 1" by Taylor Swift
"Hero" by Family of the Year
"Delicate" by Taylor Swift
"Ahead of Myself" by X Ambassadors
"right where you left me" by Taylor Swift
"traitor" by Olivia Rodrigo
"drivers license" by Olivia Rodrigo
"Maple Syrup" by The Backseat Lovers
"All Time Low" by Jon Bellion
"deja vu" by Olivia Rodrigo
"my tears ricochet" by Taylor Swift
"Party In The U.S.A." by Miley Cyrus
"One Headlight" by The Wallflowers
"Unsteady" by X Ambassadors
"Haunted" by Taylor Swift
"this is me trying" by Taylor Swift
"Somewhere Only We Know" by Keane
"So Low (feat. Spencer Jones)" by Cinematic Pop, Spencer Jones
"Fix You" by Coldplay
"People Change" by for KING & COUNTRY
"Near to You" by A Fine Frenzy
"Shake It Out" by Florence + The Machine
"Out of The Woods" by Taylor Swift
"Ghost" by Justin Bieber
"I Wanna Get Better" by Bleachers
"I Forgot That You Existed" by Taylor Swift
"Dog Days Are Over" by Florence + The Machine
"Show Me What I'm Looking For" by Carolina Liar
"Manic Monday" by The Bangles

About the Author

As a child, Cassidy Bryant wanted to grow up to be a veterinarian or a rockstar, but then her fourth grade teacher read one of her short stories and told her she was a talented writer. That day, an aspiration was born and it grew until Cassidy could no longer ignore it. Graduating Brigham Young University with a degree in English Creative Writing, Cassidy continues to write and make her dream of being an author everybody's problem. She is so excited to share her debut novel with you. To stay informed on future releases, subscribe to her monthly newsletter at cassidybryantauthor.com.

You can also support this indie author by leaving an honest review of Letters from Hadley on your review platform of choice.

www.ingramcontent.com/pod-product-compliance
Lightning Source LLC
Chambersburg PA
CBHW020932260626
47169CB00006B/1681

* 9 7 8 1 9 6 6 6 9 8 0 0 5 *